Thanks to Benoit, Eric and Mike, as always, and to Caro, for just being there. To Paul and Brenda, Adrian, Morgan, Phil, Steve and all the Kindred at Savage Garden, for answering my endless questions and helping me "What if." To Ken Cliffe and Rob Hatch for thinking of me. And lastly to Don Bassingthwaite, for putting up with my accessory impairment, and for keeping me laughing throughout what was a thoroughly enjoyable collaboration.

—Nancy Kilpatrick

Thanks to my friends for putting up with my vanishing act, to my coworkers for putting up with strange calls at the office ("Okay, so at this point there's blood everywhere...."), to Rob Hatch at White Wolf Publishing, to William Shakespeare (*Romeo and Juliet*) and Cyril Tourneur (*The Revenger's Tragedy*), and, of course, to Nancy Kilpatrick, for inviting me along for the ride, and for going all mushy at the end.

—Don Bassingthwaite

CHAPTER ONE

Two hideous gargoyles guarded the door. They were almost exact replicas of works Bianka had seen created at the end of the 11th Century. She was seven years old then, maybe eight, still human—it was so long ago. She used to sit by the clay well in the square of Venice, watching Giovanni, the stone artist, chisel grotesqueries for the churches, at least until her mother would drag her away, chastising her for taking so long to bring the pitcher of water.

Giovanni liked to work in silence, but he also liked Bianka. Sometimes he would talk to her about the gargoyles, as if they spoke to him. "They admit they are demons, you understand."

"Why does God let demons live?" she asked.

"Because only the legions of hell know how to protect the sacred."

As with much of what Giovanni said, Bianka did not understand the words, but she felt the truth of them.

"Child, the world would sully the Mysteries. These creatures stand at our doorways to confront us. If our hearts are impure, the demons rip them from our chests. If we are respectful of the Divine, we may pass through and enter the spirit realm. They can see your heart, these demons. And if you are pure, you can see theirs. Always remember that."

That was then. This was now. And the bronze gargoyles, twice the size of Giovanni's, might as well have snarled at her as she stared up the tall flight of steps before the entrance to Savage Garden.

This club, one of many along an artsy strip of Toronto known as Queen Street West, catered to punk babies, industrial and Euro trash musicians, wraithboys and gothgrrrls. And vampires. Camarilla, to be precise.

Bianka watched a human couple stop before the street-level doorway. One guy wore tight black pants and shirt, torn so that the crisp autumn air reached through the shredded fabric to caress his skin. His left ear was pierced with a small-caliber bullet. A deep scar ran the length of his face on that side, from bald head to bald chin, and she wondered if he'd been cut in a knife fight, because the scar was recent and looked to be the type made by a serrated edge. Unlike the scarred boy, his boyfriend had neatly clipped shoulder-length black hair, a pouty baby-face, and eyes that said he was addicted to coffee and heroin, not necessarily in that order.

She caught the gaze of the *enfant terrible*— thoughts too flat to decipher, too focused on his obsessions to be interesting. All she wanted was info on the easiest and most conservative way to gain access to this place, and he handed it over mentally.

She watched their taut butts pass through the doorway and climb the wooden stairs to the top. They pulled the chain at the enormous grated doors—doors that looked like the entrance to a crypt. Someone inside recognized them, no doubt. The doors opened, and they were admitted, easily passing by the gargoyles on either side.

Bianka started to laugh, letting the air stroke her fangs. Giovanni was a fool, but then he said all that long before the Kindred had formed, before the Masquerade had been created. Nobody believed in gargoyles anymore.

She grasped the hem of her ankle-length black velvet dress in her hand and started up the wooden steps. At the top, she mimicked what the two before her had done. The pale face peered out at her through the wrought iron. A face that did not recognize hers. A face that noticed the large black bird sitting on her left shoulder. A face that turned distrustful and made the mistake of looking into her eyes, eyes, she knew, that must for a split second have reminded this muscle of a pale-eyed husky—a startling contrast: dead black hair, dead white flawless skin, blood red lips, and eyes that... disappeared like the clouds....

The gate opened; the gargoyles did not come to life. She was admitted into what was probably not a sacred realm, but then, who was to say anymore....

Bianka looked briefly at the bouncer. Yet another vampire imitator, this one adorned with chain mail and shin guards, and a severe-looking braided whip dangling down his right hip. She caught his eye again, erasing the memory of her eyes, the memory of the oblivion he had for a moment visited. A visit that would last him a lifetime, that would wake him in the night with its memory, that, on his deathbed, he would remember in vivid detail.

He shivered, and the blood drained from his face. A mental shrug from her, and he occupied himself with staring through the openings in the grate and down the steps to the busy street below. "You look under the weather," she said casually. "Maybe you should take the night off."

He began to nod absently and she turned away. The music called her.

Nine Inch Nails pounded out a song that reminded her of the rhythm of the Inquisition, for some reason. She didn't want to get into that now. She had vampires to stalk.

They were scattered throughout the room, some alone with humans, some together in small groups, one or two vying for the same morsel. All doing what vampires do best, scouting out food in their territory. She caught a few eyeing each other jealousy. One, at least, seemed to be having a good time seducing the pretty Winona Ryder look-alike whose hand he was massaging and on whose neck he was nibbling. The Kindred was wearing Lord Byron drag. As Bianka passed, he noticed her. His eyes opened wide, startled, curious, enthusiastic. He couldn't have been *that* enthusiastic; his teeth did not leave the slim throat.

The walls of this dimly lit club were

midnight, except for the areas that had been painted by a local artist. A collage of vampire motifs mingled with S&M imagery. Some intuitive human, no doubt—she peered close and saw the name *Meek*. Every artist she'd met for the last nine hundred years had been like that, picking up on the vibrations of their era and recreating the undercurrents in an art form. Yet when pressed, each of them had been almost completely incapable of verbalizing what it was they had created.

The main group of Camarilla sat at one chrome table—seven of them: four females, three males. They spotted Bianka the second she walked in, of course. Several of them must possess Auspex in abundance—after all, heightened senses were not uncommon—and at least one of them wouldn't have missed her pale, almost white-pewter aura.

Fourteen pairs of eyes watched her suspiciously until she reached their table. Which one is the leader? she wondered. First guess: the female, blond and green hair, brush cut, more piercings than natural orifices in her body—Bianka did admire the tattoo of a ring of barbed wire around her biceps, though. She had the toughness, but there was something missing.

Before Bianka could closely scrutinize the others, the female said, "What clan are you, stranger? Just so we know what we're dealing with."

"Well, I'm not exactly Brujah, if that's what you're wondering."

The female jumped to her feet, Doc Martens planted on the floor, ready to attack.

A tall, slim male with crazy, quivering eyes, said, "Swan! Give her a chance to talk!"

"Why the fuck should I? Who the fuck is she?"

"Ask me nicely and I might tell you," Bianka said.

"Tell me, or I'll rip your throat out!"

"Do you always welcome help like this?"

That stopped the female, at least for a second. In the meantime, the rakish Kindred in the velvet coat and ruffles must have finished with dinner, because he came up to the table and said, "What have we here? A new beauty." He reached out to touch Bianka's face. The raven on her shoulder pecked his finger, so fast he looked startled. The tiny hole seeped blood, and he sucked on the beak-wound for a second, then, stubbornly, reached out again. This time he had the sense to stop short, not because of Ravena, but as if he'd encountered an invisible layer of protection around Bianka's body, which wasn't far from the truth. "A powerful beauty," he said. His hand moved around her face, her shoulders, her breasts, her entire body, two inches from contact, as if caressing her. This time the raven squawked, but it did not attack.

He's harmless, she told Ravena. *They all are.*

"Are you the leader?" Bianka said to the tall gaunt one.

"Yes," he nodded, his movements a bit jerky. He looked like a mortician in stove-pipe pants, long jacket—where was his top hat? "I lead the sheep to the slaughter."

Ah, she thought, a Malkavian. *This* will be a challenge!

"I'm DeWinter. This is Swan." He pointed

to the tough-looking female with the seven nose rings. "Reg," he said, indicating the dandy. He proceeded around the table, naming each of the group. When he finished, he gestured to a chair that Reg had pulled up, and Bianka sat.

"My name is Bianka. This is Ravena." She looked at DeWinter first, out of respect—if he was the leader, she needed him onside, nuts though he might be. Then she made brief eye-contact with each of the others, Swan last, and most briefly—no use challenging anybody. Yet. "I've come to save you," she added. She'd never been above theatrics.

That was met with a howl from one of them, a hiss of disgust from Swan, and laughter from a few others.

"Save me first," Reg said. His seductive sky-blue eyes tried to draw her gaze to him. She avoided eye contact, not for her sake, but for his; he might not recover. Instead, she moved her lips into a smile, and he focused on those. She knew what he saw: perfect red lips. Lush red lips. Lips on the edge of parting in receptivity. Lips that turned him on and drew him in, that silently made promises that he was busy trying to decipher.

"Save us from what?" Swan interrupted, her voice hostile.

"From yourselves, obviously."

Swan's tight mouth curled into a sneer. Her hands were bunched into fists at her taut hips, but Bianka sensed that the claw extensions weren't far behind. How to win this one over?

"Listen, why don't we start again? I'm Bianka." She extended a hand, like a human.

Swan ignored it. "Listen, bitch, I wasn't Embraced yesterday. How the hell did you get into the Box?"

"The Box?"

"Our territory."

"Ah. The enclave you call home, that the Sabbat gave you when you helped them take the city."

"You seem to know a lot about us. And we don't know anything about you, other than that you got to the Box without the Sabbat ripping out your vagina."

It was time for a bit of mesmerizing. While

Bianka spoke, she used her hands to illustrate her words. With her fingers, she formed pictures, suggestive pictures, and soon they were all watching her hands weave images that her words painted, until the colors had an impact on the listener's vision. "I just walked in. Actually, I took the train to Union Station. I didn't see any Sabbat. I didn't see anybody until I got here."

"And how did you know we'd be at this club?"

"Well, it wasn't hard. I mean, presumably you'd want to blend in, so I asked where all the Goths hang out. There were several clubs, and this is the first one I tried. There must be, what, a dozen of you in one place? I just followed my nose across the room."

"And now for the big double jeopardy question: Who is infiltrator?"

"Oh come on! What kind of paranoia are you working under—"

"Paranoia? You were sent by the Sabbat!"

"You really believe I'm Sabbat? If I were, why would I just walk in here and try to make friends with you all, especially since you're so hostile? That's not the way the Sabbat operate, at least everywhere else in the world. Maybe the Sabbat of Toronto are kind and humane. If so, I'd like to go out for tea with them."

"Maybe you didn't attack because there are a dozen of us!" Swan said.

"She has a point," Reg agreed. He gestured at Swan, and Bianka noticed his mangled hand. It would have been shocking on anyone, but on the perfect body of this neoromantic undead, that hand was like a sacrilege. She wondered if he'd been maimed as a mortal, or if it had happened after the Embrace.

"Look, I'm not Sabbat!" she said reasonably.

"And you're not Camarilla."

"I'm... kind of patchwork. Pieces, anyway."

"What the hell does that mean?"

"How can you be in pieces? You are one being," DeWinter said, looking somewhat sane, at least for the moment.

"The ones who brought me over—there were two of them. A Toreador and a Brujah. They embraced me at the same moment."

This reduced the Camarilla to silence. Obviously they'd never heard of such a thing.

"I thought you said you aren't Brujah," Swan finally snapped.

"I'm *not* Brujah. If anything, I'm a hybrid."

"She's Caitiff!" one of the Kindred sneered.

"No, I'm not."

"Why in the name of Dante would a Toreador align with a Brujah for *any* reason?" Reg shook his head. Swan gave him a harsh look. He arched an eyebrow haughtily and tossed back his blond curls with a dramatic flare.

Swan scanned the Kindred. "Anybody ever heard of a mixed blood that wasn't Caitiff?"

Heads shook. A few murmurs.

She stabbed a fingernail into Bianka's chest. "You're either Brujah or Toreador. One has to be dominant. Or you're Caitiff. Which is it?"

"Does one have to be dominant? Why?"

"Because none of us have ever heard of a vampire having two clans."

"And because you've never heard of such a thing, that means it isn't possible?"

"You better believe it!"

"I once heard of a mixed blood who was not Caitiff, but accepted by the Camarilla. He was Embraced by a Nosferatu and a Malkavian," DeWinter said.

There was silence while the others chewed over the implications of such a twisted union.

"The Beast overwhelmed him. He was killed by humans. It was many centuries ago."

"So, mongrel," Swan said, "even if we buy this stupid story, that doesn't explain why you're here, on our turf."

"I've been sent by the Camarilla—"

"We're Camarilla, in case you hadn't noticed!"

"I mean, the sect *outside* Toronto. They want you back in the fold. I've come to make the gesture."

"Well, you can turn on your velvet tail, take your fucking bird with you, and go back and tell them to stuff it!" Swan said. "They weren't around when we needed them, and we don't need them now."

"Look, I know the Camarilla left you all to fight alone—"

"Abandoned is the word. They ran scared, like the major sucks they are—"

"That may be, but you broke from them. The Camarilla never back rebels, you know that—"

"Then that's their loss. We helped the Sabbat take this city and then, when they turned on us, the Camarilla turned on us too, and left us here to rot!"

"I'd say it was fifty-fifty—you didn't ask for help."

"We couldn't," DeWinter interjected. "Once the Sabbat sealed the city, there was no way to get word out. They gave us three choices—stay here, or go. Decide soon, or die."

"Stay here, as in—"

"Stay in the Box," Swan said. "A couple lousy square miles! Home sweet home."

Bianka paused. "And the Sabbat leave you alone?"

"Sure, if we don't leave the Box. Stay in jail, do not pass Go, do not collect 200 blood donors. We're prisoners here—"

"That is not true!" DeWinter said. "When we helped the Sabbat take Toronto, and the Settlement was negotiated with them—"

"When *you* negotiated the Settlement with them—"

"We had a choice: Stay here, the area of the city they gave us, or leave Toronto altogether."

"Nice reward, huh? For helping those bastards conquer an entire metropolis. You and your friends find a wallet with three million bucks in it and the owner gives you a reward of a nickel to split between you. Seems fair to me!" Swan looked more than bitter, and the faces of several others reflected her sentiments. It was clear that this battle, within the rank and file, had been going on since the Settlement was made.

"I did the best I could," DeWinter said defensively. *"Tis a far far better thing I do—"*

"Oh, don't go off the deep end again!" Swan yelled.

"To sleep, perchance to dream—"

Swan smashed a fist on the table, rattling the

beer glasses from which they pretended to drink. "Stop it!"

Even as he spoke, DeWinter was fading. He seemed to be blending into the shadows of the room, as though he were evaporating.

Ravena squawked harshly, the sound sharp and piercing over the intense beat of the music. It didn't affect DeWinter, though.

"*I'm leavin', on a jet plane*," he sang, imitating the voice of Mary Travers.

He is a major basket case, Bianka thought. The notion that he was the leader of this disparate group made her shudder. Obviously he had some power Swan didn't, because she was the natural leader. Maybe it was just his age. Bianka guessed him to be at least 8th Gen.

As DeWinter faded physically, his voice dimmed, too, until only a slight refrain could be heard— "Don't let the hot-dog vendors step on my blue suede shoes...." and then the industrial-goth music of Nosferatu swallowed up the sound, as the air seemed to swallow his body.

Bianka glanced at Swan. "Does he do this often?"

"Too fucking often!"

Now that Swan was in charge, at least temporarily, the pressure was off her, and while still interrogative, she seemed to relax a bit. Nothing to prove, Bianka thought, and Ravena squawked.

I will watch out, she assured the bird telepathically.

"So, run it by me again. You're here to make a gesture. So make it," Swan said.

Preliminaries were over. Time to go for the jugular. "On behalf of the Camarilla at large, I've come to offer you a chance to return to the mainstream."

"The mainstream?" Swan snorted. "What makes you think we're interested in being part of that collective? Or any collective?"

A slim female whose hair was twisted into a French braid started to say, "Swan, I think we should maybe hear her out—"

Swan turned on her. "Hey, Razor, you want

command? Just say so. Next time the Sabbat are after your ass, don't come crying to me."

"I didn't mean anything, Swan. I just thought—"

"Since when do Gangrels think?"

The female crossed her arms over her chest and stared at Ravena. The bird looked back at her with some empathy.

"Listen," Bianka said, "I didn't come here to make trouble. If you're all happy living in a 'Box,' far be it from me to disturb you."

The vampire silence that followed was as loud as the music to Bianka's ears. Swan, especially, looked angry.

"Hey, we *love* it here, don't we?" Reg said. "Five parties a night. And all the death-culture you can handle." He gestured, and Bianka again noticed his hand.

"What happened?" she asked, nodding to the damaged flesh.

Reg's face closed suddenly, as if a door had shut. He wasn't about to tell this stranger anything. Before he could snap on the lock,

Bianka moved her lips in a way that caught his attention. He watched for a moment, the crimson of her lips so like blood, the movement as sensuous as any lover's kiss.

He seemed a little stunned, but said, "I met this human female—"

"Goes without saying!" Swan snapped. "You're going to tell a stranger? We don't even know her, or why she's here, and you're just gonna tell her everything?"

Reg shot her an angry look, but didn't fire back. By Bianka's best guess, they were likely both 10th Gen. But Reg was a lover, not a fighter, and Swan looked like she hadn't understood the concept of love even when she was still walking in daylight.

Ravena squawked, and Reg turned back. Bianka's lips parted slowly, from the center to the outside edges.

"Shadow. Her name's Shadow. I Embraced her."

Bianka looked around. None of the females identified themselves as Shadow. "Who...? Which...?" She felt annoyed with these stubborn Camarilla, having to drag everything out of them.

"She's not here," Swan added, hardly a gesture of goodwill, more a too-late confirmation of the obvious.

Bianka felt their coldness. No one here would offer her even the slightest bit of assistance, until she proved herself. To prove herself would require a major conjuring trick. Even Ravena felt something; the bird edged closer to her head, farther away from these suspicious Kindred.

"Do you Embrace humans often?" Bianka directed the question to Swan—no use wasting time on the others. Go for the artery.

Out of the shadows came the reply, "If you drain them, they will come."

Bianka searched the darkness. DeWinter was just barely visible, and she knew that was only because she had the power to find him—the others in the room, both vampire and human, could not.

"Shadow is a jewel," Reg was saying, "like a black diamond, her skin so dark it nearly glows beneath the moonlight, a black pearl. We met her at The Cameron, up the street. Where the Gothic Society meets."

"The Gothic Society?" What kind of weirdness were these Camarilla into?

"Reg likes to live in the past," Swan sneered.

"The past was alive with charm and grace," he said, seemingly not afraid of her. "Unlike today, when beauty is not only *not* appreciated, but attacked."

"Tell the story!" one of the males said. "Oh, the hell with it! I'm off to Death in the Underground."

"Hey Janus! Wait for me!" A short wiry Kindred caught up with him.

Bianka watched the Mediterranean vampire with the handcuffs strung around the loops of his pants stride across the room and out the door, the shorter male barely catching up.

Reg fluffed the ruffles on his shirt unnecessarily. When he was satisfied that he had everyone's attention, he continued. "After the meeting, Shadow and I wandered some of the back streets. I love the quiet; I love being alone with humans. Shadow is exquisite, a classical beauty, but exotic at the same time."

Swan gritted her teeth, "Oh for—"

"I'm telling it! In my way, all right! Anyway, every so often we'd stop at the back of a church or one of the other buildings from the last century, and she'd let me take her blood. I drank from her slowly, usually from the neck, because she enjoyed that, and so did I. A few drops at a time. It's like foreplay. You can do it all night. You should try it some time."

He gave Bianka a meaningful look. She'd only drunk like that once before, and not from a human, but from Dameon—it was an unusual Blood Bond, one established upon mutual consent. They had spent the night sipping one another's blood.... But that was then. She was not into seducing humans like that, and she had no intention of ever voluntarily Blood Bonding again unless she met someone who inspired that kind of passion in her. Reg certainly didn't. And it was beyond her imagination that anyone else could either.

"We drove around in Shadow's car all night.

It's so quiet at night, when the traffic dims, and the only humans awake are the ones who love the world of darkness. That kind of seduction, just a few drops an hour, gets me high. Lightheaded. My senses heighten, and at the same time sometimes I'm sure I can fly, like a bat. That's why I didn't notice she'd driven outside the Box. The minute I realized where we were, I made her turn the car around. It took us about fifteen minutes to get back down University Avenue to Queen Street—that's the northeast boundary of the Box.

"We parked, and I was so rattled, I had to take sustenance right away, and nearly drank her dry. I took quite a lot, and too fast. She was weak, so we went into an all-night café. We were talking, kissing, she was having something to eat... and then four Sabbat came in.

"Normally, I'd have sensed them even before they entered the building, because I can pick that up, but I guess I was still out of it, and I was also preoccupied."

"Girl-Blood on the brain!" Swan said.

Reg ignored her. His story was obviously

affecting him. He'd gone from glib to pensive, as if he wanted to look over his shoulder but was restraining himself.

"So, one of the Sabbat—Miranda, the leader—she sent Shadow home. This thug they call Tolly sat down opposite me and used a fork to mash down the slice of cake Shadow had been eating. The one they called Blue stood behind me, with a hand on my shoulder, so I couldn't escape. There was one other with them—I'm not sure who. He kind of blocked the exit.

"Miranda told me to be quiet. Something about the humans, and if I caused any trouble she'd make sure they knew about us feeding off them. It was pretty ugly."

"You mean scary," Swan corrected.

"You would have been afraid, too," Reg said. "I was outnumbered four to one, and you know how vicious the Sabbat are. I'm lucky to be here."

"I'd say," Bianka interrupted, "the fact that the Sabbat didn't kill you is exceptional. I've rarely heard of them sparing a Camarilla."

"It's the Settlement," Swan said. "We made a deal."

"Thank you," came an icy voice from the shadows, cool as a first frost.

"But the Settlement stipulates that they aren't supposed to come into the Box. I told them that," Reg whined, "but they just said I wasn't suppose to go *outside* the Box."

"So, how did your hand get like that?" Bianka prodded.

"The Punishment," the shadows said.

"Whose side are you on!" Swan yelled at the darkness, but the shadows did not respond.

The loquacious Reg stopped talking, and the others, too, were silent. Whatever happened had unnerved these Camarilla, that was clear.

"Tolly..." Reg began haltingly, "... grabbed my hand and slammed it palm up onto the table. I tried to escape, but he was too quick. He stabbed the fork he was holding through my wrist and at the same time Blue gagged me. And that bitch Miranda—she just stood there, emotionally decayed...."

Reg paused. His voice faltered. "I watched

her talons extend. It was horrible. I don't know why, but I looked up at the dozens of humans in the room for help. Maybe I was so used to being around them all the time I forgot they don't have any power—not only didn't they notice, it was as if a curtain of darkness had dropped between me and them."

Bianka nodded. Miranda might have been Lasombra, with the ability to manipulate the shadows themselves.

"I couldn't stop trembling. I really thought she was going to rip me apart. Instead, in this very calm voice, she asked my name. I told her. Then she quizzed me on the terms of the Settlement, how our leaders had helped her leaders take Toronto and, in exchange, we got the Box, and she wanted me to list all the conditions of the Settlement. Then she asked me the boundaries and as I told her, she drew a map of the Box with her claws, deep into the flesh of my hand. I didn't think I could stand the pain. Somehow, I did. No one helped me. Nobody noticed. I've never felt so alone.

"She made me admit I'd been in Sabbat

territory. I tried to tell her it was a mistake, that I'd been hungry, because I wasn't drinking more than a few drops an hour, but she didn't care. She made me draw a line on the bloody map on my hand where I'd been out of the Box. The line ended at the base of my middle finger."

Reg became very quiet. Apparently he had said most of what he had to say.

"When did all this happen?" Bianka asked.

"Nearly a year ago."

Bianka looked at Reg's hand. The map was still plainly visible, etched into livid flesh. His middle finger had been broken, bent backward at an improbable angle, and although it was clear the bone had set, the finger was contorted and that twisted the entire hand into a grotesque shape. She couldn't imagine what the Sabbat gang leader must have done to cause such destruction. It might take decades to heal, *if* it healed.

"Is that the end of it?" Bianka asked.

"No." It was Swan who answered. "Several of us caught them out on the street. It was startling to see them here in the Box, invading our territory."

"Were you outnumbered?"

A pause. "No. We were equally matched."

Bianka nodded, but just slightly. The ego of this one was at stake here, and it was best to tread lightly.

"DeWinter grabbed her arm and told her we wouldn't forget what they did to Reg," the one named Razor said softly. "Miranda pushed his hand away and said, 'You can remember as long as you want. There's nothing you can do.'"

The silence that descended was like a bomb. From the stage, the band The Dark Theater was being introduced: Vlad, the tall, lean head of the band, and Lynda, even leaner, both with matte black hair and shocking makeup. The heavy "Hell in the City" beat thundered in the air and vibrated through the floor, the sound like Dante's inferno rising up through the boards.

"So, are these Sabbat still troubling you?" Bianka asked.

"We heard Miranda went to San Francisco," Swan said. "Tolly's still around—I've seen him at the edge of the Box from time to time. Blue I don't know about. We don't know the other one, but there was some major trouble in the city after Reg was hurt, and there was a rumor, about what sounded like a Kindred disappearing in the subway, but it wasn't one of us…. He might have bit it, or they could have done him in."

They sat without speaking, listening to the music until the band finished their set. Reg's story and Swan's addendum apparently depressed the Camarilla. Even Swan, feisty as she was, looked vaguely defeated. Their dismal attitude was infecting Bianka; suddenly she needed something, anything, to dispel the gloom. And the hunger. But leaving wasn't the answer—they didn't trust her yet; if she left, it would only feed their doubts. Well, at least they would understand the power of certain drives, and she had to get *something* to ground her, because deep inside, in every conscious moment, the Beast was lurking, and it was about to exit lurk mode.

When the band left the stage and the taped music started, she scanned the humans in the room. The dance floor, encircled by prison bars with barbed wire at the top, was cluttered with bodies, like too many rats in too small a cage. They pushed and shoved and jerked in every direction, staring at themselves in the funhouse mirrors affixed to the one wall at the back. The smell of hot blood seeping through pores opened by sweat filled the air with an earthy fragrance.

Bianka stood, and Ravena flew up to a pillar overlooking the dance floor. Even after nearly a millennium of blood-drinking, it was always like the first time to Bianka. She moved as if drawn by a powerful magnet that it was impossible to fight against. And besides, she didn't want to fight it. Oh, she knew she could control this vitae lust—she would be a pretty sorry vampire if she hadn't learned something over the centuries. But why should she? This sect's misery had depressed her, and she couldn't let that happen or she would fail in her mission to save them.

As she stepped onto the dance floor, the humans parted for her, as if intuiting a presence that they unconsciously respected, or feared: A gargoyle had come to life. The Sisters of Mercy's dangerously primitive "This Corrosion" throbbed through the air and warm bodies pulsed to the beguiling beat. Yes, she thought, listening to the old lyrics, I, too, have bled all I can, and refuse to bleed anymore.

There were so many to choose from. Males. Females. One who was half of each. Tall, slim, meaty, squat. None of it mattered. What mattered was the blood.

She moved like silk through the crowd, sniffing them, the necks, between the half-exposed breasts, the insides of elbows, the groins, wherever, until the scent of one called out to her, called her as if the hemoglobin had a voice and spoke in code, on a wavelength that only her ears could hear.

The body was female, tall, as tall as Bianka, heavier, healthy. Half her head was shaved, the other half grew black-streaked blue hair down to her exposed pierced nipple. The girl—dancing alone like all the others—jerked harder when she saw Bianka, and the vampire smiled. It was so like these young humans, to meet their fate enthusiastically.

She slid close to the girl, and they danced together in a syncopated rhythm. Bianka writhed in a sexual imitation. Her hair flew about her face. She willed the girl to watch her hands, and she created patterns with both hands and hair; the dark strands were a black spider's web, and her hands the pale spider, crawling between earth and heaven and back again....

When the girl was entranced, Bianka pulled her in, swaying the human body, moving it in a sensuous alternate-beat rhythm. They moved seconds more, until Bianka had aligned their bodies, until it was one pair of hips, one set of breasts, one head....

Her lips found the thick vein between the breasts. She grasped the human's shoulders, then bit, deep, hard, piercing as quickly as a sharp scalpel slices flesh.

Bianka drank and drank. The boiling blood coated her insides, filling her with joy and hope and love for this pathetic food, for this torturous universe. Her undead cells sang out gratitude, and she heard the whisper of her own. Their voices came to her, letting her know that she was not alone.

The human, caught in feeble rapture, did not notice that her blood was being siphoned. No human noticed. When Bianka finished swallowing as much of the searing liquid as she needed, she looked up. The Kindred had noticed. Everything. Their faces said it all. They were awed that she was so smooth. So casual. So artistic. She had taken nourishment out in the open, surrounded by humans. Even DeWinter had rematerialized and stood at the head of this odd little group of castrated rebels, watching Bianka as if she were their savior.

She sealed the girl's wounds, then turned and

left the human jerking on her own to the music—a missing pint wouldn't hurt her at all.

As Bianka glided off the dance floor, back to the Camarilla, as Ravena landed once again on her left shoulder, she wondered where all the gargoyles had gone. The humans could use a few, here and there, to protect what was sacred to them. But they didn't believe anymore. Or maybe the gargoyles walked among them, and they just didn't notice.

CHAPTER TWO

Out in the hall, the stairwell door opened with a dry groan. The sound reached Lot's ears in spite of the unpleasant noise of Bishop Fletcher's nightly feeding. Instantly alert, he snapped his head up, eyes trained on the door to the hall, muscles tense and ready to send him sprinting forward if he was required. The stairwell door closed again, old springs drawing it shut. Footsteps on the worn floorboards. Lot risked a glance away from the door to check the bishop's position. Fletcher was on the far side of the room, sharing his meal, a young man taken from the street, with a couple of favor-seeking toadies. The quiet rattle of a hand on the doorknob brought Lot's attention back to the door. Ready. Waiting.

The doorknob turned, then paused. "It's Benedict," said the vampire in the hall. "I know you're listening, Lot. Calm down. I'd like to stay in one piece."

Gritting his teeth, Lot willed his muscles to relax as golden-haired Benedict pushed the door open and swept into Fletcher's throne room with the distinctive rustle of velvet on velvet. Lot wished yet again that Fletcher would listen to him and be just a little quieter. He should have been able to recognize the sound of Benedict's Teddy boy frock-coat the moment he stepped out of the stairwell. If the room didn't stink so badly, he might even have been able to smell him.

What good was he as a templar bodyguard if Fletcher paid no attention to his suggestions and took every opportunity to frustrate him?

He adjusted his gun-metal, wire-framed glasses and turned his attention back to the book he held in his cold hands. *Look you, brother,* read Vindice's lines, *I have not fashioned this only for show and useless property; no, it shall bear a part e'en in its own revenge. This very skull...*

"Benedict!" bellowed Fletcher. "Anything interesting?" The bishop's voice was thick, and Lot could just barely hear a quiet splattering sound when he spoke. He was talking with his mouth full. Lot avoided looking at him. He already knew what he would see. His face would be a mask of blood, from his rough chin to the slashing brands that decorated his cheeks. The vampires of the Sabbat might be beasts and monsters, but Fletcher reveled in taking that description to its lowest form. He lived like an animal. He ate like an animal, spraying blood and chunks of torn flesh everywhere. The fact that his lower front teeth had been knocked out in some fight, and that his lower canines had become so enlarged over the years that they protruded over his lip like miniature tusks, didn't help. In stark contrast to the simple jeans, loose white shirt, and black silk vest of his templar, Fletcher wore a soiled leather jacket without a shirt and filthy jeans without underwear. Not even his shaven head was clean. The bishop had a perpetual stubble that crawled across his scalp like a blue stain. He was big and muscular, but beefy rather than defined. If there had been such things as ogres, Fletcher would have been one.

This very skull, whose mistress the Duke poisoned with this drug, the mortal curse of the earth, shall be reve...

"Is there ever? The damn Cammies are too cowed to try anything." Benedict snorted in derision. "None of them have even reached out of the Box since that episode last year."

"What about our people?" asked Fletcher eagerly. There was a brief, oddly moist smacking sound. Lot suspected Fletcher was licking his lips or his fingers. "Did any of them do anything—?"

"Stupid?" Benedict's voice was level, but Lot knew he was disguising the revulsion he felt for the foul creature they both served.

"It's only been a couple of months since the last time any Sabbat went slumming in the Box. I think it will be a while before anyone works up the balls to risk violating the Archbishop's edict again," one of Fletcher's dinner guests, a vampire named Giles, pointed out. "Michael's ashes are still clinging to the frame of the Archbishop's door." Fletcher just snarled at him. Giles paled and bit back into his meal. Michael was a forbidden topic.

The Settlement might have been enough to keep the rogue Camarilla vampires who had sought refuge in Toronto inside the Box, but it was hardly enough to keep the Sabbat out. Officially, they were allowed to enter the Box only to punish Camarilla vampires who had broken the terms of the Settlement. Unofficially, the temptation of entering that forbidden territory, with its population of hated Camarilla, was hard for many Sabbat to resist. What Sabbat could even respect creatures so pathetic that they refused to even admit the truth of their existence, referring to themselves as "Kindred" instead of "vampire"? So Archbishop Dyce, the leader of the Sabbat in Toronto by virtue of being the strongest and most cunning of the Sabbat in Toronto, had laid down an edict: The Settlement was sacrosanct, and the Camarilla was not to be toyed with. Even if they were being punished under the terms of the Settlement, no Camarilla would be killed unless they had a killed a vampire of the Sabbat or unless they were plotting against the Sabbat. Sabbat who violated the Archbishop's edict would be punished harshly, exposed to the sun and their gray ashes pasted above the door into the Archbishop's cathedral haven.

A harsh punishment, but the Archbishop enjoyed the trophies of his conquest. And he had the personal power to enforce his edict, along with Fletcher's power as the bishop in charge of overseeing the Box and the

Settlement. It didn't stop the wild Sabbat vampires entirely, but it always gave them pause to reconsider trifling with the Camarilla imprisoned in the Box. Most very wisely chose to leave the Camarilla alone.

... shall be revenged in the like strain, and kiss his lips to death. As much as this dumb thing, he shall feel: what fails in poison, we'll supply in steel.

Fletcher's other guest, Tanz, did not quite grasp the meaning of his host's snarl, however. "I was sorry to hear about Michael," he said. "I understand he was something of a protégé of yours."

The floor creaked as Benedict took a step away from the table.

Hippolito: Brother, I do applaud thy constant vengeance, the quaintness of thy malice....

The guest continued blithely. "It must have been unpleasant for you, having to hunt down a friend."

This time, Fletcher didn't snarl. He howled and ripped twice at the arm of the young man he had been sharing. His first tug dislocated the shoulder. The second tore the arm away. Giles had forced the young man into quiescence while the vampires fed from him; Fletcher's removal of his arm brought him back into full, screaming consciousness. Still howling, Fletcher ignored him and reached over the table to swing the bleeding arm at Tanz.

Lot caught the makeshift club before it could connect. "That's a sensitive subject, Tanz," he said quietly. He dropped his book to block Fletcher's other hand and suggested, "You may wish to withdraw until the bishop has had chance to calm down. Benedict?"

Hastily, Benedict ushered the startled guests out of the room while Lot turned his full attention to Fletcher. "Calm down!" he shouted. The screaming and flopping about of the young man on the table was a terrible distraction, but he did his best to ignore him. "The Archbishop has his eye on Tanz. Hurting him is not going to win you any friends!"

"He insulted me," Fletcher growled. "You heard what he said about Michael!"

"He didn't insult you. There was nothing to what he said," Lot countered tightly. "There's nothing to any of the rumors and we both know it."

Abruptly, he released his hold on the arm-club and grabbed for the back of Fletcher's head, dropping to his knees and pulling the bishop with him. Fletcher's mouth found the young man on the table. The blood captured his attention, cutting through his anger. He shoved Lot away and wrapped his arms around the young man to feed with a savage intensity. The man's screams grew even louder for a few moments, then began to weaken again, dropping into a series of low, wracking groans.

Lot stood and watched Fletcher in disgust. He had sworn oaths to protect and serve the bishop. Fletcher might not have had Lot's fighting skills, but he had more than enough strength, speed, and ferocity to protect himself. The one thing he didn't have was control. More often than not, Bishop Fletcher was the only thing from which Lot had to protect Bishop Fletcher.

The door opened and closed. Benedict came

back into the room and stood beside Lot. "Giles and Tanz are gone."

"I don't blame them." Lot sighed.

Benedict glanced sideways at him. "He's paranoid about the rumors again?" he asked quietly.

Lot nodded. The rumors had begun just after the hunt that had captured and punished Michael. The dead vampire had indeed been Fletcher's protégé, as ruthless and cunning as a Sabbat could wish to be. Anybody who thought that hunting Michael down would have been hard for Fletcher was wrong, though; the bishop had relished the hunt. So much so that some of the Sabbat began to suspect that he had actually encouraged his trusting protégé to enter the Box just so that he would have an excuse to call a hunt. It was a serious charge. Fletcher had gone to the Archbishop in protest, explaining that his enjoyment of the hunt had been a result of Michael's betrayal, that he had only placed his loyalty to the sect above Michael's traitorous friendship. Dyce had supported him and dispensed the appropriate Sabbat justice to those spreading the rumors. Unfortunately, that had not entirely calmed Fletcher.

"Ah." Benedict looked back at Fletcher. The bishop was champing on the young man's shoulder, sucking blood from the flesh like water from a sponge. The young man's eyes were dull and empty. Benedict shuddered slightly, staring at the red smears that joined the big vampire and his prey like sticky, stinking paste. Lot wondered if Benedict had fed yet tonight. He hadn't fed yet himself, his oaths to Fletcher demanding his first attention. The scent of blood didn't affect him. He was more disciplined than Benedict, however. He caught the other vampire's shoulder and turned him away from the sight of their master's feeding, breaking the call of the blood. Benedict smiled gratefully. "So," he asked, "what do we do?"

"We serve him," replied Lot without hesitation. "Loyalty to the Sabbat requires loyalty to the bishop."

"Do you really believe that?"

Any answer Lot could have given was cut off by the sudden reappearance of the young man's severed arm: It came hurtling through the air like a gory missile to slap into the back of Benedict's golden head. Anger flashed across Benedict's face, his lips drawing back from his fangs. He started to whirl around, but Lot tightened his hand on his shoulder, holding him back. Instead, he turned around himself.

Bishop Fletcher had stood, the pale, bloodless corpse of his meal on the floor at his feet. The better part of the young man's blood brought ruddy color to Fletcher's skin. The rest stained his clothes. "Well, Lot?" the bishop demanded. His fangs bit into the words. "Do you?"

Lot looked directly into the bishop's eyes. For a vampire, the gesture was one of supreme stupidity or supreme, aggressive arrogance—or supreme trust. "I've sworn to serve you, haven't I? It doesn't matter what you do."

There was no dissembling in his words, just the honest truth. Fletcher turned his head and spat on the floor. Bloody phlegm made another greasy stain on the tired linoleum of the floor. "I don't want your approval," he snarled. "I don't need your approval."

He stomped across the room to sprawl in the heavy wooden chair that he called his throne and that gave the room its name. Lot felt his muscles trying to tense up again. He fought them, forcing himself to relax. There were other bishops who served Dyce in Toronto. Precious Annette, the mistress of revels. High Father Truth, spin-doctor, media mogul, record-keeper, and inquisitor. Caligula, his fingers buried in city politics up to the third knuckle. Stracharn, commander of the border packs at the edge of the city's sprawl. Politically, Fletcher was the weakest of them. Except in matters concerning the Settlement and the Box, the respect he commanded was practically nonexistent. The other bishops had offices—Fletcher had an old warehouse. His "throne room" was a former lunchroom. But he also had ambition, raw personal power, and an overwhelming dislike for the Camarilla that were in his charge. Fletcher wasn't long for his current position. He was foul and he was disgusting, but he had the potential to rise high in the ranks of the Sabbat.

And when he did, Lot intended to rise with him. He crossed the room after Fletcher. "But you need my service."

"You mean your Tzimisce meddling?"

Lot caught himself clenching his fists. "I mean my service," he said, his voice level. "I pledged myself to you. If that means giving you advice from time to time…" He spread his hands.

The bishop was quiet for a moment, then laughed, a short, mocking bark. "Well, aren't you the perfect templar?" Fletcher sneered at him. "A real knight in shining armor."

Benedict shifted uneasily by the door, his feet scuffing against the floor. Lot ignored him for the moment, just as he ignored Fletcher's barbed jibes. "Every bishop is served by a templar."

"Yeah?" Fletcher's sneer fell into a hard, flat scowl. "Maybe they are. And maybe their templars aren't stuck-up assholes. I don't need your advice any more than I need your approval." He stood. "Here's an order, Lot. Beat it. You've served me enough for one night. If I want you, I'll call. Piss off and hunt or something."

Lot turned smartly and walked obediently to the door. Behind him, Fletcher snapped his fingers.

"You, too."

Benedict grimaced and stepped outside. Lot followed him. Fletcher stopped him before he was through the door, though.

"Lot."

The templar turned. Fletcher was sneering at him again. He had Lot's book in his hands.

"If you're supposed to be serving me, I don't want you reading at the same time." He flicked the book at him. Lot snatched it out of the air.

"How long are you going to put up with him?"

Lot glanced at Benedict across the polished

deep blue roof of his car, then opened the door without replying and slid in behind the steering wheel. The key went into the ignition easily, like a knife into a wound, and the engine purred to life. Benedict got into the passenger seat. He looked at him expectantly. Lot kept his silence a moment longer, pulling away from the curb outside Fletcher's warehouse haven and making a tight U-turn to head north on the dark street.

"As long as I have to," he replied finally. His fingers were tight on the wheel.

Benedict snorted. He reached forward to stab at the radio. Music filled the car—a not-quite discordant blend of two stations on adjoining frequencies, one slow classical, the other hard alternative industrial. Benedict looked at Lot. Mournfully. "Something else you couldn't make up your mind on?" He reached for the radio again.

Lot swatted his hand away from it without taking his eyes off the road. "It took me a long time to get that set just right. Don't change it."

"Fine." He looked out the window. "Where are we going?"

"Hunting." In the rearview mirror, the warehouse vanished around a corner. Lot met his own eyes, dark behind his glasses, in the mirror. He considered his face. Pale skin. Strong, broad bones. High forehead. Thick, black hair, brushed back from a widow's peak. It wasn't a face that was handsome in the most classical sense, but neither was it the face of a fool. He had known what he was doing when he chose to serve Fletcher.

"Hunting where?"

Away from the warehouse. Away from Fletcher. "The Danforth." He chose randomly. "We'll hunt along the Danforth."

"Feel like a little Greek tonight?" Benedict laughed and flicked back his shoulder-length hair. A grimace snarled its way across his face, and he paused to pick at the hair on the back of his head. Clots of blood from the arm that Fletcher had hurled tangled his curly locks. "Dolmades to start?" he asked with a little wince of pain. "Then moussaka. Or souvlaki with a nice garlicky tzatzike on the side? Ouzo to finish, of course." He laughed and leaned back in his seat. "Me, I think I'll just go for a nice, full-bodied Hellene."

He flashed Lot a wide grin. Lot ignored it. Benedict sighed in annoyance and turned away. Lot watched the road and the buildings that flashed by.

Fletcher's warehouse was down on Front Street, east of Sherbourne. Once Front Street had lived up to its name as Toronto's lakefront. Now the lakeshore was almost half a mile distant, the area south of Front Street was a landfill, and Front was a mix of old, disreputable warehouses and the concrete fortresses of condominiums. To the north, Sherbourne went past the old greenery of Allan Gardens, then threaded between low restored Victorians and towering, boxy apartment buildings until it encountered the office buildings that stretched out along Bloor Street. Lot turned and drove east on Bloor Street, high over the Don Valley with its twin rivers of dull water and brightly lit asphalt, high enough to see the dark stain that was old Mount Pleasant Cemetery in the distance. On the other side of the Don Valley, Bloor Street became the Danforth. The stores that lined the avenue were squat and clean, the houses up the streets behind them comfortably middle class. This was a mature immigrant neighborhood. The families that lived here were generally fairly prosperous. Many were second-generation Canadians. It was a quiet neighborhood. A safe neighborhood.

Out of the corner of his eye, Lot saw Benedict's head swivel like a ball-bearing attracted to a magnet as they drove past a tall man jogging in the cool night air. The blond vampire's fangs were already peeking through his parted lips.

"Wait," Lot admonished him calmly.

"Fuck you and your discipline," Benedict snapped back, "I'm hungry! Did you ever think that maybe this is why Fletcher is always in such a crappy mood?"

Lot pulled onto a side street and parked. "All the time. But he's my master and you're my friend." He put his hand on Benedict's shoulder.

"Fight the beast, Benedict. Make it your servant or you will be its slave."

Benedict sighed. He dropped his head back against the headrest. "Don't pull this shit on me. I don't need it." He looked at Lot, then closed his eyes. "Discipline isn't going to save you, Lot. You're still a vampire."

"I've never denied that. Not since the moment I dug myself out of my grave during the Creation Rites. But a vampire has to have more than blood lust and sharp—"

"That's not what I meant." Benedict opened his eyes again. "You're not perfect. Unless you're careful, your discipline is going to betray you and a stake is going to slide straight into your heart." He stared at Lot, watching him. Lot stared back. Finally a smile split Benedict's face and he laughed. "Fuck, listen to me. I'm getting as bad as you. Let's hunt." He opened the car door and swung his legs out, then leaned back in to add, "And I want to see you enjoying yourself."

Lot couldn't keep back a smile.

There were more people out along the Danforth than just the jogger. Young couples moved from pub to pub. Even younger people, in larger groups, emerged from a concert. Older men (older women had better sense than to go out after dark, it seemed) walked briskly along the sidewalk. The occasional jogger or roller blader moved past more quickly. A homeless person shuffled into the shadows of a narrow, weed-choked gap between buildings. Lot looked after him. Easy prey.

Benedict followed his gaze and twitched in disgust. He swept on ahead of Lot, taking the lead in the hunt.

"Indulge yourself," he whispered. "You don't have to live on old water and stale bread." He scanned ahead. "There."

Three men had just emerged from a bar, laughing and slapping each other. One tried to pull a cigarette out of a pack. So much of his attention was on the little box that he almost staggered into the street. That set off a fresh round of laughter. The smoker managed to get his cigarette out of the pack and in between his lips, then struggled to light it while his friends urged him to hurry. All three men were large, easily as tall as Benedict and almost as broad across the shoulders as Lot. The black-haired vampire considered them carefully.

"They're more than we need," he said eventually.

"So? Do you think we can take them?"

"Of course." Lot almost felt offended. "But do we need to go to the trouble? Two is really sufficient."

"Two's company, three's dessert," snorted Benedict scornfully. "Are you afraid of getting fat or something?" His eyes narrowed in concentration. "Now, what we really need is a diversion."

"No—" Lot began, then choked off the rest of his words. *Wait until they're farther away from the bar.* It was too late. He prepared himself for a fight and watched the results of Benedict's concentration.

A woman stepped out of a doorway halfway between the two vampires and the three drunken humans. No, not just any woman—the sort of woman who intoxicated mortal men with her mere presence and inspired dreams that had messy, sticky endings. Short red hair swayed around a delicate face. The fine fabric of her blouse clung to lush breasts. Smooth, graceful legs swung back and forth like twin ceramic pendulums, high heels tapping the ground at every step. The men noticed her. One, perhaps more drunk than the others, leered openly. The woman ignored him.

Lot stepped in behind the woman. She didn't cover him physically—she didn't even come close—but her sheer presence was more than sufficient to ensure that the men ignored him. Benedict stayed behind, leaning casually against a storefront, though his face remained distant with concentration. The three men had eyes only for the woman; Lot couldn't see her face, but he suspected that she would be smiling slightly, her eyes vaguely focused on one of them. Another, the one who had been leering before, let out a wolf whistle. He stepped forward, an easy smile on his face.

The woman vanished. Lot leaped.

The gifts of the blood that came with Embrace into the afterlife as a vampire varied widely, many of them tied to the vampire's lineage and which of the thirteen great clans he was reborn into. Fletcher was a Gangrel, a shapeshifter. Lot was a Tzimisce, an old and honorable clan nicknamed the "fiends" because of their acceptance of the ruthlessness their new life demanded. Benedict was one of the trickster Ravnos, skilled in the casting of illusions—a versatile and dangerous power. Distracted by the beautiful image the blond vampire had conjured and stunned by its abrupt disappearance, the drunk men collapsed like toys before Lot's sudden attack. One fell almost instantly, the wind knocked out of his lungs. A second went down with a leg numbed by a sudden sharp jab to his thigh. The third, the smoker, was more wary and fell back, his mouth opening wide to shout for help. The bar they had left was still close. There were people within earshot.

Nothing came out of his mouth. He made no sound when Lot whirled him around, an arm crooked about his neck in a sleeper hold. Lot made no sound either, nor did Benedict as he charged up. Silence fell around Lot like a curtain when he wished, a talent he had learned from an Assamite, the dark assassins of the vampire clans. It was a very useful talent. He gestured sharply to an alley beside the bar the men had just left. Benedict nodded and grabbed one of the men, hustling him quickly off the street. Lot carried the other two.

Benedict was already feeding when Lot caught up to him. His prey's eyes were white in the dimness, rolled back in the spasms of horrid bliss. Benedict's lips were sealed to the man's throat and his own throat worked hard and fast. No blood escaped his eager hunger. He grasped the man almost tenderly, as though he were a lover.

One of the men that Lot held, the one whose legs he had numbed, began to whimper in terror. Lot tossed him back against the alley wall hard enough to daze him. He shifted his grip on the third man, holding him up by his shirtfront, allowing his unconscious head to loll back. Lot's fangs descended with the tiniest, sharpest of stings. He drew back his lips. He leaned forward. He bit down. Warm blood filled his mouth. The man in his grasp groaned, the helpless pleasure of the prey in the jaws of the predator that had always sent a thrill of ecstasy through Lot. The vampire bit down harder.

The man he had thrown against the wall recovered enough of his wits to start screaming.

Lot glanced at him without ceasing to feed. His legs still numb, the man was pressed back against the wall, his fingers scrabbling for some purchase that would allow him to drag himself away. His screams were pitiful, high-pitched and mewling. Still, they would attract attention. Lot pushed his prey away, thrusting him toward Benedict. The Ravnos flung out an arm and caught him. His mouth came away from the throat of his original victim. A single trickle of blood dripped from the corner of his lips. In his velvet frock-coat, with his curling golden hair, the flush of feeding staining his face, and a man languishing in helpless, debauched ecstasy in either arm, he looked like some demonic rake. For a moment, the man against the wall stopped screaming and stared at Benedict in silence. Then he began to whimper again. Lot reached down for him.

Desperately, the man pushed at the vampire's arm, trying to shove him away. "Please," he gasped, "I've got family at home."

"Maybe you should have been with them tonight."

"Oh, God. Jesus. Sweet fucking Jesus." The man fumbled for something at his throat. Lot saw the flash of a gold chain with something hanging from it. A little gold cross. He drew the man to his feet, brushing aside the hand that pushed at him, the hand that tried to present the holy crucifix. Lot just pulled him nearer. An ungodly stench filled the air as the man's terror emptied his bowels. Lot simply stopped breathing. He shoved the man's head back, baring his throat. The pulse thundered under his jaw and Lot bent his own head to nuzzle the throbbing vein. Rough whiskers scratched his lips as he drove in his fangs. The man shuddered one last time.

They left the bodies in the alley. Someone would find them. The deaths would be attributed to muggers or perhaps random violence, the true circumstances of the men's passing covered up by High Father Truth and his media-manipulating priests. Anyone who might claim knowledge of what had really happened would quietly disappear. Father Truth took his responsibilities seriously. Lot and Benedict walked back out to the street, warm from stolen blood and slightly drunk from alcohol stolen along with it. There were three drops of blood on Benedict's shirt, the only sign of what had taken place. The jogger Benedict had seen before passed them going the other way. Benedict gave him a lecherous smile and followed him with his eyes.

"No," Lot said firmly. "Enough."

The blond vampire walked in sullen silence until they were back to Lot's car. As the

Tzimisce unlocked the car doors, Benedict asked him, "So—do you think there's any truth to the rumors about Fletcher?"

Lot froze, then opened his door. "It's not," he replied slowly, "my place to comment. I've sworn an oath—"

"Damn your oath!" Benedict slapped the roof of the car. "Do you think Fletcher tricked Michael into going into the Box? You knew Michael as well as I did. You know Fletcher as well as I do. He's vicious. You'd almost think he was a Malkavian instead of a Gangrel. He's nuts! He wants to hunt something and humans aren't enough. He can't go after the Camarilla as long as they stick to the Settlement and stay in the Box. He can't go after Sabbat unless they go into the Box against the terms of the Settlement. If he wants a hunt, he has to manufacture a situation! Do you think Fletcher tricked Michael into the Box?" He grimaced. "Do you think he'd do it again?"

"What are you saying?" Lot paused with one hand on the open door. His eyes narrowed. "Do you think Fletcher would try to get us to go into the Box?"

Benedict shook his head. "No. Not exactly. I mean, we've already thought of it—he couldn't trick us now. But aren't you afraid he might try to pin something on us? He's dangerous, Lot."

Lot got into the car and sat there in silence. "I swore an oath."

"You made a mistake." Benedict sighed. "Hell, we both made mistakes. Fletcher's not going anywhere. He's not stable enough to hold down a position with any more responsibility. He's barely stable enough to hold down the position he has now."

"I'm not listening to this," Lot growled. He put his key in the ignition and turned it, bringing the engine to life and almost drowning out Benedict's voice. Almost but not quite.

"I think we should go to the Archbishop, Lot. I think we should have Fletcher removed before he does something really stupid." The Ravnos must have mistaken Lot's silence for tacit approval of his suggestion, because after a moment's pause he added, "And I think we should ask the Archbishop to appoint you in his place."

The steering wheel groaned under the pressure of Lot's grip. "That's treason," Lot hissed.

"No. You know I'm right about Fletcher, and I know I'm right about you. You'd be perfect. Fletcher hates the Camarilla. He was a terrible choice for bishop. You're calm—" Benedict got into the car and shot a glance at Lot's white-knuckled grip on the steering wheel.

"—Usually. You're disciplined. You'd be better for the Sabbat." He closed the door behind him. "It comes down to that, doesn't it? If Dyce removes Fletcher as bishop and puts you in his place, it might grate against your discipline and your oath of loyalty to Fletcher, but isn't your loyalty to the Sabbat more important?"

Lot slammed the car grimly into gear. Benedict looked away.

The trouble was, the Ravnos was right.

Loyalty was the mortar that held the Sabbat together. The sect had been born out of rebellion and an intense desire for freedom, freedom from manipulation by powerful elder vampires, freedom from fear of discovery by humans. The Sabbat was total freedom. Like so many of the rebellions that had striven for freedom throughout history, though, the total freedom that the Sabbat stood for had almost been its downfall. Only loyalty kept it from flying apart; most Sabbat vampires were devoted to the sect. For the cause of the Sabbat, they would repress their own desires and ambitions and surrender some portion of their current freedom in return for greater future freedom. The desire for freedom drove the Sabbat, but intense loyalty pushed it from behind. Lot had attached himself to Fletcher to further his own ambitions, swearing loyalty to the bishop to cement that attachment. If Lot and Benedict removed him now—especially if Benedict recommended Lot to fill the vacant position—he would be breaking his oath to Fletcher. If he didn't help Benedict depose the violent bishop, though... he would be acting against the good of the Sabbat.

His sworn loyalty to Fletcher or his innate loyalty to the Sabbat?

There was really only one choice. He knew it. So did Benedict. Lot wasn't sure he liked that. The blond vampire had sworn no oaths to Fletcher. His service to the bishop was solely a function of his ambition. His loyalty to the Sabbat, however, was unquestionable.

Lot pulled up outside Fletcher's warehouse haven. The room he called his own haven was inside, close to the sleeping chamber of his master. Benedict sometimes stayed at the warehouse, but not always. He had another haven somewhere else. Somewhere he could go when Fletcher became much more than he could stand. Lot looked at the Ravnos.

"Tomorrow night," he said quietly. "Tomorrow night at the Fire Dance. We'll be able to talk to the Archbishop."

Benedict nodded silently. The two vampires

got out of the car without saying anything else and went inside. The warehouse was empty. Fletcher was out somewhere. Lot was grateful for small favors.

CHAPTER THREE

As the hours of darkness wore on, Bianka talked with many of the Camarilla at Savage Garden. They were an insular group, distrustful of outsiders and particularly, as she was told throughout the night by Swan, of mixed blood Kindred. Actually, they weren't *accustomed* to outsiders of any type—she was the first that most of them had seen. Other than the Sabbat, and few of the Camarilla had even seen *them*. A more worldly group of Camarilla would have distrusted her *because* she confessed to having been Embraced by two Sires. But to this group, so bored with their prison, she was more exotic than dangerous.

The individuals formed a whole that gave off a unified vibration of despair, almost an odor. They were like caged creatures, pacing the same small territory, gazing with both fear and longing at the freedom outside their invisible walls. The group, she learned, had not grown appreciably since they had been given the Box. Only three new Kindred had been Embraced, and none of the old members had left. It was unclear, in fact *they* seemed unclear, about whether the Sabbat would allow them to step outside the Box to leave the city. She couldn't help but see them as prisoners, so long incarcerated that they didn't think clearly anymore.

Reg may have been the most honest of the group—she had always overindulged her own

Toreador energies, and felt a natural affinity toward him, more so than toward Swan. The others, including Swan, mouthed the words of rebellion, but their hearts weren't in it. The romantic vampire didn't bother with that type of artifice. He wasn't interested in politics and made that clear. He'd resigned himself to existence in the Box, making the best of a bad situation. Bianka could relate to that. He reserved his intrigue for seduction, and he even tried it with her.

She sat on a white oak church pew beneath the skylight, staring up at the full moon poised in the sky.

"A lovely pale visage," Reg said from behind her, his voice satin-seductive. His good hand caressed her long hair, stopping at her neck, parting the strands to reach her skin. He gripped the back of her neck as a human lover would. "Almost as lovely as your face."

Her instinct was to laugh. On the other hand, no one, living or undead, had spoken to her like this in... in a long long time. She reached behind and moved his hand away. "Tell me, Reg. You don't seem angry about what the Sabbat did to you. That strikes me as odd. Even Byron and Shelley let it fly on occasion."

He shrugged as he came around to the front of the pew. His blue eyes reminded her of sapphires, the moonlight glinting off them like blue sparks that refused to move too far away from the source of heat.

"The thing with the Sabbat, it's over. Like most of the recent past. Farther back in time interests me, and the future is always intriguing to speculate about—besides, you never know what can happen." He rubbed his damaged hand and gave her a captivating smile. The humans must love him.

"But since I've been here I've become like an Impressionist. All the fine aspects of life blend together and at the same time I see them separately. I'm busy studying that. Let the others shout slogans and whine about their fate. It's boring."

"An isolationist's approach? You'd make a good Inconnu."

"Absolutely. But my way of thinking makes sense."

"If you can buy into bullshit, and I don't!" Swan had come up behind him.

Watching the two of them spar, Bianka felt like she was watching the two halves of herself war against one another.

Reg didn't turn around. One corner of his mouth lifted, and the other dropped. He winked at Bianka and shook his long hair, like a lion shaking its mane, in Swan's face. She shoved him from behind, but he obviously was expecting something—his feet didn't move, just his upper body, a bit. Reg laughed, turned and headed for an Oriental beauty exiting the washroom that had "Either/Or" on the door. The human's silver-painted eyelids matched her silver acrylic nails. The claws extended at least two inches from her fingertips, and Bianka studied Reg as he watched the woman slide the nails of one hand down her throat to her breasts, which swelled over the top of a tight leather bustier. Reg would be having a good time.

"When they Embraced him, his balls dried up," Swan said, a look of disgust on her face.

"Sit with me," Bianka said, looking up, gently patting the space next to her on the bench.

Swan hesitated.

"Please? I'd like to talk with you."

Swan was suspicious by nature—Brujah usually are—and Bianka made her antennae rise up even higher. Her physical presence was powerful; she could obviously handle herself, and Bianka doubted she would hesitate to face a Sabbat one-on-one. Which made the confrontation the night Reg was maimed curious. She wanted the psychological details.

Swan sat, her legs apart, muscles tensed as if she expected the worst at any second. She pulled a skinny cigar out of the fatigue jacket she wore over a tight PVC tank top, sucked on the end, and struck the wooden match against the pew seat.

"I'm surprised you put up with this," Bianka said.

Swan's head snapped in her direction, inches

from Ravena; the lit match paused in mid-air, and the bird stared at the flame suspiciously. "What are you getting at?"

"You know what I mean. The confinement. The humiliation. You don't seem the type to balk at a brawl."

Swan laughed savagely. She lit the cigar and pitched the still-lit match ahead of her. A guy wearing K-Docs unconsciously smashed the flame with his boot sole as he passed.

"Why are you really here?" Swan looked Bianka directly in the eye. Bianka willed the Brujah's vision lower. She could feel Swan fighting, but power of 10th Gen was no match for 5th. Swan stared at Bianka's lips. The red flesh separated and spread apart slowly, exposing the tips of fangs, then Bianka pressed her lips together again, slowly, and repeated that movement.

Swan said, her voice dull, "I feel you controlling me. Stop it!"

"I'm concerned about your safety."

"Bullshit!"

"The eyes are the windows of the soul. If you look too long into anyone's eyes, you lose yourself."

"Who the hell are you? And how did you get into the Box? You're Sabbat, admit it!"

Ravena squawked twice, startling Swan, who scowled at the bird. "Yeah, up yours too, culture vulture!"

Bianka laughed, breaking the spell. "Swan, you're something, I'll give you that. You aren't afraid of anybody or anything. That's why I can't understand why you didn't take out those Sabbat who wounded Reg."

Swan sucked in her cheeks, forcing her lower lip out. It made her look tough and pouty at the same time, a bit like the corpse of a three-year-old. "Maybe I wasn't in the mood."

"I don't believe you."

"Listen, Brujah/Toreador, you tell me something, I'll tell you. That's the way I play."

Bianka folded her arms across her chest. She really did like this Brujah. Kindred with spirit always appealed to her. The Brujah in her blood felt some kind of linking here. At least Swan wasn't ready to roll over and play dead.

"Look, I'm being straight with you, because I'm straight with everybody—that's just the way I'm wired," Bianka said. "I came here to try to persuade you all to rejoin the main body of Camarilla."

"You already said that. Give me something new to suck on."

Ravena turned her head and tilted it, staring at Swan, but she didn't squawk. Maybe Swan had some avian connection besides her name. "All right, here's the situation. The Camarilla want you all back in the fold. There's a certain... guilt—"

"Right!"

"As much guilt as Kindred can feel. Maybe it's more a kind of missing a piece of the puzzle. Whatever, the consensus is that you guys were abandoned, left to the merciless Sabbat. The Sect wants you back."

Swan had watched Bianka's hands portray the story her lips told. She glanced at Ravena. The raven stared, unintimidated. Swan smiled a little, and Bianka was astonished at the change this made in the Kindred's face. The hard lines smoothed out and she went from being a dehydrated corpse to something resembling a human.

Swan reached out to touch Ravena's beak. Bianka was about to warn her—the bird had a nasty habit of snapping off digits—but contact had already been made. For the second time in seconds, Bianka was astounded. Yes, she *really* liked this Brujah, and was coming to respect her.

Ravena let herself be stroked, the beak, then the downy feathers between her eyes....

You're doing fine, she told the raven, who she could feel was tense.

Suddenly Swan stared into Bianka's eyes. Bianka glanced away. No sense losing the strongest one.

"So, half-breed, you've painted a pleasant story with your magic hands. And your black bird didn't claw me to shit. And I heard what you said before, but there's more, isn't there. I wanna hear that too."

Bianka had no reason to hide anything. And she was incapable of lying. Fortunately, none of the Kindred knew that about her. It was a fatal weakness that left her vulnerable, her one real unprotected area. She wasn't about to reveal it. In fact, she'd learned to use it, turning this weakness into a strength, because so few of the undead and humans expected honesty.

"The Camarilla can't take you back as you are. It would be a disgrace. For you. For them."

Swan's hackles went up immediately. Before she could get roiling, Bianka held up a hand. "Let me finish this. Yes, the Camarilla left you here, yes you've been virtually defenseless against the Sabbat. I know how vicious they are, and there are a hundred times as many in this city as there are of you in the Box. That's not the point. The point is, you've lost face."

Swan looked furious. Bianka touched her upper arm. Ravena bent her head down, bridging the distance between them.

Good move, she assured the bird.

"Swan, I'm not putting you down. I know you tried—I can see it in you, in everything you are. But you've got to face facts. The Camarilla in the Box have given up. And unless you show some spirit, some respect for yourselves, the Camarilla not only won't take you back, they won't *want* you back."

"Fuck them! We don't even *want* to come back—"

"That's not the point, and you know it. Each of you should have the choice."

"Why, because *they* think we're wimps?"

"No. Because *you* think that, don't you?"

Swan tore her arm from Bianka's grasp. The older vampire expected the younger, more volatile one, to bolt, or attack. But, amazingly, she stayed put, although she was seething, that was clear.

They sat listening to the music. Dracul, the German band, came over the speakers. The bass vibration rocked the floor beneath their feet as the lead singer howled and screeched and hissed to the music.

Finally, Swan turned to Bianka. The fury in her eyes was just short of explosion level. But behind that Bianka saw a deep wound. The humiliation had been almost unbearable for this one.

"Why didn't I splatter their bloody guts all over the sidewalk?" Swan said. "Because I was alone. Yeah, there were four of them and four of us. That's not what I mean."

"The others… they didn't have the will."

Swan looked like she wanted to rip out Bianka's voice box for verbalizing that. But she sat, holding onto the rage and the pain. The space around the three of them—Bianka, Swan and Ravena—became like an invisible cylinder. What was happening outside dimmed. Inside, a connection of sorts was taking place, one so delicate and fragile that Bianka was afraid to move, afraid of shattering the spell.

Finally, she touched the Brujah's thigh and let Swan look in her eyes for a split second. Only a split second. In that fragment of time, Bianka had a glimpse inside; one large pink tear welled in Swan's right eye and slid quickly down her cheek. To save Swan from too much memory loss, Bianka looked away. Ravena, though, pecked at the tear, drinking it down, and then squawked, shattering the imaginary glass that contained them.

At that moment, Reg walked up, oblivious to what had been going on. "Seen Shadow?"

"Why don't you get a leash for her!" Swan snapped, rubbing her eye.

Bianka stood. She felt drained; she needed space. The Beast was too close for formalities—she had to get out. "I'll be back," she said.

All the way to the door Ravena squawked. *I know! I just need!* Bianka stopped only long enough to have her arm stamped with a day-glo bat so that she would be readmitted to the club.

The night sang her name. But the streets were too congested. People. Cars. Smells that irritated her, that fed the Beast. She needed more space. She climbed a fire escape at the back of the building, up, past the second, third, up to the fifth and top floor, and then to the roof. She spotted the skylight below, the third floor of the Savage Garden building. Through the glass with her superior vision, she saw Swan and Reg sitting on the pew down below.

She raced across building roofs, soaring over

the spaces between. Ravena left her shoulder to flap around her head. At the speed she moved, the air up here flowed past like satin against her skin, stilling her thoughts and emotions, encouraging her to *become* the air, to become the night. And for a second the Beast vanished.

Only one thing could make this better. Vitae. She longed to be fed by the night, to drink her fill, to leave her body and mind and what was left of her soul behind and... meld.

She could smell it. Taste it. Blood, rising to meet her nostrils, to weave a path inside her, down her throat, saturating her insides, expanding her until she exploded and became the darkness. Until she disappeared!

The scream brought her to her senses, and the glass shattering.

She leapt down in a split second, roof, down to lower roof, down until her feet touched ground, then she raced inside and up the steps of Savage Garden.

Music pounded, but the humans were not moving to it now.

They had formed a circle and Bianka pushed her way through to the center.

Like a distorted *Pietà*, Swan sat on the pew, holding a bloodied Kindred in her arms. A stray bit of glass from the shattered skylight fell through the air, but most of it already paved the black floor with ice. Reg knelt before them, holding Shadow's hand; Bianka knew it was Shadow, from the description.

The Neonate's blood gushed from wounds that could only have been made with talons. Talons that knew where to cut, and just how deep. Deep enough that even a 10th Gen might not survive. There was no hope for this baby.

Bianka and the other Camarilla surrounded them, tightening the circle. A dying Kindred needed to be protected from prying human eyes. Shadow may have been beautiful, but there was nothing left of her face now that would attest to that. Gouges ran across her forehead, down her cheeks; her nose was gone. All the veins in her neck, her elbows, her wrists, all the vulnerable places where they were close to the surface, every vein had been severed. The deepest wounds were in her chest; Bianka saw her heart through the giant hole, barely beating, nearly sliced in two.

She bent low, smelling the blood that incited her lust, but instead focused her energy. "Did you see who?"

Reg was crouched down before Shadow. The expiring Kindred whispered something, and Reg put his ear to her lips. Then Shadow shuddered once, as if the cold had penetrated her bones, and she lay still as a statue.

Reg leaned back. He and Swan had obviously seen death. A lot of it. But one of their own was always more horrifying.

"What did she say?" Bianka asked—it was crucial to find out what Shadow knew.

Reg stared blankly at Bianka, missing the power of her eyes—he was already mesmerized by horror. "It was the Sabbat. Who else?" But he turned his eyes away.

Ravena squawked. *No!* Bianka admonished, giving the bird a look. Ravena did not back down easily, but tonight she did, because

Bianka would not. *Let them find out for themselves!* she told the animal.

The raven turned its back, so that it faced away from Bianka, rejecting both her and the massacre. Bianka steeled herself. This was working out to her benefit. The Camarilla were upset. They would need guidance. She just had to stay cool, get them past the distrust, and then do what she had come here to do.

Shadow's body looked shriveled already. The life-force was gone. "We've got to get her out of here," Bianka said, trying to jolt the others back to their senses. The Masquerade wouldn't hold up for long if the humans took Shadow's body.

At that moment, DeWinter stepped into the circle. His voice was controlled, authoritative, low enough so that only Kindred could hear. "Swan, carry her to the haven. The rest of you, move through the club—she drank too much and fell. She'll be all right."

Like zombies coming to life, the others began to move, doing as DeWinter had directed. Swan stood, the dead Kindred in her arms.

"I'll help you," Bianka said. And before Swan could reject her, she added, "I know you don't need my help physically. But the humans—it would be better if there were two of us carrying her."

This made sense to the Brujah. She got on one side of Shadow, and Bianka on the other. One of the dead Kindred's arms was thrown over each of their shoulders. Ravena hopped onto a shoulder.

As they moved toward the door, DeWinter suddenly appeared before them. "You know what to do," he said to Swan. She nodded.

And then he turned to Bianka. All the madness he had displayed earlier had subsided, replaced by cold logic, backed by position and authority. "And you. Don't try to leave the Box!"

CHAPTER FOUR

Out along the lakeshore, far toward Toronto's east end, vampires of the border packs had begun working almost before the sun was below the horizon. Dry wood was piled into great heaps, huge pyres that would light up the night. Raised up on bluffs, the flames of the Fire Dance would be visible from far out on the lake. That didn't matter to the Sabbat. What could humans do to them? Gasoline was splashed over the wood. There were two smaller piles and a third that was almost twice as large, the three forming the points of a triangle. In the center of the triangle was a cauldron—a real one, huge, black, and heavy, stolen from an open-air pioneer village museum—suspended by chains from a crossed tripod of posts.

Other vampires began to arrive later, filtering in from all parts of Metro Toronto. Some came thrashing wildly through the woods to the open space where the Fire Dance would be held. The overgrown night was their playground. Some came in cars, trucks, and motorcycles, roaring and bouncing along paths and roads never meant for motor vehicles. The silent darkness shattered. The vampires screamed and shouted and whooped. They laughed. A car, a big luxury model stolen for the occasion, was sent racing over the bluffs to crash in greasy flames on the rocks below. Shallow water carried burning gas along the shore in fiery threads. The Sabbat howled in joy. Some of the vampires had brought mortal "guests" with them. The humans died slowly, passed around like bottles of wine.

Lot, Benedict, and Fletcher came through the woods. The bishop led the way. His shapechanging powers were strong enough to allow him to turn himself into a wolf—though they did little to hide his true nature. The animal-Fletcher, much like the man, was big and heavy and stinking. It barely resembled a wolf at all. Instead, it looked more like a feral dog, a huge, shaggy mastiff. In any case, it was a shape better suited to the woods than human-form. Fletcher slipped through the undergrowth easily, eyes red in the darkness. Lot followed more slowly, but smoothly, sharp senses enabling him to avoid the low-hanging branches that Fletcher ducked beneath and the thorny bushes that the Gangrel skirted narrowly. At times it seemed as though Fletcher were going out of his way to make the journey difficult and potentially embarrassing for Lot. Lot knew that it would gall Fletcher that he was able to follow.

Benedict, on the other hand, was far behind. He swore loudly and often, cursing every tree branch that snapped into his face, every thorn that snagged his pants, and every patch of mud that squelched under his boots. He had persuaded Lot to carry his frock-coat for him before they were even a hundred yards into the trees.

They emerged from the woods into the middle of the Sabbat party. Fletcher turned, the gloating in his eyes dying swiftly as Lot stepped quietly into the open behind him. A growl twisted his wolfish lips. He shook his shoulders, then reared back onto his hind legs. His wolf-form fell away from him. His lips, however, remained twisted. The bishop had been in an especially surly mood ever since he had come home just before dawn last night, freshly fed, hands and face red, to find Lot still awake and waiting for him. He had gone straight to his sleeping room without saying a word.

He remained silent now as he turned to join the fray of the party. Lot took a step after him. Fletcher stiffened. "You're dismissed, Lot," he snapped. "I don't think I need your protection here." He swung around to glare at the dark-haired vampire. "Get lost."

"If you're certain—"

"I am!" Fletcher stalked away, vanishing into the crowd of vampires.

Lot watched him leave. Fletcher would enjoy himself tonight. The Fire Dance was a time for savagery. Fletcher's element. He might even forget all about his servants. Benedict came out of the woods with a final curse. Lot held out the blond vampire's frock-coat. "He's gone."

"Good." Benedict dragged a twig out of his curls, brushed off his pants, and straightened his tie and waistcoat. He had dressed his flashiest tonight. No less than Fletcher, he enjoyed a party—although his idea of a good time was perhaps a little more civilized than Fletcher's. He took his frock-coat from Lot and slipped it on, twitching the sleeves and shoulders straight. He looked around. "Then we can find the Archbishop without worrying about him."

"If we can find the Archbishop."

"He'll be around." Benedict craned his neck,

looking over the heads of the crowd of vampires. "Probably in the thick of things."

Lot grabbed his sleeve and tugged him forward. "First the cauldron."

Benedict grimaced. "Why do you have to turn everything into a ritual?"

"Because this *is* a ritual." Lot propelled the Ravnos between the piles of gas-soaked wood and toward the cauldron. Other vampires clustered around it, stepping forward and then moving away, never staying for more than a few moments. Two big vampires from a border pack, their faces and naked torsos decorated with battle scars, stood watch over the black pot. Under their gaze, Lot stepped up to the cauldron. Fletcher was just walking away. Lot avoided looking at the bishop. Instead, he bent down and slid a bone-handled knife out of a sheath in his boot. With a swift slashing motion, he drew the sharp blade down the length of his forearm. Blood gushed, pattering into the cauldron and mixing with the blood that other Sabbat had contributed. He passed the knife to Benedict, who wrapped one hand around the blade, slicing deep into his palm, letting his blood run into the cauldron as well. Every Sabbat in attendance tonight would do the same.

Benedict's cut hand was healed before they had pushed their way back through the vampires around the cauldron. Lot's arm, cut more deeply, took a little longer to heal, but when it did, there was not trace of the injury. He replaced the knife in his boot.

"There," said Benedict. "I see the Archbishop." He pointed. Dyce stood in the midst of a heavy knot of vampires, taking the remaining blood of one of the last humans present. The Archbishop was tall, with close-cropped blond hair and a face like Apollo. His mouth was pressed against the human's throat. Other vampires licked at the human's fingers, arms, and legs. There were perhaps half a dozen of them clinging like leeches to the mortal, and just as many clustered around. "Was I right? In the thick of things."

"Too much in the thick." Lot frowned. "I don't want to talk to him now. Not with so many others around."

"When then? We have to do it before the Fire Dance starts."

"After the sermon. Before the Vaulderie. Everyone else will rush up to participate. Dyce always hangs back until near the end so everyone is lost in vinculum when they watch him participate. It enhances his popularity." Benedict blinked. Lot raised an eyebrow. "You never noticed?"

"No."

"Lost in vinculum. That's the idea." He tapped Benedict's forehead. "Wait and watch this time." He glanced at his wristwatch. "It's almost midnight. Let's try to get as close to the Archbishop as we can before the sermon starts."

They were within a few feet of Dyce when a sudden flare of light lit the site of the Fire Dance. Vampires holding burning torches stood in a broad circle around the three great pyres. Every Sabbat present stopped whatever they were doing instantly and turned to face the center of the circle. Any human still alive died in that moment. The Archbishop snapped the neck of the man he had been feeding on with no more thought than he might have given to slapping at a mosquito.

Precious Annette stood beside the blood-filled cauldron. There was a book in her hands, a heavy book bound in black and filled with scraps of pasted-down paper and fragments of scribbled writings in a dozen different hands. It was a copy—or rather, a collection of copies taken from scattered pieces—of the Book of Nod. The testament of Caine, Sire of all vampires. Annette looked out at the gathered Sabbat and spoke, reading:

"Then one day our Father said to us, 'Caine, Abel, to Him Above you must make a sacrifice— a gift of the first part of all that you have.' And I, first-born Caine, I gathered the tender shoots, the brightest fruits, the sweetest grass. And Abel, second-born, Abel slaughtered the youngest, the strongest, the sweetest of his animals. On the altar of our Father, we laid our sacrifices and lit fire under them and watched the smoke carry them up

to the One Above. *The sacrifice of Abel, second-born, smelled sweet to the One Above and Abel was blessed."*

It was a familiar story, the cursing of Caine. All had heard it before, but none stirred before its majestic, tragic simplicity. Lot knew four variations of the story, alternate tales that differed in subtle ways. This was the most common form of the origin of vampires, accepted by both Sabbat and Camarilla, though the Camarilla interpreted it differently, just as they mistranslated or ignored other parts of the Book. Their ignorance was their loss.

"And I, first-borne Caine, I was struck from beyond by a harsh word and a curse, for my sacrifice was unworthy. I looked at Abel's sacrifice, still smoking, the flesh, the blood. I cried, I held my eyes. I prayed in night and day. And when Father said the time for Sacrifice has come again, and Abel led his youngest, his sweetest, his most beloved to the sacrificial fire, I did not bring my youngest, my sweetest, for I knew the One Above would not want them. And my brother, beloved Abel said to me 'Caine, you did not bring a

sacrifice, a gift of the first part of your joy, to burn on the altar of the One Above.'" Precious Annette turned slightly, shifting her gaze around the assembled vampires. "I cried tears of love as I, with sharp things, sacrificed that which was the first part of my joy, my brother.

"And the Blood of Abel covered the altar and smelled sweet as it burned. But my Father said 'Cursed are you, Caine, who killed your brother. As I was cast out so shall you be.' And He exiled me to wander in Darkness, the land of Nod."

The vampires shifted now, old anger sweeping through many of them at the injustice of devotion damned. There was no need for Annette to explain the story. The genesis of the Children of Caine was read at all sermons to stir the memories in the vampires' blood. Annette waited a moment for the murmuring in her audience to subside, then turned to a new section of the Book of Nod. She looked up.

"What are we?" she asked.

The crowd knew the answers. "We are vampires!"

"Who are we?"

"We are Sabbat!"

"What is the Sabbat?"

"Free!"

"Free from what?"

This time the crowd paused, each vampire thinking of an answer. A flurry of responses flew through the air. "From fear!" "From weakness!" "From human morality!" Then one voice rang out. "Does it matter?"

Every head turned in the direction of that voice. Archbishop Dyce's face and hair shone in the torchlight. Precious Annette nodded. "The Sabbat is freedom from all things, but especially from enslavement and manipulation. Hear, Children of Caine, the tale of Caine's Enslavement."

Annette began to read again, but this time there was no respectful silence. The tale of Caine's Enslavement had become a parable for the loathing that many vampires felt for those who would control them. Whenever it was read, the story was greeted with catcalls, hatred, and derision—directed not at the reader, but at the characters in the story. Annette's voice almost vanished into the bedlam of anger.

"One night Caine came upon an old Crone singing to the moon. Caine said to the Crone, 'Why do you sing so?' And the Crone replied, 'Because I yearn for what I cannot have....' Caine said to the Crone, 'I yearn also. What can one do?' The Crone smiled and said, 'Drink of my blood this night, Caine, Father of Death, and return tomorrow night. Then, will I tell you the wisdom of the Moon.' Caine drank at the Crone's bare neck, and departed.

"The next night, Caine found the Crone sleeping on a rock. 'Wake up, Crone,' Caine said. 'I have returned.' The Crone opened one eye and said, 'I dream of the solution for you this night. Drink once more of me, and then return tomorrow night. Bring a bowl of clay. Bring a sharp knife. I will have your answer then.' Once again, Caine took blood from the Crone, who immediately fell back into a deep slumber.

"When Caine returned the next night, the Crone looked up at him and smiled. 'Greetings,

Lord of the Beast,' the Crone said. 'I have the wisdom you seek. Take some of my blood into your bowl and mix in these berries and these herbs, and drink deep of the elixir. You will be irresistible. You will be masterful. You will be ardent. You will be glowing. The heart of Zillah will melt like the snows in spring.'

"And so, Caine drank from the Crone's elixir."

The story was approaching its climax and the anger of the vampires its crescendo. Benedict was screaming curses next to him, drowning out Annette's reading even for Lot's heightened senses. It didn't matter. He knew this story, too, and again in variations. His favorite variation was not the one that Annette read anyway. The version he preferred included an obscure stanza that described the flavor of the Crone's potion. In the midst of the screaming madness of the vampires, Lot watched Annette's lips silently, the remainder of the tale repeating itself in his memories.

The elixir was bitter, bitter beyond ashes, bitter beyond the Curse. But Caine drank from the

Crone's elixir, because he was blind in his love of Zillah, and he so desired her love in return.

And the Crone laughed. The Crone laughed aloud. She had tricked him! She had trapped him! Caine was angry beyond compare. Caine reached out with his powers, to rend this crone apart with his strength. The Crone cackled and said, "Do not." And Caine could do nothing against her. The Crone chuckled and said, "Love me." And Caine could do nothing but stare into her ancient eyes, desire her leathery skin. The Crone laughed and said, "Make me immortal." And Caine Embraced her, suckling at her withered dugs, then giving her suck at his own breast. She cackled again, laughed with the pure ecstasy of the Embrace, for it did not pain her.

"I have made you powerful, Caine of Enoch, Caine of Nod, but you will forever be bound to me. I have made you master of all, but you will never forget me! Your blood, potent as it is now, will bond those who drink it, as you did, once a night for three nights. You will be the master. They will be your thrall, as you are mine."

Annette snapped shut the Book of Nod. Majestic power surrounded her as she exerted her will over the crowd of screaming vampires, not to enslave them, but to make herself heard.

"That is the Blood Bond!" she called. "The way of the Camarilla, the way of weak, manipulating elders! The Blood Bond makes one vampire the slave of another. Will the Sabbat submit to the Blood Bond?"

"Never!"

"Our loyalty is to the sect! Our loyalty is freely given!" Annette stepped up to the cauldron. "This is the sign of our loyalty: the vinculum that ties one Sabbat to every other! The rite of Vaulderie!" It seemed impossible that the shouting of the vampires could intensify, but it did. Annette brought her wrist to her mouth and tore at the skin with her teeth. Blood seeped down, dripping into blood.

"This is my blood. Drink and be strong." Someone handed her a cup and a dipper. She stirred the dipper in the cauldron and brought it up, pouring red blood from dipper to cup in a dark stream. Abrupt silence fell over the crowd.

"This is your blood." She raised the cup to her mouth and swallowed. Three times. Drinking deep. She lowered the cup and smiled. Her fangs had emerged and redness spilled over her chin.

"I drink and am strong in your strength." She flung her arms out and her head back, calling to the sky, challenging the cold stars. "Let the Children of Caine defy their damnation! Let all participate in Vaulderie and know the strength of unity!"

A renewed roar surged out of the vampires and they rushed forward, eager for a turn at the cauldron of mingled blood. Lot grabbed Benedict. "Dyce," he reminded him firmly.

"But the Vaulderie—" Benedict's fangs had also descended. The Ravnos was caught up in the sheer thrill of the sermon and the rite of shared blood.

"Will wait. There's lots of blood. If the Archbishop can be patient, so can we." He propelled Benedict toward Dyce. The Archbishop was alone, pacing slowly after the other vampires. "You talk."

Benedict stumbled, then recovered himself. The Archbishop had already turned, looking at both of them. He continued to walk. "Your Grace," Benedict said hastily.

Dyce nodded. "Benedict of Ravnos. Lot of Tzimisce." He reached out to pull Benedict into a casual embrace as he moved. "You'll share in the Vaulderie with me?"

"We would be honored, your Grace, but there is something else we want to discuss with you. Our master—"

"Bishop Fletcher."

"Yes. The bishop." Benedict threw Lot a quick glance as if appealing for support. Lot nodded back. *Get on with it.* They were drawing near to the fringes of the crowd around the cauldron. They were going to miss their chance. Benedict smiled at the Archbishop. "Lot and I are concerned that Fletcher may no longer be capable of fulfilling the demands of his position."

Dyce's face remained clear, but his eyes became as dark as a stormy sky. "Does this have anything to do with the rumors about Michael?"

"Yes, but—"

"I have answered those rumors already, Benedict. I find no wrong doing on Fletcher's part—he carried out the task that was demanded of him with speed, efficiency, and commendable devotion. He is a true servant of the Sabbat. As am I—and as, I hope, are you." The Archbishop raised a single eyebrow.

Benedict folded like cheap paper. Lot stepped in quickly. "We don't question your judgment, you Grace. We only want what's best for the sect. Bishop Fletcher's stability is what concerns us."

That gave the Archbishop pause. "In what way?"

"He's sharp. He's violent. He's prone to sudden outbursts."

"None of which are uncommon among vampires. Particularly among the vampires of the Sabbat."

Lot clenched his teeth. "We're worried that

Fletcher's outbursts and violence might damage the Settlement."

"There is nothing that the Camarilla of the Box could do to us, Lot—even if the Settlement did collapse. Even if they had the strength to try something. Which they don't." Dyce looked at Lot directly for the first time. "The Settlement and the Box are not the center of my universe. You're a levelheaded vampire, Lot. I know that. But Fletcher is ideal for his job. He's strong—and, yes, he's violent. The packs are afraid of him. And as long as he's bishop, I know where he is and what he's doing. If he wasn't bishop—" Dyce waved his hand. If Fletcher wasn't a bishop, Dyce would have no way of keeping tabs on him. "Do you have evidence that Fletcher's instability is damaging the Settlement or the Sabbat?"

"No," Lot admitted slowly and regretfully. "Nothing definite. Nothing hard."

"When—if—you have evidence, come to me again. I'll listen. Now," he wrapped his free arm around Lot. "Join me in the Vaulderie, brothers." He kissed each vampire on the forehead and led them forward. The crowd parted before them, red-masked vampires granting their leader clear passage to the cauldron. Precious Annette stood there smiling, cup and dipper in hand. She poured a dipperful of blood into the cup and offered it to Dyce.

He shook his head. "More." Annette filled the cup to the brim. Dyce took it.

"Benedict?"

The Ravnos took the cup and drank. He passed the cup to Lot. It was a large vessel. There was still a lot of blood inside. Lot drank. The cup was still half-full. He returned it to Dyce. The Archbishop raised it over his head. "*And Caine said to dark-winged Uriel,*" he shouted, quoting again from the Book of Nod, "*Not by God's mercy, but my own, will I live. I am what I am, I did what I did, and that will never change!*" The Sabbat howled back at him as he lowered the cup and drank from it, swallowing deeply, not pausing. When he took the cup away from his mouth, he raised it high again, and turned it over. Not a drop of blood spilled out. The howls of the Sabbat were deafening.

On cue, the vampires who had been holding the torches moved in, thrusting fire into the waiting heaps of wood. The gasoline splashed over the piles ignited first, with a hiss of greasy flame, then the wood itself, with a snap and a roar and an explosion of heat. The torchbearers swept in to take their turn at the cauldron as the other vampires began to race out through the heat of the three fires and into the darkness. Chaos bloomed, shadows and dancing light flickering across the swarming Sabbat. Fire was a vampire's enemy, as irresistible as sunlight. The Camarilla feared fire. The Sabbat played with it, fighting their fear. Only in true strength and true courage was there true freedom! Music shrieked and thundered out of the darkness beyond the light. Hard rock, fast, heavy, pounding. Sabbat danced through the edges of the fires, in and back. Some grabbed flaming brands and waved them, juggled them. Spilled blood hissed on burning wood. Ashes made dark patterns on bare skin.

Lot lost the Archbishop in the confusion. Benedict was gone as well, lost to the Fire

Dance. Lot let him go. They had their answer from Dyce. Evidence or nothing. But there was no evidence, only their own feelings. He turned—and met Fletcher's gaze.

The Gangrel stood perhaps fifteen feet away. Rage darkened his face. His jacket was gone. His bulky torso gleamed in the firelight. Great claws sprouted from his fingertips. His teeth, fangs and tusks, parted in a bellow that was barely audible over the pandemonium between the fires. Lot froze. Fletcher couldn't have failed to see his two servants standing with the Archbishop. He couldn't have failed to guess what that might—did—mean. They were conspiring against him. Unless Lot could convince him otherwise.

He walked forward calmly, slowly, nonthreateningly. He watched Fletcher carefully as he did so. Very carefully. The sharpness of his undead senses went beyond normal sight. When he wished to, Lot could see auras, the energy that surrounded every creature, mortal or immortal, revealing emotions, temperament, and health. He watched Fletcher's aura now. It flared smoky crimson, jagged and sharp, licking out toward him like a living thing. He took another step closer. The bishop's aura collapsed back as he tensed his muscles, ready to leap. Lot flung out an open palm. "Wait!" he shouted, hoping Fletcher would hear his voice.

He did. The big vampire's aura flared again as he spat, "What were you doing with the Archbishop?"

"Talking. He asked Benedict and I to join him in the Vaulderie." Fletcher hissed. His aura shifted, still rage crimson, but shot through with the pale green of distrust. Lot amended his explanation. "We wanted to explain the incident with Tanz and Giles to him. In case Tanz had talked to him. We wanted to make it clear that nothing happened. You didn't harm Tanz in any way."

The veins of green spread steadily through Fletcher's aura during Lot's impromptu explanation, but at least they displaced the crimson. The agitation of Fletcher's aura slowed as well. Jagged slashes faded and became smoother. Sharp lashes that might have been attacks before became gentler, more probing. Fletcher was calming down. Lot took another cautious step closer, ignoring the intangible tendrils that caressed him. If Fletcher had been able to see auras, he would have been driven into an absolute fury by the degree to which his own aura betrayed his thoughts.

"Really?" Deep blue, suspicion, whispered along the edge of the bishop's aura. "And what did the Archbishop say to you?"

"He defended your position." The truth, more or less. It was safest to cling to a story that had some basis in reality. "We put forward our arguments, Dyce listened, and then he told us that he would do nothing unless evidence was put before him." Lot spread his hands. "And there's certainly no evidence that you abused Tanz."

"Because I didn't." Fletcher's aura glimmered around his body, not jagged, not reaching out. It was, however, still deep blue. He was suspicious, but at least Lot had talked him out of his murderous rage. Suspicion he could cope with. Lot allowed his vision to drop back into the realm of the strictly physical. Fletcher wasn't finished yet, though. "If Tanz had a complaint with me, he should have challenged me to a duel."

"Tanz hasn't gone to anyone yet," Lot lied. He hoped that Tanz would never mention Fletcher's rage last night to anyone at all. "We beat him to the Archbishop."

"You know what I mean." Fletcher frowned, almost a snarl. "You're always trying to protect me." He thumped his chest. "Maybe I want a fight."

At least he was no longer angry. "I swore an oath to protect you," Lot said tiredly. "It's my duty."

Fletcher snorted derisively. "So you'll keep me away from every danger? How about this, then?" He snatched a chunk of wood out of the nearest fire and tossed it from hand to hand. Flames licked close to his filthy face. "Isn't this dangerous?" Suddenly, he flung the burning wood at Lot. The dark-haired vampire knocked it out of the air. The flames singed his shirt and ignited a patch of grass where the wood landed. Frenzy-driven Sabbat flocked to this new plaything, gleefully stamping it to death. Fletcher laughed. "You want to be my follower and guardian? Then follow me and protect me as best you can. Just make sure you don't get hurt in the bargain!"

He turned and plunged through the edge of the fire behind him. Lot hissed. It was a challenge he couldn't refuse. Fletcher was testing his loyalty. Lot no longer felt especially loyal to the bishop, but he had sworn an oath—and if he didn't follow, Fletcher might very well turn murderous again. Steeling himself, he ran after him.

Most of the Sabbat playing the game of the Fire Dance were lost in frenzy, drawing mad courage out of their very fear. They laughed and yelled. Fletcher laughed and yelled as well as he sprinted through flames and leaped high over the bonfires, running back into the shadows to cool himself. Lot ran and leaped in silence. There was no madness for him. His discipline held his fear in check, blunting the edge of mad courage. He knew exactly what he was doing. It was dangerous. Very, very dangerous. More than a few Sabbat had died during Fire Dances. Many more had been hideously scarred and maimed. But he had no choice except to follow Fletcher's near suicidal lead.

The ultimate goal of the Fire Dance was to leap as high as possible, soaring over the burning pyres. Usually on these occasions, Lot made a few passes above the fires, then sensibly returned to the sidelines to watch others risk horrible injury. Fletcher often lasted until near the very end of the Dance. He was in fine form tonight, leaping like an Olympic athlete with a grace and speed that belied his bulk. Lot followed him easily at first, tireless undead muscles thrusting him onto the air to hurtle the fires. Some of the Sabbat began to pause, watching the contest between bishop and templar.

Over an arm of flame, into the darkness. Back, over another arm, then over the very center of one of the two smaller bonfires.

Throbbing music pulsed through Lot's body, the tribal rhythms of the Sabbat. More fires, plunging blind into darkness, leaping bedazzled into the inferno. Back and forth several times over each of the smaller fires, through a hail of juggled torches. Then, suddenly, Fletcher was springing high, almost taking flight. Caught in the rhythm of the chase, driven almost to trance by the music, discipline pushing him after Fletcher, Lot sprang, too.

It was the largest of the three bonfires and they were throwing themselves up over the furnace of its heart. Lot watched Fletcher soar, an arcing dive that carried him high. His own leap wasn't enough. Senses confused by the pace of the madcap pursuit, he had leaped too low, expecting one of the smaller fires. Hot flames licked at his clothing. He came down inside the fire, feet crashing through burning logs, throwing him to his knees on red embers and white-glowing coals. Desperately, he thrust himself out of the conflagration, rolling on the ground beyond. His nerves screamed at the kiss of the flames. He panicked, thrashing on the ground, shrieking and beating at the fire that clung to him until it was out and his clothes and charred skin smoked in the night air.

Fletcher looked down on him mockingly, then vanished, hurling himself once more into the Fire Dance amidst screams of enthusiastic praise.

Hatred and anger blossomed in Lot's heart. Benedict came rushing up. "I didn't see you go down," he apologized. "I was on the other side of the Dance."

"I want him," Lot spat. "I want him, Benedict. Dead. Humiliated. The oath is broken." He tried to stand and couldn't. He needed blood and rest to heal the burns on his legs. Benedict helped him up.

"Monomacy?" the Ravnos asked. "A duel?"

Discipline reasserted itself. The duel of Monomacy would be stupid—Lot had as good a chance of losing as Fletcher. He refused to allow such a creature to kill him! A duel wasn't enough, either. He didn't just want Fletcher dead. "I want his position. I will be the next bishop and I will see him kneel to me before he dies!" He snarled as he took a tentative step. Pain. Even with Benedict's support, the walk back to the car would be torturous.

"How are you going to get it? The Archbishop won't just give the job to you, even if you defeat Fletcher in Monomacy."

"We embarrass Fletcher. We frame him." Lot began cold calculations. "The Archbishop knows he may be incompetent. All we need is evidence. We can make it up if we have to! If we can show Dyce that Fletcher has lost control of the Box—"

"He'll depose him!"

"And if I'm the one who shows him that Fletcher is a failure, Dyce is sure to appoint me in his place." Lot smiled grimly in spite of the pain. "We need to know more about what's happening in the Box. We need to find something we can exploit."

Benedict grinned in the darkness. "Leave that to me." He pulled a little cellular phone out of his pocket, unfolded it and dialed a number. When someone answered, he said one word. "Nightbird."

Lot watched Benedict from inside the car as the Ravnos talked with a shadowy figure half-hidden in a doorway nearby. The cooling body of a young blond woman lay across Lot's lap. He brushed his fingers idly through her hair. Blood filled his body, but it hadn't been enough to heal his wounds completely. He needed a day of sleep before he would be able to walk properly again, and so he had elected to wait in the car. The vehicle was parked southwest of King and Bathurst, almost inside the Box, but just barely still outside.

Money changed hands and Benedict slipped away from the doorway. The shadowy figure came with him: a woman in tight-fitting black clothes, with French-braided, black-dyed hair. A Camarilla vampire. Lot rolled down the window. Benedict smiled again. "Lot, this is Razor, code name Nightbird. She spies for me inside the Box. I was able to convince her to make a short trip outside tonight. It seems we may not have to work very hard to bring our favorite bishop down." He stepped back and pushed the Camarilla vampire forward. "Razor, tell Lot about Bianka."

CHAPTER FIVE

The sun hovered just below the horizon. Two dozen Kindred clustered on the tar roof.

Yes, they keep a distance from one another, Bianka told Ravena. *Like birds of prey.*

The building, three blocks east of Savage Garden, housed the Cameron—a hotel on the upper floors, a bar on the main floor, and a separate room within the bar that, Bianka was told, was where the Toronto Gothic Society met. Several of the Camarilla lived here, although Bianka was not sure which ones. They kept their safe havens a secret—even from each other, it seemed. She, as an outsider, was not going to be privy to that kind of information.

The roof was like the majority of those below it, and the ones above—Bianka had seen most of them earlier in the night. This one, though, differed in one way—a brick chimney shaped like a cross rose five feet up toward the sky. The smoke stack was large enough to hold a body, arms spread wide, legs together, crucifixion style. A body like Shadow's: dead. A mangled body that had already begun to stink of decay. A body that, when the sun seared it from directly overhead, would receive those rays at the bottom of the stack and disintegrate almost instantly, turning muscle and organs and bone to dark ash.

Ravena flew to the top of the stack and perched on the edge of the rough brick, overseeing the proceedings. The raven's head jerked this way, that way, like a sentinel's, not so much guarding the proceedings as guarding Bianka from something. Maybe it was the Final Death that clung to the air, or maybe it was just the monstrous violence of this night, but something invaded Bianka, like air pollution; invisible, but you knew it was there and that it was hurting you badly.

Shadow's body had been stripped of clothing, to hasten the disintegration process, apparently. Around her neck, though, hung a silver new moon. Bianka had heard Reg tell one of the others that Shadow loved this piece of jewelry—it had been a gift from him to her, when she was still human, when he was drawing her blood on a nightly basis.

The Kindred presented one face, a solemn visage, and Bianka was surprised.

"Yeah, it's unusual," Swan said, and Bianka whirled around as if the Brujah had read her mind. "Till I got here, I'd never seen Kindred give much of a damn when one of us bit it."

She looked hard at Bianka, as if for confirmation or denial, and Bianka nodded.

"Were you... close?"

"With Shadow?" Swan laughed. She picked up a pebble and hurled it, the power of her muscle sending the stone four buildings over. "No way. I told you, Toreador and Brujah don't mix." She eyed Bianka suspiciously, as if either the blood in her veins was a lie, or the lie was about the blood in her veins.

Reg, dressed in a flowing black and gold opera cape studded with bugle beads, quoted passages in a theatrical manner from various works of literature that obviously meant something to him. Whether or not they had had meaning for the departed was unclear.

"'To sleep, perchance to dream.' All of life is but a dream."

He waved a hand in a grand gesture. "We are today, 'As one dead in the bottom of a tomb.' They have taken her from us. They have ripped her heart from her chest, and our hearts are torn out as well. 'Death is the ugly fact which nature has to hide, and She hides it well.'"

The melodrama in his voice was mixed with something close to true feeling. Bianka had never experienced anything remotely like this. The faces of the other Kindred said they were taking all this seriously, not mockingly, as she would have expected.

Above, the eastern horizon, or as much as the buildings would let her see, had turned pale, nudging the darkness into the western sky. Bianka did not have to look to know the earth was spinning toward that sunrise. Any minute it would sear the line separating sky and earth, then soon afterward scale the heavens, frying Kindred in its path. Why in hell these fools were risking incineration was beyond her.

"'Dry sorrow drinks our blood. Adieu, adieu!'"

The heat and pressure from the sunrise grew intense. Bianka was about to bolt. She turned to Swan. "We're all going to be crispy if this keeps up."

"He's almost done."

"How do you know?"

Reg's voice billowed. *"Between the idea*
And the reality
Between the motion

And the act
Falls the Shadow—"

"He's started quoting Eliot," Swan said. "He hasn't read any human who's lived in the last hundred years except Eliot. When he gets to *Ash Wednesday*, he's at the end of his repertoire."

Bianka let a smile slide across her face. At least Swan was not completely buying into all this.

Finally Reg did finish, with a rousing,

"Because I do not hope to turn again
Because I do not hope
Because I do not hope to turn."

A long moment of silence filled the too-bright air. Ravena glanced at the sky and squawked loudly, the sound echoing down and up from the stack. Finally, one by one, the Kindred approached the chimney. Amazed, Bianka watched as each of them tossed on top of the corpse something that belonged to them—not an object, a part of the body. Locks of hair; fingernails; toenails; an eyelash was plucked by Janus, the lanky Mediterranean who had left Savage Garden earlier. Ear wax, saliva and other bodily juices, including bloody tears dropped from Reg's eyes. Even Swan brushed her upper arm as if dead cells could fall from the dead onto the dead. This odd ritual was like something communal, something that the Sabbat would contrive.

Only Bianka was left. It wasn't their stares that forced her to the chimney, but the awareness of the sun and the scant seconds remaining. Shadow lay as Bianka had seen her earlier when she'd looked into the chimney—classical death pose, arms folded over her chest, a flower, wilting, clutched in her hands. Naked but for the silver crescent around her neck. The bloody wounds had stopped seeping and the coagulated blood had jelled and hardened. By the time the sun hit, that blood would become paper thin and crackle, like brownish-red cellophane. Clearly rigor mortis had come and gone and the corpse was supple again.

Ravena squawked. *All right!* Bianka said, because she could think of no alternative. She reached out and stroked the raven several times. A short tail feather loosened. Bianka placed it in her mouth and pulled it out by the quill. She released the moist feather and it fell rather than drifted down onto Shadow's remains.

The air had become oppressive. It was past time to go. They all needed to surrender to the weight of sleep and save themselves from the torture about to descend. And if they didn't move now, there would be several dozen piles of ash and a crowd taking the journey to Valhalla with Shadow's soul.

Reg lifted a large sheet of glass over the chimney, ensuring that the body would fry fast. And he did it not a moment too soon.

As light broke the horizon, Kindred ran moaning and screaming to the door leading from the roof. Swan bolted through the opening, and Bianka raced behind her to the escape. Suddenly Swan turned.

From blackness, dozens of eyes stared out at Bianka, like a Lovecraftian monster.

"Let's go!" Bianka cried, feeling the heat rippling over her skin. Pain shot through her, and her back spasmed. But the Kindred, with Swan in the doorway, stood their ground.

"You did her, didn't you?" Swan said.

"Me? No. I was inside the club, remember?"

"You came in later, *after* she fell."

"It wasn't me. Let's talk about this inside."

Suddenly, they pulled the door closed. Bianka grabbed for the handle—and it wasn't there. She wasted precious moments trying to wedge her fingers into the crack around the steel door as they bolted it from inside. But those seconds were gone—the fireball in the sky forced her to act.

She leapt to the fire escape, unfortunately on the east side of the building. Some demented artist had studded the wall with half a dozen two- foot-long orange roaches that the sunlight glinted off. Finally she hit the sidewalk. Ravena flew past her head, squawking wildly. *I know!* Bianka shouted. *But where?*

Ravena, by instinct, led her to the door of the bar at the front of the building. Only in passing did Bianka catch a glimpse of more of the orange roaches affixed to the gray brick wall at the front; they were too reminiscent of death and burial for her taste at the moment, not that she had a moment. The black fire door was barred, and chained with a heavy chain and enormous padlock. In a split second, Bianka had snapped enough links and torn the bar from the latches.

She was inside, behind the closed door, her clothing smoking, the flesh of her arms and neck scorched. And she was rattled.

Ravena flew ahead, into the darkness, while Bianka tried to relax.

"Nice work. At least your Brujah side isn't dormant."

The sound of Swan's voice was like claws on a blackboard. Before she could stop herself, Bianka lunged in the direction of the voice.

She wanted blood. Redeeming blood. Blood in revenge. Blood for the nourishment. Blood to heal. Blood, just for the taste of it. For the kill!

Time stopped and sped up. Claws tearing. Teeth snapping.

Red rage washing her like violent waves in a storm.

And then it was over. The hands restraining her. The awareness of the dark interior. Sounds returned, voices, Ravena warning her to calm down, or else. Air, not enough of it, reaching Bianka's lungs. Her limbs throbbed with thwarted energy.

"Chill, half-breed." Swan's voice. She sounded anxious in the darkness, but undamaged. The sound grated like a serrated blade dragged along Bianka's jugular.

As her vision returned, the red evaporated and the darkness illuminated. Eyes, dozens of them, watching her, with curiosity, with suspicion, with hatred. With lust for her blood.

"Bring her," DeWinter's voice said. His was a dark shadow against blackness. She recognized his eyes. Neither distrust nor trust. He turned, and the others dragged her below ground.

When night descended, it was as if a curtain rose; the world as Bianka knew it existed once again.

She found herself in a box. Memory flooded her of what occurred the night before, and she was surprised that they hadn't bound her—the lid lifted easily enough—or killed her outright.

This subbasement was dirty and smelled of mildew. The walls were damp to her touch. Nothing here but more boxes. Her macabre sense of humor took over—these Camarilla were certainly theatrical. Coffins for the undead! How original! Maybe she'd find Dracula himself, if she searched every one. Where were those holy wafers, anyway?

"I must apologize."

She spun around to find DeWinter behind her. Ravena had perched on a beam above and from this angle, it looked like the raven stood on his reedy shoulder. Clearly, the leader of this disparate desperate band had the power to rise earlier than the rest.

"Swan... gets ahead of herself sometimes."

Bianka was about to tell him which level of

Hell he and his wimpy troupe could descend to when Ravena squawked.

Damn you! Bianka told the raven. To which Ravena uttered almost a serious chirp. *All right. I'll be good.*

"I'm the victim here, so you'd better fill me in. What the hell was that all about?"

"Swan doesn't trust you. Nor do some of the others. That's understandable, don't you think? You come from... where? Telling us you were sent to save us—"

"You don't believe me?"

"I believe you were sent here." He paused. "You're Inconnu, aren't you?"

If only she hadn't been cursed with this damned inability to lie. Sometimes the truth made things worse. She glanced around the room, trying to find an evasive half-truth to shell out.

"They're still sleeping," DeWinter said. "If you're going to trust anyone, it will have to be me."

Right, she thought. Trust you. Trust you to flip out every hour on the hour, whenever the cuckoo makes an appearance. But she knew she had to gain the trust of at least the apparent leader. Swan was something else, and she had no clue how to reach that stubborn Brujah without wiping her memory clean, which seemed very appealing at the moment.

"Yes, I'm Inconnu," Bianka said. She waited, but DeWinter stood like one of the posts, silent, blending into the dismal basement. But she saw that his eyes were wild, as if he were about to frenzy. Or worse, lapse into the paranoia she could already see tying him in knots.

She wove her words with hand pictures, elaborate gestures that blended with her voice, and she watched him watching her hands, reading her lips, avoiding her eyes. "I came for the purpose I stated. You could rejoin the Camarilla. You should. This is no way to exist. Hiding in fear that the Sabbat will wake up on the wrong side of the coffin and take it out on your merry band of blood sippers. You're Kindred. You're not meant to be restricted to just a few city blocks. You don't have enough breathing room, let alone hunting territory—"

DeWinter held up a hand. "I don't need the lecture—I've heard it before. I've even said it myself. And I don't want the visuals, so save your charming ways for the Neonates who can be easily enchanted."

Clearly, he was sharper than she thought.

"And I already know all this, far better than you do," he said. "All of us in the Box know it. But we made a deal with the Sabbat—"

"That was then. Now it's time to break the deal."

"Why should we give up Toronto to the Sabbat?"

"You don't *have* Toronto. You have eight square blocks. You have nothing."

DeWinter turned suddenly and stared up at Ravena, as if he felt the bird's beak boring into his back. He snapped his head around. "Inconnu don't meddle. In fact, they don't even interact. And, if I recall anything of history BB—"

"History 'BB'?"

"Before the Box. The Inconnu, you tend to side with the Sabbat, if you side with anybody, and you don't usually side. In fact, you don't usually do much of anything."

"That's true. But the Inconnu have disputes as well. There are some of us who believe it's important to build a base of trust between the Kindred."

"Before Gehenna, am I right?"

DeWinter wasn't as crazy as he seemed, she was sure of it. She wanted the trust of this leader—it was the only way the plan would work.

"Look, I want to be straight with you," she said. "I came here because there are forces at play, larger than either of us, larger than what's happening in this city."

"It's hard to believe that a few dozen Camarilla have anything to do with the greater scheme of things."

"That's why you stay here, under the thumb of the Sabbat. You can't see your place in the big picture. You're like a band of Anarchs. Lost. Alone. Disconnected. You don't even have an order to this... society of yours."

Her words struck DeWinter where it hurt.

He didn't even try a defense, like, *I'm the leader here*. It was clear to both of them that his hold was tenuous. Who was there to lead? And where to? She could see all that in his dark eyes, eyes glazed and pitted with madness, ready to erupt at the slightest dis-ease.

"A puzzle can never be completed if some of the pieces don't fit," she said gently. "You, here, you're a piece of the puzzle. You need to find your place. For the greater good." She took a step toward DeWinter and watched him fade in and out, as if fear of her words was diminishing.

"I'm only trying to get you out of here," she said, with her words, with her hands, with her lips moving in a sensuous way. "How can that hurt you? Surely you can't be happy, living like caged animals."

"Since when is happiness a goal, half-breed? Or don't you read any Zen?" Swan's sarcastic voice saturated the subbasement.

Bianka felt the little blood in her veins cooking. Every instinct in her insisted she rip this Kindred apart. The threat of last night could not be overlooked. She turned slowly to face her adversary.

Ravena cried out a warning, but it wasn't that Swan was about to attack. The alarm was strictly for Bianka, and the raven clearly meant: *control yourself!*

Swan's face showed strain. Her body, though, was balanced, in a tough, defensive stance. She was a fighter, and prepared, Bianka knew, but not about to go on the offensive. She expected retaliation—what Kindred wouldn't? That gave Bianka an edge. An edge she wanted to keep. You can always settle a score, she told herself.

"All right, Sister Brujah," she snarled at Swan, "listen up good, because you owe me one, which I should take out of your tough little hide by stripping it from your body with my teeth. Nobody would deny me that revenge, and we're virtually alone here now—"

"Except for our fearless leader." Swan nodded at DeWinter. Her voice, though even, was a bit high in tone, and Bianka knew she had her running.

Bianka felt DeWinter behind her. His energy vacillated between hot and cold, and being around him made her jittery. She would have to rely on Ravena to keep her posted, in case he turned against her.

"We'll do it here, and we'll do it now," she told Swan. Fear flashed in the Brujah's eyes. But Bianka did not intend a physical confrontation. Not just yet, anyway. "Tell me you want to stay caged in, a rat, feeding on the homeless, the junkies, the hungry Goth babies. Tell me you feel proud of yourself, living like scum under the boots of the Sabbat. Tell me you don't give a damn about the rest of the Camarilla, what they think of you, what you could get from them. Tell me you don't want a change, that you want to stay in the Box for eternity, subsisting on the crumbs the Sabbat deign to leave you, hoping they don't come in here and destroy you in your sleep. Tell me all that, that you're incapable of even a small act of defiance, and Ravena and I will be on our way. I can write you off, a small band of anarchs, on the verge of extinction. The prey of the Sabbat. Anarchs so cowardly they don't deserve to exist."

The silent air in the chamber became heavy and still. Eternity pressed in from the moist stones, an eternity that could whimper omega as easily as it could shout alpha. Bianka waited. She had no idea which way Swan would fall, but she knew that as important as it was to have DeWinter back her, Swan was the one who could rouse these pathetic Kindred to action. She might be off the wall in her own way, but she was stable in her fury. DeWinter was apt to fade when the going got tough, and it was already getting tough in the Box. Shadow's death proved that.

Around them, the others began waking. Lids of wood and metal were thrown open, clanging against the earth floor, the cement walls. Reg was one of the first to emerge, and he looked savagely hungry.

When ten Kindred stood behind Swan, each with that wasted, starved look in the eyes, that predatory stance that said only vitae mattered at this moment, Bianka expected the tension to break Swan. And it did.

"We need blood. Now. Talk's cheap, and you can buy it even cheaper at midnight, upstairs." She spun on her heels.

The others followed her quickly up the stone steps, leaving only Bianka, Ravena and DeWinter in the basement.

"She is… feral," he said. "But her heart is gold. 'I've been searching for a heart of gold. And I'm growing old.'"

Bianka watched DeWinter fade in and out like an old black and white movie flickering in and out of focus. His madness pivoted on fear. He couldn't help her. And she couldn't help him. She had never seen so many twisted Camarilla in one place before, and it was like entering an asylum for the insane. Somehow it resembled a real society, but the rules were askew, and nobody seemed to know them, let alone follow them.

Ravena floated down and perched on Bianka's left shoulder. The bird caught her eye. The message was clear—the raven was anxious.

Don't worry, Bianka reassured the raven, *I don't trust any of them any more than they trust me.*

At midnight, Siouxsie and the Banshees' latest slid through the speakers. It was background noise. The Toronto Gothic Society was holding its monthly meeting at The Cameron and, unknown to the humans present, there were real vampires in their midst. Vampires who pretended to be part of the neo-Goth scene. Vampires who used these 'friendships' to scout out food. Where are the gargoyles when you need them, Bianka wondered, or at least that's what she thought the humans should be wondering.

The room was a Victorian parlor, with red-velvet and walnut sofas, mock gas lamps on the walls, and gilded mirrors. Groovella and Morpheus seemed to be the leaders of this society, exquisitely clothed from head to toe in black with splashes of red for effect. The twenty or so Goths were dressed in layered black velvet dresses, or brocaded coats, leather appliqués, white and silver lace trim—Suzie, a pretty blonde in the corner with a French accent, tatted mercilessly throughout the proceedings.

Announcements were being made, about the annual gothic picnic; about Mitchell's gothic radio program and his guest of the week, a local cult author named Amarantha Knight; about the new Dracula play in the park and the costume contest; about the Prisoners of the Knight convention and that David and Penny were now selling the T-shirts....

While these humans went about their business, Bianka watched the Kindred, chatting with the living, pretending to drink, seducing—Reg already had a new conquest, a lovely woman named Mari Anne, with long brown hair, wearing a black leather corset over her satin dress—she looked as if she'd stepped out of a tintype.

That the Camarilla struggled so desperately

to fit into human society had always amazed Bianka. It was like a kind of envy for a state they had left behind. In many ways, the Sabbat were more realistic about what they were. They knew they were vampires, and that humans were their prey. Bianka could easily empathize with that position. From the moment she'd been Embraced, she had understood that she was among them, but not of them. Despite the blood of the Toreador riding her veins, seduction of humans was not high on her list of priorities. Oh, she could do it, better than most, but something in her wanted the blood simply, and without fuss, and normally that's how she took it. Like now. From the red-headed wraithboy from whose wrist she had been surreptitiously drinking for the past hour.

She hadn't even needed to mesmerize him. He identified her as what he thought of as a human blood-drinker, and offered his blood. Why should she refuse the fiery-haired human? He had already been hurtling toward unconsciousness. Like several of the others, he had been drinking absinthe, homemade no doubt—the devil's brew had been illegal in most parts of the world for most of this century. Bianka remembered the scent, though, of wormwood, and the sweet sugar cubes on the little spoons hooked to the rim of the glass so the bitterness of the beverage could be cut. She had watched many of the Romantics whom these humans emulated drink their fill of absinthe, and endure the madness that followed.

The intoxicant in the blood she consumed caused Bianka to weave through a mild hallucination; she imagined for moments that she was in another century.

Groovella, with graceful movements of her black fish-net gloved hands, and expressions in her liquid black eyes, gestured toward Bianka. The jet coating on her long nails glittered in the candlelight. "Tell us something about yourself."

Ravena ruffled her feathers in amusement, and Bianka could only half stop the smile crossing her lips. An Inconnu. Telling anything about herself. What irony!

But Bianka was here, playing the part: The Newcomer. Time to Talk About Yourself. Out of the corner of her eye, she watched Swan enter the alcove where the meeting was taking place. Ravena was watching too. Closely.

Bianka placed the wraithboy's wrist in his lap. "Cool!" he murmured.

"The architecture," Bianka said. "The Gothic doorways, that lead inward, through levels, descending, downward, always to a new layer. There is no end to Dante's Heaven or Hell."

"That's very interesting," an ethereal woman who called herself Angel said. "Go on. Please."

They were starving, these mortals. Caught in a time where mystery and magic had been pressed flat by steel and chrome. At least these babies found something in the past to cling to. And for a moment, Bianka felt a stirring that could have been some mild mothering urge, like a bird feeding her young.

"When you descend one more rung, you cannot go back. That's the fear, and it is real. There is no stasis in eternity."

"'He not busy being born is busy dying.'" DeWinter's voice glided around the mock gas lamps like vapors.

"Entropy is not an end result, but a phase," Bianka told them, "and each level brings its own birth, death and rebirth. You go in, but you will not come out, at least not as who you were."

The Goth babies hung on her words. They needed to understand the cycles. And oddly enough, so did these lost Camarilla. The eyes of the Kindred were just as hungry, not for vitae, but for another substance.

"The arches draw you when you are ready to be drawn. And you think you have a choice, but you really have none. Your only choice is to be aware of what is happening or to be unaware."

She glanced at the wraithboy beside her. "Fate, so compelling, operates exclusive of living... and dead." Bianka turned to Swan. The Brujah's eyes glowed. She had fed recently. She was receptive. "Carl Jung said it best. 'That which is not brought to consciousness is acted out as fate.' And fate can feel like a box, imprisoning you. Do you understand me?"

Silence filled the room as the audience digested the meaning of the words.

And when the sounds of movement and speech again grew and filled the space, one voice, close by, drifted past Ravena, who tilted her head as if to hear it better, and the sound entered Bianka's ear. It was Swan's answer to so many questions. "Okay, half-breed, show me the way. I'm ready to descend."

CHAPTER SIX

Benedict's fingers drummed a staccato beat against the car door. The Ravnos looked at the shadowy doorway across the street and grimaced. Tonight the doorway was empty.

"Where is she?"

Lot leaned back and waited silently, listening to his carefully tuned radio.

Bianka.

He grinned to himself. The information Benedict's spy had brought them last night was exactly the sort of thing he wanted. A Camarilla vampire stirring up trouble in the Box, undermining the authority of the Sabbat. And not just any Camarilla vampire—a vampire who had slipped into the Box from outside as a representative of the greater body of the Camarilla. And the young vampire Razor called Shadow, dead, the victim of Sabbat intrusions into the Box. He and Benedict wouldn't have to frame Fletcher. The big Gangrel really had already lost control of the Box. All they needed now was hard evidence.

The sooner they had it, the happier Lot would be. After talking with Razor last night and hearing her descriptions of the vampire who wove stories with her hands and was accompanied by a raven, he and Benedict had returned to the haven. Both of them had been immensely pleased with themselves. That had lasted until they were standing outside the door of the warehouse. Benedict had glanced at Lot.

"He'll know something is up."

Lot had shaken his head. "No."

"He's not stupid."

"He'll expect a certain amount of anger. We'll give that to him. We'll be surly but obedient—or rather, I will be." Lot considered the door, as rough and solid as Fletcher himself. "He defeated me in what was essentially a duel. He's proven his dominance. You can behave however you want. As long as I'm subservient, he won't suspect a thing. I can probably avoid him altogether for the next couple of days unless he feels like gloating."

"He might."

"Let's hope not."

As it turned out, when they had gone inside, the warehouse was still empty. Fletcher had not yet returned from the Fire Dance. They went to the rooms where they slept. In spite of being exhausted and wounded, though, Lot still lay awake for a long time, listening for Fletcher to come home. He did, finally. Just a little before dawn, Lot had heard the warehouse door open, and Fletcher's heavy footsteps as he entered.

The door closed. Lot had turned on the thin pad that he used for a bed: Though other vampires, like Benedict, might sleep in real beds, with mattresses and bedclothes, Lot felt no need for them. He was utterly unconscious during the day, deep in the insensate sleep of vampires. Comfort meant nothing. The thinness of the pad also kept him close to the dirt that was scattered under it. The earth of his homeland—actually fine, dark alluvial soil from the river that flowed through the city where he had been born. That was the curse of his clan. Like the vampires of legend, they needed the soil of their homeland in order to rest comfortably. With that soil under him, it didn't matter what Lot slept on. It would have felt like a bed of feathers. He had closed his eyes.

Then Fletcher's footsteps had paused outside Lot's door for several long, unnerving minutes. Lot could smell the wood smoke that clung to the bishop. Wood smoke and blood. Fletcher had been feeding recently and well. Lot remained still. After several minutes, Fletcher had moved away. When the sun had set that night, Lot had gone immediately to Benedict and they had left the warehouse without even looking for Fletcher.

Tonight they had a mission. Razor was going to take them inside the Box. Forbidden territory. They were deliberately going to violate the Settlement. Lot told himself that they had a reason for it, a purpose for so flagrantly disregarding the orders of the Archbishop. They were going to prove Fletcher's incompetence. It was for the good of the sect.

He was still nervous. He refused to let it show.

Benedict's drumming fingers fell silent. "She's not coming."

"Wait."

But doubt hung over him as well. What if Razor wasn't coming? What if the other Camarilla had gotten wind of her treachery? They might be waiting just inside the Box. They couldn't kill intruding Sabbat, but it was within their rights under the Settlement to punish unwarranted trespassing. Of course, the intrusion was warranted—the Camarilla were plotting rebellion. Except the first Sabbat that they would contact to protest an intrusion, warranted or otherwise, would be Fletcher. Benedict and he would have to defend their actions to the bishop. At worst, the bishop would punish them. Lot could foresee no mercy from him. At best, Fletcher would learn of the mysterious Bianka's presence and her efforts to stir up the Camarilla. He would uncover and put down the rebellion and look like a hero in the eyes of the Sabbat. And Lot could foresee no mercy from him even in the better situation. They had to be fast tonight, fast and stealthy. They couldn't be caught or even seen. They had to get their evidence—and take it to the Archbishop directly.

Benedict waited. They both waited.

Finally, Benedict glanced at the clock in the dashboard of the car. "She's an hour late."

Razor wasn't coming. For whatever reason. Lot made a decision. He started the car and pulled out onto Bathurst Street, heading north.

Up along the western boundary of the Box. Benedict stared at him in shock. "What are you doing?"

"Razor isn't coming. But we need to go in."

"Without her?" Benedict yelped. "We're driving in?"

"No. If we drove, we might get trapped in the car." Lot crossed Queen Street, a dark and yawning canyon at Bathurst, and continued past the Box's northern boundary. He turned east onto Dundas a few blocks later. They drove through Chinatown. "We'll go on foot. We'll be able to move around more easily, and fight if we need to. But I don't want to walk into the Box where we were supposed to meet Razor. If the Camarilla is expecting us at all, that's where they'll be."

Off of Dundas and south on University Avenue, broad and spectacular with memorial monuments marching up the grassy center meridian like a parade, hospital, offices, and institutional buildings crowding the sidewalks to watch. They passed Queen Street again, gaudy and alive at this end. A block and a half south of Queen Street, Lot made a fast left down into the parking area of the Toronto Hilton, pulling up in front of the attendant's booth. A young man with the bleary eyes of a night-shift worker leaned out. "Guest parking only," he said mechanically.

Benedict leaned across Lot to wink up at him. "We're checking in." He placed his hand quite visibly on Lot's leg.

The young man flushed and raised the gate for them. Benedict sat back. Lot nodded. "Quick."

The blond vampire shrugged. "It was either that or kill him." He smiled. "But I may come back another night."

Lot took a parking spot. He turned off the car, then paused. He glanced at Benedict. "Ready?"

Benedict drew a deep, completely unnecessary breath. "As I'll ever be. Let's do it." He opened his car door and got out. Something about him shifted as he stood.

By the time Lot was out of the car and looking at him under the orange-tinted lights of the parking garage, it was as if he were facing an entirely different person. Lot had been able to convince the Ravnos to leave his frock-coat and teddy-boy clothes at home tonight. Instead, Benedict wore a blousy, white Romantic shirt with tight fitting breeches. His hair had been tied back in a pony-tail. The clothes, however, were not what made the difference. Benedict had spun an illusion over himself, very simple and very subtle, but also very powerful. His cheek bones seemed higher and his nose sharper. His eyes were dark, his jaw thin. Lot could see Benedict beneath the illusion, but only because he knew to look.

There were no illusions for him, though. Benedict could maintain his own disguise with little effort, but casting such an illusion on another would have been almost as taxing as creating the woman had been two nights ago. Lot relied on more mundane methods of disguise. A tight ribbed-knit T-shirt that revealed his muscular build far more than he was really comfortable with. Torn jeans. His black hair was ruffled forward and down over his forehead and eyes. He had taken off his glasses as well. His vision had been heightened in death along with his hearing and sense of smell and he could do without the glasses, but it did become a strain after a while. Benedict looked him over appraisingly. "You should dress like that more often. It makes you look a lot younger."

Lot snorted. They took a flight of stairs up out of the parking garage and into the hotel's lobby. Ignoring the stares of the hotel's more conservatively dressed guests, they walked out and onto University Avenue. Across the street, the Sabbat's territory ended and the Box began. Lot didn't hesitate. He dashed into the traffic on University and across. Benedict followed a little more carefully. "What now?" he asked apprehensively once they stood on the other sidewalk.

"We go in. Side streets first. Queen Street is the busiest part of the Box. We'll check it out last. Watch for Camarilla."

The blocks closest to University were little different from the grand avenue itself. Dull, boxy gray buildings that spoke of the drone of monotonous bureaucracy. More government offices. Faceless, nameless architecture. The people were faceless, too. They looked away from Lot and Benedict. That wasn't unusual in itself. Toronto was a cold city even in the summer, icy with defensive politeness. Nobody stared. Nobody made eye contact. People had a tendency to ignore those around them, not even acknowledging their presence. That cold politeness made it easy for the Sabbat to exist in Toronto. Nobody noticed anything.

The people on the side streets at the eastern fringe of the Box, however, actively avoided Lot and Benedict. They turned their heads. They stepped off of the sidewalk or pressed up against the cold gray buildings. One man crossed to the other side of the street. It was as if they were frightened, not of any savage menace that might cling to the two vampires, but of an awareness that they were unnatural, that they did not belong in this gray, mundane twilight. Benedict turned to stare after the man who had crossed the street. Lot looked straight ahead and kept moving.

Within a block and a half, the character of the buildings had changed. Parts of the Box had been Toronto's garment district until only a couple of decades ago. Cold gray buildings took on character and warmth. They were still solid and imposing, but there was a humanity to them now. People had worked in these buildings. People had designed and built them. Now people played in them. Where garment factories and fabric wholesalers had been were restaurants and nightclubs. The area still had something of an industrial feel, but the lights were bright and the night alive. The spicy smells of Caribbean cooking drifted out of a red brick monstrosity. Dance music filtered from the basement of a tired yellow heap. Further along, a gas station had been turned into a trendy diner and a run-down diner into a boutique of nostalgia and kitsch. A few buildings were newer, all steel and glass and organic curves, urban renewal mocking the faded industrial zone.

Lot led the way west, then south, and slowly back east again. The Box encompassed surprising diversity for such a limited area. The old industrial structures of the garment district. Elderly tall and narrow buildings with stores and bars on the lower floors and cramped apartments higher up. Aging homes looking distinctly out of place. The southern reaches of Chinatown. Toronto's theater district, just inside the Box on the north side of King Street. A small auto-parts dealership next to a large jazz bar with people laughing and talking in the cool night air on the patio. Away from University Avenue, the people were as different as the buildings, it seemed—almost different from the standard character of Toronto altogether. They seemed at ease here. They were loud (comparatively loud, for Toronto). They were casual. They greeted strangers. Couples kissed on the street corner.

Benedict walked with a stunned look on his face. "The Camarilla have it good! Why did we give them the best part of Toronto? This place is prime grazing land."

"I don't think it was the best part of Toronto when we put them here." Lot paused and looked around. They stood on the corner of John and Nelson, under a sign advertising ice cream and fruit ices. An awning just up the street was striped in warm sunny yellow that reminded him of the warmth of his living days. Further up was a café specializing in gourmet desserts. Beyond was a club with the fresh, cool atmosphere of the Rocky Mountains. Beyond that club was a stretch of pubs, coffee shops, and more cafés, all the way up to the lights and noise of Queen West itself. "Maybe some Camarilla with more sense than the others decided to do something with their time and attract potential prey. Maybe some humans with more sense than others realized this area was safer than other parts of the city and moved here on their own."

"Why would the Box be safer than other parts of Toronto?" snorted Benedict. Lot gave him a steady stare. Benedict just raised an eyebrow questioningly. "Well?"

"Maybe," Lot suggested, "because there's no

Sabbat here?" Benedict flushed, stolen blood coloring his cheeks. Lot ignored him. "Let's go up to Queen Street."

"Haven't we seen enough?"

"No." Lot shook his head and started walking. "We haven't seen nearly enough."

"Like what haven't we seen? We've been back and forth through the damn place. We must have seen everything there is to see in the Box."

"Wrong. Think about it."

Benedict's eyebrows furrowed, his illusory disguise wavering slightly as he thought. Then his lips drew back in a sudden snarl. "We haven't seen any Camarilla!"

"Exactly. Where the hell are they? I've been watching for them." Lot didn't bother to ask if Benedict had been doing the same. He suspected that the Ravnos had forgotten their reason for coming here as soon as he had started watching the people. "There hasn't been any sign of them. If we'll find them anywhere, though," he stopped for a traffic light, "we'll find them here."

Queen Street West stretched out to their right and left, east and west, like a serpent writhing through the night. The intersection of Queen and University was the snake's mouth, drawing in the bland city for the street to digest. Lot had occasionally stood on the other side of University Avenue and looked down Queen Street, stretching his senses to watch the odd, unpredictable events here. There was a strange atmosphere to Queen West, a mingling of frantic energy and hip lethargy. People raced between pleasures, lingered where they found sensual solace. Live fast, die young, leave a good-looking corpse—or just imitate one while you were alive. So many young people dressed in black, as if they were mourning their passing youth.

Goths and Goth wanna-bes weren't the only ones on the street, though. Queen West was a magnet for the people who didn't fit in anywhere else. Ravers. Slackers. Club puppies. Kids who didn't look old enough to be out this late, their skateboards clattering over the slabs of the sidewalk. Urban primitives with as many piercings and tattoos as Lot had ever seen on the most demented or artistically inclined of Sabbat freaks. And the street catered to them. Lot and Benedict crossed the street and turned west, walking into the heart of this dreamworld. Odd little bookshops. Music stores with cluttered walls and low-budget decor. Trendy clothing stores and boutiques with blown-glass globes suspended in their windows like flashing raindrops. Cafés. Coffee shops. Bars. All open late. Vampire hours, Lot supposed. The most unusual stores and shops were clustered on the upper floors of the old buildings, selling items that would never be in great demand from the general population but that were precious commodities here. Antiquarian books. Music that was like a fading whisper of pain and loss. Clothing of unbleached cotton, white linen, blackest velvet, multi-hued polyester, dark rainbows of silk—the fashions of the past three decades and the last two centuries. Incense, oils, candles, chalices and consecrated knives. Dark, dark bitter coffee, milky spice tea, forbidden liquors, forbidden drugs.

But there were no vampires. The members of the Camarilla were nowhere to be seen.

After a few blocks, Benedict stopped, clenching his hands in frustration. "This is futile!" he hissed.

"They have to be here somewhere," Lot pointed out. "They can't have left. We just have to keep looking."

"The longer we spend in here looking, the better the chances that the Cammies are going to find us. Maybe it's time we changed our strategy." He swept his arm about, indicating the crowds of humans along the nighttime street. "With all this traffic, why don't we just sit and wait for one of the Camarilla to come to us?"

"Isn't staying still going to give them a better chance to spot us?" asked Lot. Benedict grimaced. Lot grinned. "It's a good idea, Benedict. We just need some cover. Like there."

He gestured up the street to the sidewalk patio of a bar. There were enough humans squeezed into the little enclosure for the two Sabbat to blend in easily, but not so many that their view of the street would be obscured. Benedict nodded. They moved in. Choosing the right table wasn't difficult; they simply approached one occupied by two women. Lot let Benedict walk up to them. "Do you mind if we join you?" he asked charmingly. The women looked at him... and smiled, entranced by the Ravnos' charisma. Lot found two vacant chairs and dragged them over. The women were introducing themselves. One, named Mary, was a pretty black-haired woman wearing a short dress. The other, Laura, was a brunette with a rich, throaty voice. Both had eyes only for Benedict. Lot didn't mind. He signaled for the waiter. "Smithwick's," he said, choosing randomly from the list of beers on tap. Drinks would provide them with further cover. "Benedict?"

The Ravnos took Mari's hand and brought it to his lips flirtatiously. "A bloody mary." Laura looked jealous. She glanced at Lot. Lot smiled back at her. She glanced away again. Lot let his smile collapse—just as well. He watched the street and let Benedict entertain the women. They would keep Benedict entertained, too, at least for as long as he cared to play with his food. Lot didn't care to hear any more of the blond vampire's complaints. They would stay in the Box tonight until they learned something that they could use against Fletcher.

Last call had been announced before Lot finally spotted one of the Camarilla.

The Kindred was thin and there were handcuffs slung from the waist of his tight jeans. He was walking east on Queen, quickly, almost eagerly. Lot watched him over the rim of his beer glass. The beer brushed his lips, but didn't enter his mouth. If either Mary or Laura had noticed that the level of Lot's beer had not gone down in all the time he had been sitting there, in spite of all the sips he had apparently taken, they didn't comment on it. Lot considered going after the scrawny Camarilla. He might lead them to something. He was definitely going somewhere, and he hadn't noticed the two Sabbat at all. Lot glanced back the way he had come.

Camarilla advanced up the sidewalk like a motley army.

Lot gasped, then almost choked as beer washed into his mouth. "Benedict!" he spat. "Cover!"

"What?" The Ravnos looked up lazily, then focused on the approaching Camarilla. "Shit!" He grabbed for Mary, pulling her into a sudden, passionate kiss—and putting her body between him and the sidewalk. Lot seized Laura's arm and dragged her toward him. The brunette resisted, but there wasn't much a human could do against vampire strength. Before she could make a sound, Lot had his mouth on her neck and his fangs in her throat.

The fight went out of her and she surrendered to him. Being fed upon was indescribable ecstasy for a human. Lot let Laura collapse against him, holding her as if they were lovers. He shifted his mouth so that it looked more like he was kissing her. At the same time, he peered around the curve of her neck, past the veil of her hair, to watch the passing vampires. There were so many that the entire undead population of the Box must have been gathered together. No wonder he and Benedict had been unable to find any Camarilla! He scanned the air for the play of their pale auras. Violet excitement and yellow idealism. His eyes narrowed. They didn't suspect a thing, but probably because they were worked up about something. Like the scrawny boy with handcuffs who had gone before them, they were on their way somewhere. What had gotten them so excited?

A flare of color caught his eye, a virtual rainbow of an aura. Glittering gold. Spirituality. Brilliant red. Happiness. Pale blue, calm, but also purple, aggression. Someone who knew what they wanted and had just gotten it. The central knot of vampires shifted as it passed the patio. Lot caught a glimpse of the vampire who radiated that marvelous aura. Long, straight black hair falling to her waist. She wore black as well, not consciously or with Goth attitude, but as if the color were natural for her. She was tall for a woman. There was a strength to her. Lot caught only a glimpse of her face: high cheek bones and pale skin, an expression of quiet triumph that match her aura.

Bianka. The troublemaker.

He stared after her. She moved like nobility. Confident. She was talking to a tough-looking blond woman Lot recognized as Swan, a Brujah and one of the erstwhile leaders of the imprisoned Camarilla. He thought about trying to listen to what they were saying, but all that filled his ears was the rush of his own blood. Bianka's hands moved as she talked, floating and folding like delicate white rice paper.

The parade of Camarilla was past them before he realized that Laura was light and cool in his arms. Her heart still beat, but only faintly. He had drawn more and more deeply on her blood as he watched Bianka... he shook his head... as he had watched the Camarilla pass. And he and Benedict couldn't afford to leave dead and drained evidence of their visit to the Box behind them. He doubted if the Camarilla, trapped in such a limited space, ever killed their vessels. They were more likely to let them live so they could feed again. Dead bodies would betray them, the mark of Sabbat intruders. Lot licked Laura's neck, sealing the wounds he had made, and pushed her away. "Benedict," he whispered.

The Ravnos looked up. He had been feeding on Mary as well, but the black-haired woman was only swooning instead of near death. Benedict glanced at Laura's pale body. "Finish her."

"I can't." He slipped Laura back into her own chair and let her head fall forward onto the table. He took her friend's hand, drawing her unfocused attention to her. "Mary, Laura's had too much to drink," he lied. "Call a cab. Take her home."

No vampire mesmerism, just simple suggestion. Mary nodded sleepily. "Okay." Lot smiled at her and stood, pulling Benedict away from the table, then out of the patio onto the sidewalk, after the Camarilla. Benedict grinned at him.

"Hungry?"

"What?" Lot blinked. "No. I mean—"

"Eyes bigger than your mouth." Benedict

looked after the Camarilla. None of the other vampires looked back. The possibility of being followed had probably never even occurred to them. "I saw Razor with them. No wonder she didn't show up to meet us." He frowned. "I wonder where they're going."

Without a word, Lot started down the street after the Camarilla, keeping clusters of humans between himself and the other vampires. It wasn't hard to follow them. They walked like they owned the street. Back past the bookshops and clothing stores, cafés and bars. Past the point where he and Benedict had walked onto Queen West. Further east, past the point where life began and into the realm of office supply stores and empty, soulless buildings. The Camarilla approached University Avenue—and then descended into the subway station beneath Queen and University.

Benedict cursed. "They're leaving the Box!"

"Not necessarily." Lot bit his tongue. "If they get off at King and University, they'll still be inside." But King and University was only one stop south. Why would the entire Camarilla board the subway only to ride it four short blocks south?

"They're leaving. You know they are." A broad grin split Benedict's face. "Fletcher's out on his ass as soon as the Archbishop hears about this!"

Lot stared at the entrance to the subway. "We still need proof. We don't know where they've gone. From the subway, they could get practically anywhere in Metro Toronto. We don't even know if they've gone north or south."

"Put out a call for a hunt. The Sabbat will find them."

"That will tell Fletcher something's up, though." He looked over his shoulder, back along Queen West into the heart of the Box. "They all came walking along together. We need to find out where they came from. Maybe we can get more answers there."

Whenever people handled something, they left traces of themselves behind, like spiritual fingerprints. Lot could sense these traces, an extension of his ability to see auras. Mostly this power was good only for discrete items, things that Lot could run his hands over, feeling for the spirit's touch. Occasionally, though, the power could be adapted to other uses.

Lot and Benedict stood outside the bar with the patio once more. Mary and Laura were gone, maybe in a cab, maybe hustled away by the concerned staff of the bar. Lot didn't spare them much more than a thought. He knelt down on the sidewalk, pressing his fingertips against the pavement. He closed his eyes. He could feel the passage of the Camarilla vampires, but only faintly. This was a busy street. People passed over this spot constantly, each leaving their own trace behind. The concrete had soaked up so many auras that it was hard to draw out any single one. And, of course, the Camarilla had themselves passed this spot many times during their long imprisonment in the Box. They had left multiple impressions on the sidewalk, dim, pale, and depressed. Lot frowned. He needed to look for something unique.

Something like Bianka. He drew on his brief memories of her—her hair, her face, her shining aura—and tried again.

The record of her passage was a comet across the sidewalk. Lot opened his eyes and stood slowly. The connection was still fragile. If he lost it, he might not be able to pick up the Camarilla's path again. He nodded to Benedict and they started walking, Lot concentrating on the traces left by Bianka, Benedict keeping people out of his way. It was a good system. It worked. Lot surrendered himself completely to Benedict's watchful care. He didn't think about what lay in front of him. He barely thought about where to place his feet. He filled his mind with Bianka.

Her passage was like her aura. Strong. Vibrant. Complex. Assured. She had set her foot here, had stepped on this crack in the concrete. She had paused briefly there, the pattern of her being leaving a little pool of influence behind. The pause was in front of a store window. Lot imagined her looking through the glass, and he glanced in that direction, as if his gaze were hers. A book on architecture. His feet carried him along. Almost he felt the urge to walk backward, to place his feet in Bianka's very footprints, literally retracing her footsteps. His contact with the foreign vampire, however tenuous or indirect, felt good. He...

Benedict grabbed at him, yanking him back. Lot blinked. Bianka's path shattered, his connection to her passage lost.

A big delivery truck thundered past his face. Benedict was screaming in his ear. "Damn it, Lot! What the hell were you doing?"

"What?" Lot looked around, a bit dazed. They were at a broad intersection, busy with cars and trucks even at this time of night. Queen and Spadina.

"What the hell were you doing? You just took off. I could barely keep up with you!"

"I—"

Bianka.

He shook his head. "I guess the connection

was too strong. I'll be more careful next time."
He knelt own again, touching the sidewalk and
feeling for the lingering trace of Bianka's brief
presence here. There was nothing. Lot shifted
his hand and tried a second time. Once more,
nothing. He clenched his teeth. "I've lost her."
He slapped his palm against the concrete.
"Shit!"

Benedict was silent. Lot glanced up to find
the other vampire staring at him in concern.
"Are you sure you're all right?"

"Why wouldn't I be?" Lot stood and sighed.
"All right. We know she came this way. I almost
walked right across the street, so—" They
waited for the light to turn green, then crossed
themselves. On the other side, Lot tried feeling
for Bianka again. Still, nothing. Traffic at the
intersection was even heavier than traffic along
the sidewalk. Bianka's passage had left no trace
here. Lot looked at Benedict. "Any ideas?"

The Ravnos grinned and pointed. "Let's try
there."

Just down the street was a brick building,
painted gray. Affixed to the side were the

DON BASSINGTHWAITE AND NANCY KILPATRICK

effigies of a number of big, orange cockroaches. Coming out of the building was a group of Goths in full regalia. A couple even wore false fangs, dainty ivory points that flashed when they laughed. A "vampire" club. Lot smiled. It would be just like the Camarilla to have been hanging out here. Vampires masquerading as humans masquerading as vampires.

Benedict caught his arm as he walked forward. "Are you sure about this? If we go in there and there are more Camarilla around—"

Lot shrugged off Benedict's hand. "We saw them leave. There can't be any more of them—the Box wouldn't be able to support that many vampires. I can't believe it supports as many as it does."

"But if there are?"

"We take prisoners and interrogate them." Lot turned back toward the club grimly. "We need to know what's happening."

They walked into the club as if they belonged there, as if they came here every night. Nobody stopped them. Hardly anybody even spared them a second glance. The place was like a cavern inside. Black. Huge. The lights were angled so that deep shadows fell across the walls, disguising the true size of the place. The music system was somehow contrived to echo as if the club were immense and utterly empty. There were people inside, however, crawling through the darkness like flightless bats. The sense of vampires was everywhere, but Lot could find no indication that any of the Camarilla were actually in residence. The undead had gathered so frequently here that the atmosphere of the club was stained with their presence. He considered the humans in the club. Could one of them know...?

Something flickered at the edge of his vision, a shadow in the shadows falling against one wall.

He turned. Nothing.

Something flickered again, further along the wall this time.

"Benedict!" he murmured, grasping for the blond vampire's hand. "We're not alone." He felt Benedict stiffen, but resisted the urge to glance back at him. He kept watching the wall. The flicker of movement came again, half-glimpsed, almost his imagination. It moved around a corner, through a dark doorway shrouded by a partially drawn curtain. Silently, Lot crept after it, pulling Benedict with him as he stalked through the club. People stepped out of his path instinctively, as if they could sense that he was a hunter. By the doorway, he released Benedict and gestured for him to stand on one side of the door. Enough light reflected from off the club's dance floor that Lot could see through into the room beyond. It was styled like a parlor. He could see the shapes of sofas and the faint shine of wall mirrors. Nothing moved, but the flickering shape had not emerged. He made a sharp gesture to get Benedict's attention, then held up three fingers. Countdown. Three... two... one...

He stepped through the doorway and into the room, ready for a fight. Benedict followed him a half-second later. There was a little gun in his hand, a pearl-handled derringer. Lot wasn't sure if it was real or an illusion, but

Benedict held it as if he meant to use it and that was what mattered. The Ravnos felt along the wall. Mock gas-lamps flashed to life as his hand encountered a lightswitch.

As if throwing that switch had also activated some intricate machine, a tall, gaunt vampire stepped into the room, drawing the curtain and closing an inner door with quick, precise movements. "Good evening." He turned to regard the two Sabbat and the tiny pistol Benedict held pointed at his chest. "You can put that away."

Lot snarled. "DeWinter."

"Lot." The elder Camarilla walked past him to sit on a sofa. Benedict's derringer tracked his every movement. DeWinter ignored him. "Bishop Fletcher is well?"

"Well enough." Lot found himself answering hesitantly. His blood urged him to attack his enemy, but he struggled against the impulse. DeWinter wasn't upset at their presence? Had he been expecting them? Lot had encountered him before, though they had never actually spoken. Fletcher talked with the thin vampire from time to time, the two meeting at a prearranged spot to stand on either side of the border between their territories and discuss Sabbat intrusions into the Box or Camarilla offenses against the Settlement. Fletcher had taken Lot with him most of those times. DeWinter, the bishop had said, was a Malkavian, one of the vampires cursed with madness from the moment of their Embrace. It took a mad vampire to recognize one, he supposed. "What do you want?"

"What do *you* want?"

"Wrong answer," growled Benedict. He scooped up a heavy marble ashtray and flung it at DeWinter.

The vampire vanished. The ashtray skimmed through the air where his head had been and smashed into the far wall. "Stop that!" Lot snapped at his friend. Benedict grimaced, fangs showing. "We need answers from him!"

"Like where to find the others and their charismatic new leader?" DeWinter was back, sitting on the sofa as if he had never moved. Lot cursed silently. None of the mad vampire's appearances and disappearances tickled his senses at all. Usually he could see right through such tricks! "That's why you're here, isn't it? You're after Bianka."

"Maybe."

DeWinter's eyebrows rose. "I hope you are, because otherwise you're in violation of the Settlement. I'd hate to have to report you to Fletcher. He's not especially stable, you know."

Lot gritted his teeth at the ironic truth in DeWinter's words. "Yes," he said, "we are looking for Bianka. You were expecting us?"

"Very little goes on in the Box of which I'm entirely unaware. In spite of what the hot dog vendors and Razor think." He held up his hand to forestall Benedict's shocked outburst. "Don't worry. I haven't told anyone." He turned back to Lot. "But you're too late to stop Bianka."

"So we noticed," Lot replied dryly. "We watched her lead the Camarilla down into the subway. Presumably she's taken them out of the Box."

"A clear violation of the Settlement if she has."

"A very serious violation." Lot watched DeWinter carefully. "There are going to be severe repercussions."

"I expect so. I hope that Bishop Fletcher— or perhaps his Grace, the Archbishop—will take into consideration that many of them were essentially pressured into going along with her?" DeWinter pressed back into the stiff, hard back of the sofa. "She's taken them," he said briefly, "to the Capel crypt, an old mausoleum in Mount Pleasant Cemetery. I don't expect them back until tomorrow night."

His candor stunned Lot for a moment. The old vampire was betraying his companions, very casually, very easily. DeWinter might have read his thoughts because he glanced sideways at the Sabbat and added, "You won't mention this to them?"

"We'll see," Lot said coolly. He didn't want to owe DeWinter any favors. The mad vampire had practically handed him something to hold over his head.

"I'm sure you'll make the right decision." DeWinter shifted slightly and caught Lot's eye.

"I notice the bishop isn't with you tonight. That's odd for such a hands-on kind of man."

Lot didn't answer him. There wasn't any need. The point was made—DeWinter had something to hold over Lot's head as well. DeWinter glanced away again, looking down at his hand as he ran his fingers over the burgundy velvet of the couch, drawing and erasing patterns in the nap of the upholstery. "This is what I suggest you do: Take the information I've given you to Bishop Fletcher. Surprise the others in the cemetery. Make sure that you capture Bianka. Without her, the others will fall like leaves." He stood and walked toward the parlor door. "Fletcher knows how to contact me if he wishes to talk."

As soon as his hand touched the doorknob, he was gone again. The door opened, seemingly of its own occurred. The curtain twitched aside. Benedict spat on the rug of the room. "Bloody hell! What do we do?"

Lot gestured him to silence. DeWinter might still be in the room. He stretched his enhanced senses to their limit, seeking some trace of the mad vampire. There was nothing, but Lot knew now that he couldn't fully trust his senses when it came to DeWinter. Without another word, he led Benedict out of the parlor, out of the dark club, and down Queen Street West, out of the Box. Only when they were once more on the far side of University Avenue, in the parking garage under the Toronto Hilton, did he say anything. "I'm going up there."

Benedict grinned. "Alone?"

"No. Freon and his pack owe me a couple of favors. I'll take them. Maybe I can find another pack willing to help me as well." Benedict wiggled his eyebrows hopefully. Lot shook his head. "Not you. You have to stay around the warehouse so you can cover for me with Fletcher if he asks where I am."

"Damn!" Benedict smacked the roof of the car.

"Everyone has his place, Benedict." Lot opened his door. First to the warehouse. He wanted to get out of these ridiculous clothes and retrieve his glasses. Then to Mount Pleasant cemetery. Then... he smiled to himself. Then to the Archbishop, with all of the damning evidence against Fletcher that Dyce could ever need.

CHAPTER SEVEN

Bianka led Toronto's Camarilla along the eight blocks of Queen Street West, past the trendy ethnic bars and restaurants, and odd-spots—the store front composed of nothing but rusted bicycle parts—past the many Goth clubs like Velvet, beyond Central Billiards, by the windows of the cutting-edge boutiques like Siren, and Dead or Alive, past Bakka Books and Pages, the used CD shops, CITY-TV's sandblasted Baroque building, past X-Rays and the Queen Mother Café…. The street vibrated with the life of the under-thirty alternative-fashion elite, hip business people, artists and spike-haired street youth begging for change to feed their ferrets.

As the Kindred neared University Avenue—the eastern edge of the Box—Bianka felt their tension mounting.

Getting them to this point had not been easy. It had taken from midnight until six a.m. last night, sitting and talking with Swan, to get the Brujah settled into the idea of rebellion. And that was just the beginning.

Tonight, the Camarilla met at Savage Garden, near the western limit of the Box. With Swan onside, it had been easier to convince them that existence in this capsule was not what being a vampire, being a Kindred, was all about. Too many members of this cowardly rebel faction of the sect were

Neonates, Embraced just before, or just after the Camarilla had helped the Sabbat take the city. They were like creatures born in captivity. It was all they knew, so they didn't miss the outside world. But some remembered. Swan was one; Reg another. And half a dozen more. Their mounting fervor was enough to sway the emotions of the others.

Oddly enough, DeWinter had kept quiet while Bianka and Swan talked. Toward the end, he mumbled something about hot-dog vendors knowing, or not knowing, the truth, and whether or not it was out there, hidden away in a file with a big "X" on it. Bianka felt he wasn't so much acquiescing as tolerating her plan, perhaps because he knew just how tenuous his hold on the leadership of this group was.

When the others agreed by vote to leave the Box, he decided to stay behind. He did not forbid them to go—that would have been too much of a showdown. But he couldn't bring himself to go with them—that would have been a betrayal in some way, a diminishing of his power. Bianka figured it was just as well. She didn't need him quoting either Dylan Thomas or Bob Dylan to the hot-dog vendors enroute.

At the corner of Queen Street and University Avenue, just outside a Georgian historical residence called Campbell House, the group as a whole came to an abrupt halt, as if collectively they'd hit an invisible wall. Bianka turned and stared at them in astonishment. The mixture of excitement and fear on their faces was reflected in the energy pulsating from the group. It was obvious they were terrified of leaving home.

Ravena danced on Bianka's left shoulder, eager for action, and this time it was Bianka's turn to tell the bird to cool it.

"Where are we going?" the slim woman named Razor asked. She pulled the end of her long hair, twisted into a French braid, over her shoulder. On her right cheek, a stylized bat had been tattooed. A small ring pierced the bat's nose.

"We're descending," Bianka said, and gave Swan a knowing look.

Descending was into the subway, and Bianka

led the brood deep into the bowels of the sandy earth that composed this city, past the pastel tile walls of the tunnels to a glass booth with metal turnstiles before it.

A quick glance at the cashier inside the booth from Bianka, and each Camarilla mimicked depositing a token in the fare box. Further down via an escalator—so far so good. They were holding up. But then, technically, they were still in the Box.

As a unit, they walked to the side of the platform that was still in their territory, the side where the south-bound train stopped. Ravena squawked in disgust.

Reg eyed a gaggle of pubescent girls in tartan mini skirts. Their legs were long, but so were their necks, and Bianka wasn't sure which part of their anatomies attracted him more. They stood on the opposite side of the platform that separated the north and south tracks, but Reg didn't make a move in their direction. The lanky Camarilla named Janus was busy strolling the edge of the platform along the yellow rubber strip that let the blind know they were going too far. He read the subway ads for current movies, pantyhose and classes in philosophy and Advanced French.

"When was the last time you came down here?" Bianka asked Swan.

The Brujah made a fist and hammered the metal lid of a trash bin back in place, denting the tin in the process. Ravena made a sound low in her throat, and Bianka grinned.

Yes, my dear feathered friend, the Camarilla are nothing if not civic-minded.

"I come down here sometimes."

"To the other side of the platform—out of the Box."

Swan scowled at her. "Of course I've been on the other side of the platform!"

"When's the last time you took the train?"

Swan's brows knitted together in annoyance. She shrugged and sneered, as if it was a stupid question, and turned away, ostensibly to see who was coming down the escalator.

That elaborate pride, Bianka knew, would

keep Swan on track. Without the Brujah's total commitment, the Camarilla would flee at the speed of light.

The train finally barreled down the track toward them, whistle blowing, a sound like an electric whip cracking preceding it. Bianka shepherded this motley crew onto the middle of the train like a mother hen with chicks.

They held up well between Queen and King. But the second the train pulled out of King station, the south-western tip of the Box, panic exploded.

The calmest of them fidgeted uncontrollably. Others began yelling, hassling passengers, trying to pry open the doors. One broke a window, ostensibly by accident. Another ripped the emergency strip from the wall.

Ritz, a voluptuous Gangrel, straddled the lap of a startled businessman, well, his briefcase, since he didn't have time to move it off his legs. She brushed the few hairs on the top of his head aside and planted her teeth in a vein in his forehead.

A six-foot-two blond Kindred named Marcus

used his rapier to thrust and parry with a group of young hockey players, who thought it was pretty funny.

Janus had cornered two gay men, slid his hands down to their respective crotches and grabbed on, to the delight of one, and the chagrin of the other.

Razor was busy trying to pull open the door to the booth where the second conductor sat, struggling to keep it shut. The conductor was too stunned to press the emergency button, fortunately, and Bianka managed to peer into his terrified eyes just long enough to put him to sleep at the controls. Then she hissed at Razor, who threw back her head, laughed, and exposed her fangs to a woman with a three-year-old clinging to her in horror.

Bianka and Swan glanced at each other for a fragment of a second. In unspoken agreement, they surged into action before any of the Camarilla frenzied. It was all the two of them could do to catch the eyes of the terrified passengers and lull them, meanwhile grabbing Kindred by the scruff of the neck as they would children throwing a tantrum and hauling them down the car to the rear. It took two stops—humans entering and exiting with looks of anger or terror on their faces—to get the Kindred settled at one end of the car, and another two stops to get them under a viselike mental control. And then they became exactly like children, in a new place, eyes round, glancing at everything for the first time. Enthralled.

They studied the walls, the seats, the floor, the ceiling fans. It was as though they had been in the Box for so long, they had forgotten this world of freedom existed. Sights, smells, the feel of the metal poles and the brown and orange plastic seats, the glass in the windows, the swaying of their bodies as the train rumbled forward, the view of the blackness of the tunnels, the sound of metal scraping metal as the wheels rounded a curve in the track, announcements on the PA system, the salty-sweet scent of popcorn from the three-year-old's bag, the chimes as the doors opened and closed, passengers entering, exiting, seated, standing, laughing, arguing, reading, kissing in the train going in the opposite direction, dressed formally, informally, for business, for sport, for dancing... all of the normal aspects of subway life in Toronto, and these poor Camarilla saw it all as bewitching and exciting and captivating. And it made Bianka sad. Whatever else occurred, she longed to free these tormented souls.

Finally they reached Davisville Station, and she herded them out onto the exposed platform, then up the narrow escalator single file and finally onto the busy street.

They all felt it, but Reg was the first to verbalize the fear that threatened to crush them. "We're in Sabbat territory."

The others glanced around as if the danger of the situation had suddenly struck home. They'd violated the terms of the Settlement. It had been fun. But now it was serious.

"If they find us... " a statuesque blonde said, her voice cracking.

Their fear became palatable.

"Follow me," Bianka snapped, taking charge

before they ran screaming into the night, drawing to them the thing they feared most, attracting the attention of the Sabbat.

She led them south quickly, to the northeast corner of Mt. Pleasant Cemetery. Her plan had been to take them through a main gate, but they were too jittery to walk another block— they'd never make it that far without a scene.

"Over the fence," she ordered. They paused, too long. Finally, she turned to Swan. "Don't be afraid."

The challenge to the Brujah was the right way to proceed. Swan didn't hesitate, but leapt the wrought-iron fence in one bound. Reg eased between the stone embankment and the last spike of the fence. One of the others pulled two of the rails apart, and a dozen Camarilla slipped through. What must have been a Nosferatu began burrowing under the metal.

Once they were all inside the grounds, Bianka climbed the fence and Ravena flew over the top. She led them further at a good clip, away from the distractions of Yonge Street, the traffic, the lights, the scent of human blood. The fear of the Sabbat.

The cemetery was peaceful. This, the oldest part, lay dense with Celtic crosses, marble tombstones whose dates the elements had rendered indecipherable, and elaborate pillared crypts from the last century. They passed one crypt, a small imitation of the Parthenon, and Janus said, "Hey, they left the door open! They going in or coming out?"

"Good Evening!" Reg said, in a Bela Lugosi imitation, bowing grandly, as if calling to the dead.

Razor leapt up the steps and pushed the gargoyle face on the door. The iron door opened and she peered inside. "Nobody home."

"Just as well." Reg sounded relieved.

Bianka moved them across the vast lawn, between graves, under the rustling dying leaves and toward a building that stood taller than most of the crypts. By the moon, its shape was clear but odd—rounded at the top, square at the bottom, turrets along the roof, and a spire—it looked like a small castle. Moonlight glinted off the upright rectangular window panes and the matte metal of the grated door.

Over the door, carved into the stone, was the name Capel.

Bianka mounted eight stone steps and at the top broke the chain holding the door closed. She pushed inward on the iron and held it open. Silently, the Camarilla entered one by one. When they were all inside, Ravena flew in and up to a ledge just beneath one of the stained glass windows, above the small marble alter. When Bianka entered, she saw expectant faces turned in her direction. Already some of the Kindred had seated themselves on the Oriental carpet on the floor. Several others perched on the altar, and the ledge just behind it, below the ledge on which Ravena sat. Janus was helping Razor pry open one of the drawers. Inside, they found a mahogany coffin, and they opened that as well.

"I hate it when they use embalming fluid," Janus said. He lifted one of the deceased's arms, too high, and it broke away from the rest of the body like the leg comes away from the trunk of a roasted chicken. Razor laughed. The tall lean vampire tossed the arm back into the coffin and shut the lid. He must have had the power of speed, because he was, in an instant, seated on the closed lid.

As Bianka pulled the metal door shut, the clank felt loud and heavy in the enclosure.

"How come you brought us here?" Swan demanded.

"Well, it's safe, for one thing," she assured the Brujah. "No humans. And no Sabbat."

"How can you be sure the Sabbat aren't here?" Reg wanted to know.

"Why would they be here?" Swan answered for Bianka. "They hunt most of the night; there's no blood in a graveyard at night. And they certainly can't be here in the day any more than we can."

"How come you know this place?" It was the lean male seated on the coffin asking.

"I don't believe we've been introduced," Bianka said, using this formality because he had a defiant nature, and she wanted him as an ally, or at least not as an opponent. And because she didn't want to answer the question.

"They call me Janus."

Bianka nodded. He looked to be of Greek descent, wavy black hair, earthy, soulful eyes. She figured he must be Tremere. He was the most high-strung of this group, ultra sensitive to sounds, to vibrations. Even before Ravena squawked, he looked up, as if sensing the shift in the bird's vocal cords.

"So, how do you know about this place?" He wasn't about to be distracted.

"I've been here before," Bianka said, and left it at that. Fortunately, so did the others.

"You've come a long way tonight," Bianka told them.

"Yeah, at least five miles on the subway," Janus said.

The others laughed, and Bianka joined in. The laughter was cathartic. They were all too tense.

She took a seat on the floor, next to Swan. "As I said earlier, this is a small action, but it's a big step as well. The Camarilla outside the

Box will know about your defiance—I'll make sure they do. They're eager to help you, but you've got to help yourselves first, and show them you need and want help."

"So, how long are we staying in this mausoleum?" Reg asked, looking around at the carved stone interior. "I mean, it's lovely and everything, if you like crypts. Of course, I once made love in a crypt, when I was still human—"

"Oh, please!" Swan said. "Not that story again!"

"Let him tell it," Razor said. "It's always different."

"Yeah, every time we hear it, he manages to come one more time."

The others laughed, and Reg did as well. Bianka was glad he wasn't offended. The mood was good, humorous. This minor act of rebellion had not only lifted their collective spirits, but it seemed to give them confidence. What before had been cutting remarks between them now came out as playful banter among comrades.

The Kindred laughed and joked the night

away and about an hour before dawn, as the sky was lightening, Swan said, "If we're going to make it back to the Box, we'd better go now."

"We can stay here during the day," Bianka said.

Immediately she felt unease spread through the group.

"That's not a good idea," Reg said. "That increases the chances of the Sabbat finding us."

"Look, the subway is closed by now. If we leave, and we can't find a cab, we'll be on the streets—it will take us a good hour to get back, and that's at top speed. And there's a better-than-average chance that the Sabbat will spot us."

This sobered the group quickly.

"If we stay the night," Swan said philosophically, since she clearly saw that leaving now was no alternative, "we can all say we were in Sabbat territory for a day. At sunset, we'll head out, catch the subway—better yet, cabs—and be back in the Box before the Sabbat have a chance to brush their pointed teeth."

The agitation did not quite die out, but with

Swan's support it leveled enough that a consensus was reached: The Camarilla would stay the day.

They got busy blocking the stained glass windows with their shirts and untied bandannas from their heads to avoid the colored light that would filter through. Swan used the carpet over the grated door. Once they were in total darkness, feeling the pressure of the impending daylight, they settled back like children, too tired to either worry or protest further.

Ravena squawked, but softly. Only Janus turned to stare at the bird.

I'm going to, Bianka assured the raven. *They need to be soothed.*

"The Camarilla have a long and complex history," she said. "And so do the Sabbat."

Eyelids split apart and sleepy orbs turned in her direction. Other eyelids grew heavy and pressed together. They were hungry, these babies, and needed feeding.

"Once, shortly after the Inquisition, when the Masquerade had just barely gotten underway, I remember being in Barcelona, walking Las Ramblas, the market area, shortly after the sun set. The street then was earth, and the stalls wooden, the area congested with animals and humans. I stopped by the well— it's a fountain now—and watched as a Camarilla and a Sabbat headed toward one another, unaware, from opposite directions, one from the north, one from the south. Neither noticed the other—I guess they weren't very strong in Auspex powers."

Janus laughed. Bianka heard several sighs as the Kindred nudged close to slumber.

"By the time they reached the fountain, both males had spotted the enemy, and me, of course. They weren't particularly interested in me, which was just as well, and I suspect that because I didn't move to one side or the other, that reassured them."

"You're Camarilla," Swan yawned. "Why didn't you side with your Sect?"

Bianka looked up at Ravena. DeWinter, apparently, had not told the others she was Inconnu. Now might not be the best time to spring it on them. Evasion was not a lie, and a half truth sometimes went further than the full truth. "In the early days, lines were not yet clearly drawn," Bianka said. "The Masquerade was implemented slowly, carefully. There was a lot of confusion."

Swan seemed to accept this, or at least she did not question it.

"They were dressed in the skins and leather of the day. Both had just awakened, it seemed—it was not one hour after sunset.

"I watched both take a fighting stance. 'Out of my way, thin-blood drinker!' the Sabbat demanded, as they do.

"'Your way?' the Camarilla cried, equally obstinate. 'Your way is the other way, Kindred.'

"The Sabbat snarled, 'Kindred!' as if it were a curse, and spat at the Camarilla's feet. 'You weaklings dance to the tune the humans play. You live in a dream. A fantasy. Wake to your true nature, Camarilla! You're a killer, like me. A vampire. Or can't you say the word?'

"The Camarilla stood his ground. It was clear he had a cloaking ability. Even as I watched him, his brown body seemed to blend with the earth tones of the merchant's stalls. The Sabbat, on the other hand, seemed to possess the powers of the wolf. Before my eyes, he began to change form.

"That the humans in the square were able to pass by all this without noticing amazed me. I don't know what they saw. A shadow? A large gray dog? Probably one of the two Cloaked the Gathering.

"'Yes, I'm a killer, but I have reason as well,' the Camarilla countered. 'I can choose to kill, or choose not to kill. You have the same choices, friend, if you choose to exercise them.'

"'I am not you *friend*, fiend! We are sworn enemies. And don't try to drag me through the maze you weaklings love to build with words. Our nature is to hunt! Vitae is what drives us! You are a disgrace!'

"They went back and forth like this for some time, posturing, threatening, trying to Dominate, but being careful not to push too hard. Finally, it got late enough that the humans had vanished and there were only the three of us, the two of them still going at this verbal combat. Suddenly, the Sabbat turned to me and said, 'You, girl! Tell us which one has the right of way!'

"This startled me. Of course, I'd been wondering for hours why these two refused to come to blows. After all, they *were* sworn enemies. I'd seen many fights that led to death on one side or the other. And now this Sabbat was asking *me* to intervene? My amazement doubled when the Camarilla said, 'Yes, you saw the whole thing. We will abide by your decision.'

"They were like drunken soldiers, too tired or off-balance or stubborn to fight, or so it seemed. I was never so bloodthirsty that I needed to see Kindred and Vampire at each other's throats, so I took the diplomatic route and said to the Camarilla, 'I believe you were headed east,' and to the Sabbat, 'and you west.'

"'And?' the Sabbat said fiercely.

"'And since you've come from opposite directions, and are headed in opposite directions, neither of you has to move for the other.'

"The two thought about it for a few minutes. In unison, both turned, the Sabbat toward the west, the Camarilla toward the east. Both proceeded on their way, as if this encounter that had lasted for nearly twelve hours had never been. Astonished, I watched them both until they vanished from view. It was only then that I understood that they had not wanted to fight but felt compelled to put on a performance, perhaps for my benefit, perhaps for their own."

Bianka looked around the crypt. The Camarilla slept, stretched out, curled into a ball, entwined one with another, on the floor, on ledges—Janus lay atop the coffin. Swan, fists balled, sat propped against the cool stone wall, eyes closed, succumbed to the weight of near-deathlike sleep.

This place spawned memories, too many, too powerful, and although they were not recent, they still held the power to resurrect pain in her.

High up on the ledge, Ravena flapped her wings once, then curled them around her body and tucked her head down beneath one.

Yes, Bianka told her, *they will need all the sleep they can get. And so will I.*

Bianka should have been the first to awaken, but it was Janus. And he was screaming.

Even before the Camarilla could get to their feet, Sabbat swarmed over them.

How in hell did they get here so fast? Bianka said, but there was no time for Ravena to offer an opinion.

A clawed, fanged, filthy creature had Reg by the throat, bashing his head against the stone walls of the crypt. Swan fought two of them, but she'd been taken by surprise, that was clear. They had her down on the floor at an awkward angle, biting her, tearing the flesh from her body, although she managed to kick one in the groin, and he howled.

Ravena flew between the violence, hysterical, searching for the exit, finally crashing against a stained glass window hard enough to break it until she was outside, swooping back into the fray, and then out again.

Screams and the scent of blood flooded the death chamber.

Desperate to stop the carnage, Bianka searched for the leader. And found him.

He had two Camarilla off their feet. One he grasped around the waist and clutched against his hip. The other, a petite female just under five feet tall, he held upside down by her ankle. Just as Bianka stepped toward him, a hulking monster with blood-stained fangs attacked her. Her steely glance sent him crashing backward as if she'd struck him physically.

In an instant, Bianka stood before the leader. "I'll give you what you want. The Camarilla aren't responsible for being out of the Box. I'm the one you want. Stop them."

He was her height, wearing glasses with round lenses and gunmetal frames. Through those lenses, he stared straight into her eyes. She was astonished that he didn't capitulate to her powers. She had meant to Entrance him.

But he was not Entranced. And that left her stunned and helpless.

He dropped one Camarilla and tossed the other on top of

Reg, who lay moaning from his wounds. For a second, he stared at her and she saw something in his look. It might have been respect, maybe because she stood up to him, maybe for some other reason. Maybe it wasn't there at all.

A Sabbat, drunk on Camarilla blood, stumbled past, and this leader yanked him back. "Freon, end it!" he said.

The Sabbat looked at him like he was crazy, but the leader shook him hard, bringing him to his senses. Together the two of them shoved, hauled, and hurtled the half dozen Sabbat warriors out the door of the crypt.

For the most part, the damage had been done, and it was almost too late. Bianka looked around. Camarilla lay in pools of their own blood, stripped of their flesh, gouged. But the wounds would heal. None were fatal. None, she knew, were as bad as they would have been in a few more moments.

"And you are?" the Sabbat leader asked.

She turned back to him. "Bianka."

He looked as if he knew that already. She wasn't surprised. Word traveled fast through Sabbat circles. Especially when it came from the Camarilla, and she knew they had been betrayed.

She couldn't drain his mind. She would have to try seduction, although she was not proficient at it when Sabbat were concerned. "I brought them here," she said, using her hands like paintbrushes, her lips curling around the sounds that came from her. "I convinced them to leave the Box."

She watched him watching her. Maybe she could charm him.

He snatched at her, grabbing both wrists in one of his hands. No, that wouldn't work. She felt more helpless than ever. It had been a long time since she'd met one of the undead she could not control.

"Am I suppose to believe you hypnotized them?"

"No. I didn't say that. But I... convinced them. Look, let them go."

He laughed. Still holding her wrists, he shoved her hard against the stones. "Don't make me laugh, Camarilla. Why should I let any of them go? You've left the Box, invaded our territory—"

"Because if you free the others, I'll stay willingly."

"You'll stay anyway, or didn't you notice you're already a prisoner?"

He might be stronger than her physically, but she had many centuries under her belt, and a few tricks up her sleeve.

"Lot, I can't hold them back much longer," the Sabbat at the door, the one the leader had called Freon, who had helped clear out the crypt, said.

Bianka willed him to look at her, for only a split second. No permanent damage. Just enough to display her powers.

The one named Lot saw his friend wilt, as if exhausted, too tired to think of the battle.

Lot twisted Bianka around, so her back was to Freon, blocking her view. "Don't look at her eyes!" But it was too late. Freon slid to the floor in the doorway and was snoring within seconds. Ravena, still flying haphazardly around the room, swung low over Lot's head.

"What the hell did you do to him?" Lot shook her, hard enough so that her fangs clacked against her lower teeth.

"Let them go!" she cried. "I won't do that again to any of the others. I give you my word. Just let them go. You've punished them enough. I'm to blame. You have me. I'll stay of my own will."

He stared at her, balanced between two points, deciding. A quick glance at the torn and bleeding Camarilla surrounding him seemed to help him decide. In a low voice, he said, "All right. My men will take them back to the Box, under guard."

"Can you guarantee they won't be harmed further?"

"No one could guarantee that. I'll order them not to kill them—it's all I can do."

She knew it was as much as she could get.

"Undo what you did to Freon."

She smiled slightly.

"Do it!" He raised a hand, as if to hit her.

"I can't. He'll sleep, probably most of the night. I didn't take much of his memory. Maybe a day or two."

He didn't hit her, but he didn't lower his hand right away. He stared at her as if she were a dangerous animal. He was wary now, ready to do her violence—the violence going on all around them encouraged that. He also looked at her with disbelief—how had she altered Freon, a hardened warrior, but not him? It was a question she asked herself.

Lot had one of the vampires take Freon back to his haven. To the other four, he gave specific instructions. Bianka could tell from their faces that they had no intention of obeying beyond a fine line; they would not kill the Camarilla, but they would do as much damage short of death as they could between here and the Box.

She just hoped that the numbers—one Sabbat to two Camarilla—would make their job more difficult.

The Camarilla were hauled up and out of the tomb, cuffed, slapped, punched along the way. Swan was one of the last, her face bloody, her look fierce yet unreadable. It could have said betrayal. It could have reflected gratitude that an exchange had been made. Bianka had no time to study it to find out.

Ravena, still flapping around the inside of the crypt, soared low, beak open, shrieking. Lot pulled a dagger from his belt.

"No! Don't harm her!" Bianka yelled, and smacked his arm away.

He shoved her back by instinct, and she hit the stones hard.

To the outside! Go! she ordered the raven.

Ravena squawked, and it meant only one thing: She would not abandon Bianka.

Suddenly, Ravena landed on Bianka's left shoulder. Her wings folded back and she settled. Determined.

"Don't harm her, and I give you my word, I won't try to escape," Bianka said quickly.

Lot watched it all. Oddly enough, he seemed half amused, half awed. She saw him slide the heavy knife back into the sheaf at his waist. "Are you Gangrel?"

"No," Bianka said. She reached up and stroked Ravena's belly feathers, still looking at Lot. He was watching her. Intent. Curious. Amused. And another look Bianka thought she saw but didn't understand at all: delight.

A peculiar feeling descended over her. One she didn't recognize and couldn't identify. Suddenly, though, she saw this Sabbat in a different way. There was a strength about him, more than just physical, that appealed to her. Strength based on fairness and sanity.

"Come on," he said, heading toward the door.

"Where are we going?"

He didn't answer.

"Can I bring Ravena?"

He looked half-amused, half-annoyed. "Why not? I've never interrogated a bird."

CHAPTER EIGHT

The attack came off almost exactly as Lot had planned it. He had his Sabbat recruits gathered and in place well before dawn. Convincing Freon to join him had been as easy as he expected, and Freon had known another Sabbat pack that would be willing to help for the privilege of kicking some Camarilla ass. Lot's price—that they not tell anyone about the Camarilla's escape for two nights, giving Lot time to go over Fletcher to the Archbishop—had been accepted eagerly by both packs. The contempt that the Sabbat showed for the Camarilla had surprised Lot. Did they really despise them that much?

Once they were in the cemetery, Lot had sent a Nosferatu skulker up to eavesdrop under the windows of the big Capel tomb. The ugly, twisted vampire had come back nodding. "They're in there. They got the windows and doors covered against sunlight. Sounds like somebody's telling them a bedtime story."

"Now?" Freon had asked, flexing his thin white hands.

Lot had shaken his head and ordered the Sabbat to find refuge for the day in the crypts nearby. The Sabbat were fierce and the Camarilla degenerate, but the vampires inside Capel's crypt still outnumbered those outside two to one. They would attack at sunset, defying the last moments of twilight, and catch the Camarilla still rising from their sleep. Surprise and confusion had always served the

Sabbat well in the past. Together with some of Freon's pack, Lot had stretched himself out in the narrow confines of a small mausoleum. A couple of handfuls of his native soil, collected from the warehouse along with his glasses and regular clothing, made the tomb comfortable. The day passed quickly and the gathering darkness of dusk brought him instantly to full alertness.

They crept up on Capel's tomb in absolute quiet. Lot's power of silence choked off the squeal that opening the old metal door might produce. The Camarilla lay like mushrooms in the darkness inside the crypt. Lot raised his hand....

One of the Camarilla shifted in his sleep, then sat bolt upright, eyes still closed, and screamed in terror, as if from a nightmare. Lot snarled. The screaming vampire threw his timing off, but the Sabbat knew a natural signal when they heard one. Instantly, they were among the startled Camarilla, roaring and hissing and screeching and bellowing, keeping their opponents off balance. Freon and the other pack-leader were struggling with a Camarilla wildcat, but they had her down quickly and kept her down. The Nosferatu who had eavesdropped on the tomb last night had his warty hands on a pretty-boy vampire. He grinned hideously as he bounced the Camarilla's handsome face off of a wall. There was a bird, a raven, in the crypt as well, shrieking in panic and flapping through the air, adding to the chaos.

Two Camarilla charged at him. Lot had moved his knife from his boot-sheath to a sheath on his belt where it would be easier to reach. His hand moved toward it. One of the Camarilla took the bait. She slapped at Lot's hand, but met only air. Lot ducked down, seized her ankle, and straightened up again. She fell, cracking her head hard against the floor, then she was dangling limp from Lot's raised hand. Lot caught the other Camarilla with a lightning-fast knee to the stomach. The force of the blow probably would have killed a mortal, rupturing vital internal organs. Vampires didn't use their internal organs much anymore, but the blow still hurt. The Camarilla doubled over. Lot caught him by the waist with one arm, hoisting him up, ready to throw him.

Then the sea of battle parted. Bianka stood there, challenging him. "I'll give you what you want," she said.

Lot paused, listening to her words, but barely hearing them.

She was beautiful.

Now that he was looking at her directly instead from the side, he could see her face. Her lips were full and as red as rose petals. Her cheekbones were high, her eyebrows fine and arching. Her eyes, though... her eyes were pale, pale blue. They lent a wonderful eeriness to her face, an otherworldly look that set her apart from the violence in the crypt.

Then Bianka blinked and the spell was broken. Lot focused his concentration on the moment, trying to put her out of his mind. There was a strength to Bianka, and she was beautiful... strength in beauty, beauty in strength.... He felt himself falling into her again. No! She was his enemy. Still, her suggestion had merit and it coincided with what DeWinter had asked of him. He could take Bianka to Dyce and let the other Camarilla go. If the Archbishop decided to punish them later, that was out of his hands. Lot threw aside the two Camarilla that he held and grabbed Freon as the pack-leader came past. "End it!" he ordered.

A harsh shake emphasized his words, then Lot turned back to Bianka. Freon began sweeping the other Sabbat out of the crypt. Lot shoved any Sabbat that came within his reach toward the door as well. Bianka was looking around, sorrowfully surveying the damage that had been caused to the Camarilla. The Sabbat had remembered Dyce's edict. None of the Camarilla were dead, though most were injured, some horribly. Bianka seemed to be the only one to have emerged unscathed. That wouldn't last for long once the Archbishop had her in his hands.

Blood tangling that fine black hair, blood seeping over those perfect lips, bloody tears of agony staining those pale eyes...

Lot tore himself away from the vision his imagination had created. He was strong! He forced his discipline into a hard edge. "And you are?" he demanded harshly, just as if he didn't know her. He was reluctant to betray the roles that DeWinter and Razor had played in bringing about this savage attack.

"Bianka."

It was all he could do to keep his face and body rigid. Her name, from her lips, in her own voice! No. No! There could be no weakness. Fortunately, Bianka didn't give him a chance to reply. She started to talk again, offering excuses for the Camarilla. She began to gesture, weaving patterns with her hands to enhance her words, just as Razor had said she did. Lot grabbed her wrists to stop her.

Did she know how soft and smooth her skin was? Discipline, he reminded himself. You are Sabbat. She is Camarilla. She has violated the Settlement. The Archbishop would judge her. Lot's rights and duties were clear. But... he kept talking to her. He couldn't stop himself. Something in the pit of his stomach drove his voice onward and all that his discipline could do was mold it. "Am I supposed to believe you hypnotized them?" Harsh words again, the words of Sabbat to Camarilla.

"No. I didn't say that. But I... convinced them. Look, let them go."

His mouth twisted with black humor. "Don't make me laugh, Camarilla." He couldn't bring himself to say her name out loud. It was as if the syllables might shatter his tenuous control. He despised himself! He pushed Bianka roughly against the stone wall of the crypt. "Why should I let any of them go? You've left the Box, invaded our territory—"

"Because if you free the others, I'll stay willingly."

Was she mocking him now? "You'll stay anyway, or didn't you notice you're already a prisoner?"

Freon called something from beside the door. His attention on Bianka, Lot didn't catch what the other Sabbat said, but he saw what Bianka did. She glanced at Freon, meeting his gaze.... Hastily, Lot snapped a warning to Freon, simultaneously stepping around to put himself between the Sabbat and Bianka. He was too late. Freon crumpled to the floor. Lot cursed silently. The power of command—but Bianka had spoken no words, given no suggestions to Freon's conquered will. She was powerful. Was that what this demonstration had been intended to prove? That she could escape any time she wanted?

If she could command Freon from across the room, why had she not tried to do the same thing to him while he was staring into her pale eyes from mere feet away? Or had she? Was that why he wanted to let her go?

Anger slowly edged through his passion. As unwelcome as his feelings for this mysterious foreign Camarilla were, he felt strangely and suddenly violated. His rage as he shook her was genuine. "What the hell did you do to him?"

"Let them go! I won't do that again to any of the others. I give you my word. Just let them go. You've punished them enough. I'm to blame. You have me. I'll stay of my own will."

He froze. Could he believe her? Part of him,

his anger, said to kill her now. Another part, his discipline, calmly pointed out the wisdom in what she said. A willing prisoner would be far easier to handle than a prisoner who was trying to escape. A third part, the weak, despicable kernel that spoke out of his chest, murmured support for his discipline. If Bianka did have the power to knock him unconscious or manipulate his emotions with a gaze, why hadn't she pressed her advantage?

His hands clenched around Bianka's arms as he listened to his own conflicting feelings. Anger locked against discipline locked against... against something pathetic and weak! Lot growled, as much at himself as at Bianka. He wasn't weak!

One of the Camarilla on the blood-stained ground groaned. It was the pretty-boy that the Nosferatu had been slamming into the wall. Lot glanced down at him. The Archbishop would want the Camarilla returned to the Box, wouldn't he? After all, he liked his captive vampires; wouldn't preserving them make him happy? Lot wasn't sure which part of him made the suggestion—he hoped it was his discipline—but it made his choice easier. "All right," he murmured to Bianka. "The Sabbat will take them back to the Box, under guard."

"Can you guarantee they won't be harmed further?"

So much concern from a vampire. He wanted to laugh. He wanted to pull Bianka into an embrace. He chose to laugh. She was talking about Sabbat and Camarilla. She might as well having been talking about wolves acting as shepherds. "No one could guarantee that. I'll order them not to—it's all I can do. Undo what you did to Freon."

She just smiled at him. His rage surged again. His hand rose over her... but he held back, forcing himself not to harm her. He lowered his hand, but only slowly. He felt ashamed of himself. It wasn't entirely shame that his discipline had failed him, either. He had one of Freon's pack take her fallen leader back to their haven. The rest of the Sabbat he ordered to escort the Camarilla back to the Box—as discretely and gently as possible. He backed up his commands with a snarl and a flash of fangs, the kind of straightforward command that the Sabbat could recognize and respect.

He was watching them haul the last of the Camarilla away when a piece of darkness detached itself from the shadows near the tomb's roof to dive at him, shrieking. The raven. Bianka's raven. Instinctively, he snatched the knife from his belt, ready to ward the bird off. Bianka shouted and shoved at his arm. She was only trying to protect her creature, he knew, but that shove almost woke the beast in him again. It was only with supreme self-control that he pushed her away with his free hand and not with the one that held the knife.

When he looked at her again, the raven had settled on her shoulder. Words came into his head. Without thinking, Lot spoke them. "Are you Gangrel?"

He regretted it instantly. It was a stupid question. There were a hundred questions more important, questions that he should have asked her. Instead he was asking her clan, like one human asking another what her sign was. He struggled to control his embarrassment. Bianka watched him and said, "No." She didn't offer him any other answer. The matter was at an end. Lot almost smiled with relief—then suppressed that, too. Bianka was still watching him. He pulled her toward the door. She asked where they were going, but he kept his silence. She wouldn't want to know. She didn't ask again, but she did add, "Can I bring Ravena?"

The bird. "Why not?" His mouth twitched, a smile trying to force its way onto his face. "I've never interrogated a bird." Bianka didn't laugh. Neither did he. He steered her out of the crypt and pulled the grated door shut behind them. "This way." He set off across the dark grass of the cemetery. He had come to the cemetery with Freon's pack last night, riding in the back of the pack's big van. His own car was still at the warehouse. All of the Sabbat had parked at the far eastern end of the cemetery, then approached Capel's crypt on foot. That was a long hike, and he wasn't even sure if the cars would still be there. The Sabbat might have collected them to transport the Camarilla back to the Box. The cars might simply have been towed during the day, in which case he felt real pity for the night watchmen at the impound yard. In any event, He didn't feel like wasting time looking for the cars. He wanted to get Bianka to Dyce, though they would have to stop briefly at Fletcher's warehouse first. Lot hoped fervently that the bishop would be out.

The subway, he decided, would be too conspicuous, too open. What if Sabbat spotted him with Bianka? A cab down Yonge Street would also be too conspicuous. The Sabbat haunted Toronto's main street just as the Camarilla haunted Queen West. There were other options, though. He would take her through the old, moneyed residential area just south of the cemetery until they hit Bloor Street and he could hail a cab. From there they could reach the warehouse easily.

He glanced at Bianka in the dim moonlight. She kept her eyes on the ground, stepping carefully. The terrain in the old part of the cemetery could be treacherous. Many graves here had subsided, leaving unexpected dips and hollows. Fallen, broken, and vandalized gravestones had been replaced with little granite markers set almost—but not quite— flush with the earth. Flat moonlight and the neglected grass of the lawn hid dips and markers alike. The moonlight also turned Bianka's hair into a blue-black curtain like a nun's wimple. Almost he reached up to brush it aside so that he could look at her face.

Ravena, her black eyes glittering, cocked her head to look at him.

Lot's hand fell back. They walked on in silence.

CHAPTER NINE

Bianka followed Lot through quiet residential streets. The homes here had gone from large to opulent, the lawns spreading wider and the number of trees lining the streets surrounding them increasing until it felt as if they were walking through a park and not a neighborhood.

Eternity, she thought, *is a long time, and yet*

there are occasions when time seems too short. Like now. She was headed to someplace where she would likely be tortured, and possibly killed. She shuddered. Ravena edged closer, brushing the feathers of her right wing against Bianka's cheek.

Thank you, my friend, she told the raven. But that was little comfort against the inevitable.

Over the centuries of her existence, Bianka had witnessed too many atrocities committed by her kind to count. The violence that humans did to one another paled in comparison. The Sabbat were the worst, because they had nothing to lose. There was no pretense, no efforts to blend in with or imitate humanity as the Camarilla tried to do. Their codes and rules didn't lack ethics, but their values were such that the Sabbat were not responsible for the very same things the Camarilla felt responsible for. Normally, this did not trouble Bianka. She had been around long enough to find elements of both the Sabbat and the Camarilla appealing, and revolting. Being outside their realms had advantages. She had a cool overview of each that was in no small part tinged with a feeling of superiority.

But she wasn't feeling superior at the moment; she was feeling afraid. Witnessing what the Sabbat had done in the crypt felt like perverse foreplay. She knew that once she reached wherever Lot was taking her, to whoever he served, it would be her turn to suffer. They couldn't know that she was restricted to telling the truth. Truth wasn't all it was cracked up to be. Sometimes lies were preferred by the asker because they made more sense, or kept things simpler. What she knew deep in her heart was that they were going to torture her, whether she told the truth, or lied—if she had been capable of that, which she was not. They would torture her simply for the pleasure of it.

"Is it much further?" Bianka asked. She really meant, how much more time do I have before I must face my own death. She struggled to keep the fear out of her voice. There was no sense in letting this Sabbat see her as weak. The Sabbat despised weakness, and he would use it against her, of that she was convinced.

Lot turned to look at her. His dark eyes took in her face, her body. He was distant, haughty, the way a conqueror is with the conquered, but that interest she'd seen earlier was still there, and it made her wonder what he was about.

"Don't tell me you're tired, Camarilla," he said sardonically.

Tired was not something those in her state experienced very often. At least he had a sense of humor.

"Not tired. Hungry. There aren't any restaurants on this route."

One side of his mouth turned up, only a fraction, but she saw it before he looked away. "You should have stayed home last night; then you wouldn't have this problem."

Bianka's senses came alive. There was a human on this street. She felt his presence, felt the lure of the blood. Lot sensed him too.

She touched Lot's arm and said softly, "I'm

very talkative after I've had a bite. Let me take him."

He ignored her but didn't move to brush her hand away.

The human came into view, a heavy man of about forty, in a uniform; not a policeman, a security guard, hired by this wealthy neighborhood to protect its privileged residents.

Bianka watched him. The blood traveled through his veins at a sluggish pace. It would be old, likely disease-laden from too much drink and tobacco, but fast food was better than none.

As he strolled toward them, he squinted—his eyesight wasn't what it had once been, obviously.

They were dressed outlandishly for this well-heeled area. Bianka, in one of her ankle-length midnight-velvet dresses, a silver cross at her throat, a bird with wings that glittered like diamonds on her shoulder. Lot looked more "normal," in the human sense of the word: comfortable jeans, a loose white shirt, black silk vest. It was the dangerous and illegal weapon hanging from the sheath attached to his belt that put him out of sync with this upscale area.

The guard had no gun, but he did have a walkie-talkie, and automatically his hand reached for it, resting there. Just in case. Not that it mattered—he would be unconscious before he could pick it up.

Only when Lot caught her hand did Bianka realize her nails had dug into his flesh deep enough to draw blood. He took her hand and held it, as if they were lovers, out for a stroll. The real reason he held it was to restrain her. It was like being caught in a vice; the pain stunned her. The bones in her hand were a millimeter away from being crushed. She couldn't speak, could barely keep walking. The pain sliced through the desire for vitae.

As the guard passed, Bianka dimly heard Lot say in a cultivated voice, "Nice evening. Are you going to the costume party too?"

The guard hesitated, then a relaxed smile creased his face. "Nope," he laughed. His hand slipped from the walkie-talkie. Bianka stared at his throat, the flesh constricted by the tight collar, the vein bulging up, so tempting. She leaned toward him.

"Well, have a good evening anyway," Lot said. He tugged on her hand, reviving the pain, sending shooting bolts of it up through her arm, to her shoulder, making her gasp, causing her vision to blur. She realized he was again dragging her along the street.

She felt her teeth ache, the roots throb. Her throat felt so parched she could hardly breathe. Normally, she controlled her hunger quite well. But for some reason, maybe because she felt so vulnerable, because she *was* so vulnerable with this Sabbat and what she would soon face, the Beast danced in circles around her, which made her even more insecure.

"Blood!" she panted. It was all she could manage to say.

"We don't feed prisoners."

She turned on him and lashed his face with her free hand, knocking off his glasses. Ravena flew straight up into the air. Bianka tore at him, the blood haze coloring her vision, her nails strong as claws. Every drop of energy in her was directed toward destroying this creature that stood between her and life-sustaining food.

The battle was short. He had fed recently, and a lot. She was no match for him, tonight.

Moist dirt and slippery grass pressed between her lips and their basic scent filled her nostrils. She realized she was lying face down on a lawn, Lot on top of her, pinning her, holding her while her body thrashed against the earth. Somewhere above, Ravena dive-bombed him, and he had to press Bianka's neck down with one hand and ward off the bird with his other.

"You and your friend better both calm down," he snapped, "or what you drink will be raven blood!"

The thought of him harming Ravena was too much. Slowly the tide of red faded before her eyes. Aches and pains from the struggle began to enter her consciousness. It took some time to get a grip. Finally, he pulled her to her feet.

She stared at him, panting, her hair askew, her face smudged, spitting sweet grass and tangy earth from her mouth. Ravena still swooped low, and Lot blocked the bird with his forearms. All the while, he held onto Bianka as if she might be entertaining thoughts of getting away. She felt insulted.

"Look, you don't have to hold me. I gave you my word I'd come with you and not try to escape."

He looked at her, incredulous. "That's suppose to mean something to me, Camarilla? You'd say anything to save your skin. But your skin is mine, now, beyond saving."

Ravena squawked harshly and attacked again. Bianka could see that Lot was contemplating reaching for his dagger.

Stop it! she commanded. *He's not harming me, and you're going to get yourself killed!*

It took a long time to calm Ravena down, but finally the raven came to rest on Bianka's shoulder. Its normally fast-paced heart pounded even faster, and she felt its muscles quiver and its wings struggling to relax. The bird looked at Lot suspiciously, and he returned the look.

"I need blood," Bianka said simply.

"Don't we all." A light went on in the window of the house before which they had fought. He pulled her along the street, in the direction they had been heading.

After they'd walked another block or so, she yanked her arm from his grasp, tearing the sleeve of her dress in the process. He let her go, but it was clear he wouldn't let her move very far away.

"I'm surprised," she said, when she'd gotten full possession of herself. "That was a very Camarilla thing to do back there, with the guard. Wouldn't you normally just rip out his jugular and leave his carcass in a tree?"

He said nothing, but she read into the silence. "You've got some agenda going, don't you?"

He turned and stared at her.

"You sent the others away on purpose. This slow route to wherever we're going—why not the subway, or a taxi, if you're so eager to interrogate me? There won't be any Sabbat wandering these streets, will there? Nothing to hunt out in the open, and the doors are all barred with high-powered security systems."

She had touched a chord, that was certain, and pressed it a little harder. Maybe he would slip and tell her something. "You want to interrogate me alone, don't you? But that's not the Sabbat way. Who do you answer to? And why are you breaking the chain of command?"

He looked like he wanted to tear her limb from limb. Ravena felt the tension and began twitching beside her. *Steady*, she told the bird. Suddenly, Bianka stopped under a streetlight and forced him to meet her gaze. He still wasn't affected, and that still surprised her. And maybe because she couldn't control him, she realized suddenly that she trusted him in some strange way. That trust washed away some of her own fear.

"I'm not Camarilla," she said sincerely.

The look on his face was priceless, and if the situation had been less dangerous for her, she might have laughed. "You're not Sabbat," he said as a statement, not a question.

"No."

It's all right, she assured Ravena. *I know what I'm doing. I think.*

He ran a hand through his black hair, from the widow's peak back. She watched his broad features shift around as he struggled to come to terms with this new and voluntary information. "You're not Caitiff. You're not repulsively thin-blooded."

"Thanks. And no, I'm not."

"Then what are you?"

"I am Inconnu."

He blinked once. "Unknown. Unknowable. Why tell me?"

"I'm not telling you because I'm afraid of you. I know you're stronger than I am, right now anyway. And I know that you, or someone like you, will torture me, probably kill me before sunrise. You need to know that I'm Inconnu, if you're going to help me. And I need your help."

He laughed in a humorless way. "I think you're confused, Inconnu. You're my prisoner. You're going to help *me.*"

"Get power. Yes. I see you want power. I also see you're ready for it, and you deserve it, that's clear. Am I some means to that end?"

He hesitated, thrown off-guard by her direct statement, which showed him that she saw him clearly, maybe too clearly.

He needed time to think, she knew. He turned and started walking. This time, though, he did not hold her. Maybe it was a test. He wanted to see if she would bolt. She knew that even if she was able to, she wouldn't have gotten three feet before he tackled her. But she couldn't run. She'd given her word. He couldn't know that, and she wasn't about to tell him she was restricted to truth—it would be giving away all of her power, and she was helpless enough.

She followed along until she caught up, then walked by his side in silence, down past a mansionlike house, into a ravine. The woods were lovely and quiet, only their feet on the path, the rustle of the leaves they brushed. Above, a swelling moon lit their way. What a romantic setting, she thought, wondering what had made her think that. But ahead of her, Lot's broad shoulders and narrow hips caught her eye, the way he strode along the path, his hair swaying, the curves of the muscles of his arms… She felt young, foolish. Almost human.

The lights of the city grew brighter as they came up out of the ravine. Once they reached the street, where they might be seen, Lot hailed a cab immediately, glancing in all directions to make certain that there were no probing Sabbat eyes in the vicinity.

"I don't think you can keep me a secret for long," Bianka said. "The guards who took the Camarilla back will be returning soon, and they'll have stories to tell."

"I don't need to keep you secret for long, just long enough. Get in," he said. And added to the driver, "Keep your eyes on the road!"

Ravena flew up into the air. "She doesn't like moving vehicles," Bianka explained, knowing the raven would fly beside the taxi.

In the back seat he ordered, "Lie down." He *really* didn't want her to be seen. Whatever his plan, she knew she was a pivotal part, at least until he got what he wanted from her. When her use value was up, so would be her existence.

She lay her head in his lap, and curled her legs up onto the seat. The scent of the cabby's blood filled her nostrils and she hugged herself as a spasm of intense hunger clutched her stomach. When it passed, she opened her eyes to find Lot staring down at her. He looked confused. He also looked fascinated.

She parted her lips and watched him watch her mouth. The slight and subtle movements of her fleshy lips intrigued him throughout the long ride through the city streets. The half-formed words. The expression of emotion. Opening, closing, enticing. She didn't for a moment think he was Entranced, at least not in the sense that humans were, and most of the undead. But something kept him watching her lips, scanning her face.

She wanted to trick him. To deceive him. To force him to a weak point so she could escape; and yet she could not escape, because she had given her word. That made her feel bleak.

Hopeless. But that was not all she felt. Bianka was unnerved to realize that she just wanted him, near her, touching her. Close.

The moment she became aware of that odd desire, his dark eyes locked onto hers and she knew he could see her longing. Just as she could see his.

CHAPTER TEN

He still wanted to touch her hair. And when she looked into his eyes... he stared back for a few moments and then forced himself to look away.

Lot met the cabby's gaze in the rear view mirror. The human was watching them with interest. What would he see? A man and a woman, her head in his lap. Lot held back a snarl and just glared at the man until he dropped his eyes and looked back at the road.

The drive back down to the warehouse didn't take long. The light of the streetlamps flashed on Bianka in much the same way the moonlight had, but it was harsher and gave her more of an edge. At the same time, though, the cold light seemed to make her vulnerable. Was she trembling, or was that just the motion of the taxi?

If Bianka was trembling, she was right to be afraid. She had guessed that she would be tortured tonight. Lot didn't intend to torture her. Maybe once he would have. Before he saw her. He had to ask her a few questions now, though—that was why he had brought her back to the warehouse. Things he had to know before he could present her to Dyce. The Archbishop, however, might very well torture her. He might hand her over to High Father Truth. That wouldn't be too bad. Truth worked quickly.

But Inconnu. He never would have guessed. If that was true, then Bianka was very old and very powerful. She probably had the ability, as she had demonstrated in the crypt with Freon, to escape whenever she wanted. That would be the best thing she could do for herself. The Sabbat didn't trust the mysterious members of the Inconnu. When it encountered them, the Sabbat did its best to destroy them, either as unknown and therefore dangerous quantities in the war with the Camarilla, or... Lot glanced out the window. Or as stepping stones to power. A younger vampire who consumed the heart's blood of an older vampire, literally drinking them to death, took on the power of the older vampire. It was a way of becoming closer to Caine. The Inconnu were almost always ancient. Self-protection was one of the reasons they usually isolated themselves from other vampires.

Bianka had left the protection of that mystery, though. If he released her now, she might still be able to flee back to it. Except that he couldn't. His loyalty to the Sabbat demanded that he present her to the Archbishop as a criminal guilty of inciting the Camarilla of the Box to rebel and as an

Inconnu, a possible threat to the Sabbat as a whole. His need to revenge himself on Fletcher demanded that she be given up as proof of the bishop's incompetence.

He avoided looking back down at her again.

The trip to the warehouse was over far too quickly. Lot slid out first, standing quietly beside the cab for a moment and reaching out with his senses to search for any signs of Fletcher's presence. There were none. The bishop was gone. Ravena was there, though, perched on a faded sign as if she had been waiting for them. When Lot pulled Bianka out of the cab, the raven fluttered down to perch on her shoulder once more. Lot shoved some crumpled bills at the driver then drew Bianka into Fletcher's haven.

He left her in the big, echoing main room of the warehouse. There were moldering old crates here, left over from when humans used the warehouse. Lot had never looked to see what was in them. He sat Bianka on one.

"I'll be right back. Don't move. Don't try to escape," he said, without trying to restrain her.

"I gave you my word."

"I wish you hadn't." The words came unbidden. Lot turned away quickly.

Benedict was upstairs in Fletcher's throne room, lounging on the bishop's throne and reading one of Lot's books. "This is great stuff!" he said without looking up. "Listen: *Enter the Duke's Bastard meeting the Duchess.*" His voice dropped, then rose as he read the appropriate parts. "*'Had not that kiss a taste of sin, 'twere sweet.' 'Why, there's no pleasure sweet, but it is sinful.' 'True, such a bitter sweetness fate hath given: Best side to us is the worst side to heaven.'*" He turned the page. "How did the attack go? Do we have guests?" He glance up, smiling. The smile vanished as he looked at Lot. "What the hell's wrong with you?"

Lot told him about the attack, about Bianka and the deal that she had offered him, and about how he had accepted it. He didn't tell him about his feelings for Bianka or about her affiliation with Inconnu. As best he could, he kept the story simple and detached. He didn't fool Benedict for a moment.

The Ravnos stared at him, then laughed and reached out to rap on his head. "Hello? Lot? Discipline? Loyalty? Patience? Duty?" Lot pushed his hand away irritably. Benedict snickered. "Lot is like a roomful of dead air. You're not Lot. Prove you're Lot. Tell me to wait. Say 'calm down.' Say 'have patience.' Then I'll believe you."

"Benedict," Lot growled. He grabbed for his friend.

Benedict slipped under his grasping hand and slid off the throne, dodging around to its other side. "I see!" he gasped dramatically. "The Camarilla has kidnapped Lot and sent an impostor home in his place." Lot circled around the throne. Benedict circled as well, keeping the big chair between them. "Do I have to summon him back? *In the beginning there was only Caine*—and he didn't even have a copy of Penthouse. *Caine who was cursed with the lust,*" Benedict pumped his hips with a mocking grunt, "*for blood. Caine grew lonely in his power. He saw in his the blood the potence of fertility —* oh yeah, give me that potence, baby!"

Lot leaped across the throne, crashing into Benedict and knocking him to the floor. "Stop it!" he snarled. "Just stop it!"

Benedict grinned up at him. "You poor son of a bitch. You've fallen in love with her, haven't you?"

"No!"

"Yes." He shook his head in disbelief and quoted, "*Embrace not Love, for Love in My Embrace will grow cold, wither, and die.*"

"That means don't make humans you love into vampires." Lot let his grip on Benedict go slack. "But at least you're getting the words right."

"Now that sounds like the Lot I know." The blond vampire shoved Lot off of himself and stood up. Dust and dried blood clung to his frock-coat. Benedict brushed at it. "You idiot. Are we still going to take her to Dyce?"

"Yeah," Lot replied miserably. There wasn't much choice, was there? "Where's Fletcher?"

"Out hunting."

The outer door of the warehouse crashed

open suddenly. Benedict winced. "Or perhaps not."

Lot was already gone, dashing back downstairs and out into the main part of the warehouse. Fletcher was there, staring at Bianka. Lot's entrance brought his head up. The bishop's eyes narrowed as he regarded his templar. "I don't suppose," he said slowly, dangerously, "you would know anything about a rumor I've just heard, would you? It seems that the Camarilla left the Box last night and stayed the day in an old tomb in Mount Pleasant. Apparently, they've been returned to the Box and their leader captured. Rumor has it their leader was a woman with long black hair and her captor a certain Sabbat templar."

Someone—one of Freon's pack, one of the other pack—had started bragging too soon. Lot choked off the sick feeling that surged in his stomach. "There wasn't time to come get you when I found out," he lied quickly. "I got the packs together and—"

"You could have called." Fletcher's voice was silky.

"I tried. There was no answer."

"Why didn't Benedict tell me about this? Weren't you two out together last night?"

"I just found out about it all myself." Benedict appeared, walking calmly, as if nothing was wrong. "It happened after we separated." He looked at Bianka and whistled. "My, my—" He walked up to the silent vampire, circling her. "Pretty birdy. At least we've got her now, right Fletcher?"

The bishop didn't respond. He was still staring at Lot. "If you couldn't get in touch with me, you should have waited. We could have gone into the Box after them later."

"I thought the Archbishop would want hard evidence."

"Fuck the Archbishop!" Fletcher spat. "I'm in charge of the Box, aren't I? Remember, *you* serve *me*." With each word, he jabbed a finger hard against Lot's chest. His face was inches from Lot's. The other vampire could smell the stink of old blood on his breath. Lot's knife was still at his belt. For a moment, he felt the urge to draw it and plunge the steel into Fletcher's chest. "How did you find out they were leaving?"

He couldn't admit to being in the Box. "Nightbird told me," he said quickly.

"Nightbird?"

Benedict came to Lot's rescue again. "Nightbird. My spy in the Box. I've told you about her. Forget about it." He put his hand on Fletcher's arm, shoving it away from Lot's chest. He jerked his head toward Bianka. "We've got her," he said again, emphasizing the words, driving them into Fletcher's brain. "And with the evidence she can give us, we can collect the other Camarilla anytime." The Ravnos looked at Lot. "Why didn't you tie her up?"

He knew perfectly well why Bianka was loose. Lot had told him. The question, the Tzimisce realized, was meant for Fletcher. Benedict was trying to take the bishop's mind off Lot. "She gave me her word she wouldn't try to escape."

The plan worked. Fletcher snorted. "And you believed her?" He turned away from Lot, back to Bianka. "Do you really intend to keep your word?"

Bianka looked up at him. Her eyes were defiant. *Take him now!* Lot urged her silently. *Do what you did to Freon!* But Bianka just looked and answered Fletcher's question. "Yes."

The big Gangrel's hand shot out, backhanding her viciously. "I don't believe you," he said with perfect calm.

"Believe it or not." Bianka was calm as well. Blood trickled over her lip. Lot's hands clenched in instinctive anger, ready to strangle Fletcher. "It's the truth."

"We'll see." He turned, walking toward his chambers. "Lot, come with me. There are some things I need and then we'll get the truth out of her."

Torture. Lot felt chilled. Fletcher's brand of torture was nothing like High Father Truth's. Fletcher didn't care about the truth, and he didn't work quickly. Helplessly, he started to follow the bishop. He cast a quick glance back at Bianka—just in time to see her stare into

Benedict's eyes and murmur something. The Ravnos blinked.

"Wait," the blond vampire called after Fletcher, "I'll come with you. If she tries to escape, Lot will be able to restrain her more easily than I could."

"Fine," Fletcher yelled back. "Just hustle your butt."

Benedict hurried past Lot without even looking at him. Lot watched him in astonishment for a moment, then dashed back to Bianka. "Why did you do that?"

Bianka turned her face up toward the shadows of the high ceiling. A moment later, Ravena came gliding down out of the darkness. "I need you to let her out," Bianka said urgently.

"After all the trouble of bringing her here with you?"

"I knew you wouldn't harm her." Bianka bit her lip. "Even if you tortured me. But Fletcher—" she shuddered. "He would hurt Ravena just to hurt me. I could stand anything else, but not that." The Inconnu raised her hand and the raven hopped onto it. Bianka looked into its eyes. "You have to go."

The bird squawked quietly in defiance of her command. Bianka shook her head. "Go." She gestured for Lot to kneel down. He did. Bianka set Ravena on his shoulder. The raven glared at him, then pecked viciously at his cheek, drawing blood. Bianka hissed. Ravena withdrew into a sullen calm. "Just take her to the door," she begged. "Let her escape. If she won't—"

Surprisingly, the vampire bit back tears of concern. Lot nodded and stood. "I don't have your skills, but I have a little talent for working with animals." He touched her hand. "I'll do it." Cloaking himself in silence, he walked quickly to the warehouse door and opened it. Ravena flapped her wings and screeched with rage, but no sound escaped Bianka. Lot turned his head and met her black gaze. Some vampires could actually speak to animals. He presumed that was how Bianka communicated with Ravena. He could only communicate emotions and needs easily; anything more was difficult and he had no time for it now. He sent three simple thoughts into the bird's mind. A sense of flight. And a sense of terrible urgency—if he didn't return quickly, bad things would happen to Bianka. And, finally, calm protection. He would safeguard Bianka as best he could. That seemed to surprise Ravena. It surprised him a bit as well, but it was enough to convince the bird of his sincerity. She ducked her head once in that sharp, avian way, then launched herself into the night in a silent flurry of feathers. Lot closed the door and ran back to Bianka. "It's done."

"Thank you." She hesitated, then added, "There's something else I think you should know. I can't lie."

"What?"

"I'm incapable of lying." She pressed fingers to his lips, forestalling his questions. "I can't tell you why right now, but if there's anything that happened tonight that you don't want Fletcher to know, you'll have to make sure he doesn't ask me about it."

There was a clatter and a crash and a curse from Fletcher as something fell to the floor out in the hall. The Gangrel and the Ravnos were returning. Lot stepped away from Bianka. She composed herself, a mask of calm settling over her fear with such resignation that Lot's heart almost broke. Fletcher and Benedict entered, each laden with a number of items. Chief among them were chains, ropes, a thick whip, and a blowtorch. The bishop dropped his load on a crate beside Bianka. He handed a long length of heavy chain to Lot. He didn't tell him what to do with it, but Lot guessed what he wanted. He started to throw a loop of chain around Bianka's wrists. Fletcher stopped him.

"Take off her dress first."

Lot let go of the chain. It slithered to the ground, rattling like a lethal metal serpent. Bianka wouldn't look at him as he drew her to her feet, turned her gently around, and unfastened her black velvet dress. Like the chain, it fell to the ground as well. The sound of its falling, however, was a mournful whisper. Bianka stepped out of the pool of black fabric. Wearing only her shoes, socks, panties, and brassiere, she held her wrists out to him. Lot tried to ignore her body as he bound her wrists, and then her ankles. He couldn't, however. The smooth, pale perfection of her face and neck extended to the rest of her body as well. Light, tight muscles slid under her skin.

"Shoes," snapped Fletcher. Lot knelt and humbly tugged Bianka's shoes off of her feet. His hands trembled as he removed her socks. Her feet were delicate, almost too perfect, like fine porcelain models of real feet with all the flaws corrected.

There was an old block and tackle up among the rafters overhead. A cable with a heavy hook at the end descended through the shadows, dangling cruelly. Fletcher gestured for Lot to hang Bianka from it by her wrist manacles. Hopelessly, he did so, grasping her by her slender waist to lift her up, fumbling to raise her arms into position with his other hand. Finally, though, it seemed as if Bianka was beginning to resist what would happen to her. Her arms sagged and flopped. But Fletcher was still watching him and eventually he had the chains looped over the hook. He released

Bianka as gently as he could. Her toes were just fractions of an inch above the ground. Her entire weight hung from her wrists.

He tried to remember if there was anything that he had told Bianka tonight—or that she had guessed—that would betray him to Fletcher. The long cab ride, the secrecy in bringing her to the warehouse. That was suspicious, perhaps, but not incriminating.

Fletcher had the whip in his hand. He swung it through the air experimentally, making it crack and hiss. Then he snapped it at Bianka. A streak of red appeared across her back. It was that red that finally reminded Lot thought of something that Fletcher could not be allowed to discover.

The blood of ancient vampires was potent. If Fletcher were to taste Bianka's blood, he would realize her age and strength. Likewise, if he were to find out that she was actually Inconnu, he would probably be able to guess at her power. If he did, any thought of torturing Bianka for information would vanish from his head. He would fall on the helpless vampire and drink her heart's blood greedily. Bianka would die. Fletcher would be more powerful than ever. Neither could be allowed to happen. Hastily, Lot stepped up next to the bishop. "Fletcher, did you hear what happened to Freon tonight?"

"She did something to him. He passed out."

Good. Fletcher didn't know what had really happened. That gave Lot his opportunity. He nodded toward Bianka. "During the fight, he bit this Camarilla bitch." It didn't seem likely that Fletcher would ever assume Bianka was anything but what she seemed, but it didn't hurt to reinforce the bishop's ideas. "Her blood is what made him pass out. I smelled it. She's carrying some kind of disease." Diseases of the blood that affected vampires weren't entirely unknown, though fear of them was usually disproportionately large when compared to how uncommon they were. Among the Sabbat, such diseases were especially feared. It only took a single carrier participating in the Vaulderie to infect most of a city. Fletcher twitched and nodded without questioning him. He swung the whip again and again, but didn't pay any attention to the blood that patterned Bianka's back.

Bianka bore the whipping silently. The force of Fletcher's lashings set her swinging in the air, rocking back and forth, chains biting deep into her wrists. Sometimes the tip of his whip wrapped around her body to leave angry marks on her belly and sides. She remained quiet, however, refusing to cry out. The hard lines of her clenched mouth and tightly closed eyes told the true story, however. And Fletcher hadn't even begun to question her yet.

Pain and terror echoed across Lot's soul with each swing of the whip: pain felt for Bianka.

Finally, Fletcher lowered the whip. A human in his position would have been breathing hard, sweat dripping from his body. Fletcher removed his leather jacket. His inhuman torso was still dry. The vampire stretched, however, loosening stiff muscles. He watched Bianka. Lot watched her, too. The blood that had been running from her whip-torn back was slowing as the worst of her injuries began to close. She was healing with the speed of any vampire. Lot ground his teeth in impotent frustration. She had told him earlier tonight that she was hungry. He had not let her feed, had denied her blood. Now Fletcher was forcing her to burn the blood that was left in her body. He would allow her to heal, then whip her again, repeating the process until she had so little blood left that she was utterly dry and helpless.

Bianka must have realized the same thing, because her face suddenly twisted in concentration. She was willing the healing to stop. Fletcher noticed. He set down his whip and picked up a plastic bottle of some clear liquid. "Keep healing, Camarilla. Won't it be nice not to hurt anymore?" He removed the cap from the bottle and raised it up, splashing the clear liquid over her shoulders and back. Bianka screamed piercingly for the first time and twisted in her chains. Her wounds closed almost instantly as her body reacted to this new pain.

The scent of vinegar stung Lot's nostrils. Bianka's shrieks tortured his ears. He wished he could look away. Fletcher picked up the whip again.

The bishop whipped Bianka twice more, each time allowing her to rest and heal. After the third whipping, however, she could no longer heal. The wounds left by the whip were bloodless. Bianka's eyes were wild, her fangs extended, her lips drawn back savagely. Fletcher retrieved a cage from among his torture equipment. Inside was a small white rabbit. When he reached into the cage, the rabbit cringed away from him, red showing around its little eyes. Fletcher grabbed it roughly. The rabbit kicked and scratched at him, but he ignored its struggles, holding it up in front of Bianka. Her eyes locked onto it instantly. Her tongue strayed out of her mouth and licked at the air in a desperate struggle to reach the creature's blood.

"It's yours," said Fletcher, "if you answer some questions."

"Anything," Bianka rasped. Her voice was barely human.

"Did you lead the Camarilla out of the Box?"

"Yes!" Her body jerked forward, jaws snapping hungrily. "Now feed me!"

Fletcher laughed. "I have more questions. Did they come willingly or did you force them to leave?"

"I convinced them to leave."

"Did you force them or did they follow willingly? Answer the question." Fletcher waved the rabbit, baring its furry throat.

Bianka's mouth clamped shut, but an answer forced its way out. "They followed willingly."

Fletcher laughed with evil triumph. "Yes!" He spun to look at Lot. "We've got them. Their asses are ours! They left willingly." Lot didn't answer, but he didn't have to. Fletcher was already turning back to Bianka. "Why did they leave the Box?"

"Rebellion." Her answer was a snarl. Her eyes followed every movement the rabbit made in Fletcher's hand. Every twitch. Every kick. Every random swing.

"Is that all?" Fletcher demanded. Bianka didn't answer. "I said, is that all? Was rebellion the only reason the Camarilla left the Box?"

Bianka still didn't answer. "She's too far

gone," Lot whispered to Fletcher quickly. "Give her the rabbit."

Fletcher's mouth twisted with disdain—Lot wasn't sure whether for Bianka's weakness or his show of compassion. He held up his free hand. Talons sprouted from his fingertips. He flipped the rabbit upside down, holding it by its hind legs. One talon ripped down the length of the rabbit's belly. The animal's guts spilled out, blood pouring down the length of ropy intestines, past straining lungs and a still beating heart, to splatter on the floor. Fletcher held the mutilated animal in the air for a moment longer, then dropped it to the floor. It struggled amid its own innards for a few moments longer before dying.

Bianka went mad, screaming incoherently and struggling in her chains. The combination of hunger and unreachable blood was perhaps the cruelest torment one vampire could devise for another. Fletcher watched her with all the care of a scientist evaluating an experiment. When her flailing began to slow, he gestured Lot forward.

"Hold her legs." The Tzimisce grabbed her around the knees. Bianka was strong in her hunger—it was all he could do to hold on. Fletcher grabbed her around the neck, the crook of his beefy arm restraining her head like a collar. She still snapped at him, spittle flying.

"And lift!" the bishop ordered. Lot lifted. With his other arm, Fletcher slipped Bianka's wrist chains free of the hook. Then he pitched her forward. Shocked, Lot released his hold on her as well.

She hit the floor hard, her jaw cracking. The dead rabbit, blood steaming, was a couple of feet away. Gibbering in starvation, Bianka dragged herself toward it. Her fingers dug into the floor. Trembling muscles tensed. She slid forward. Again. The rabbit was right in front of her. She buried her face in the mess, licking the blood from the concrete floor, a beast feeding.

Lot looked away.

"We'll let her recover a bit," Fletcher said, "then we'll start again." He picked up his blowtorch and a metal pail full of rusty old nuts and bolts.

Lot couldn't stand it. "I'll be in my room if you need me." He walked out, away from the bishop.

Benedict came to him a little while later as he sat on his thin pad of a bed in the darkness. "Fletcher's starting in on Bianka again."

"Will you help me fight him, Benedict?" Lot's voice was harsh. It had taken a lot of effort for him to restrain the beast inside, to walk away from Bianka's torture without howling and leaping at Fletcher. It had taken all of his discipline.

The Ravnos stepped back, startled. "What?"

"Will you help me fight him?" Lot looked up. In his anger, his fangs had descended and every word was accompanied by a whispering hiss. "He has to be stopped. Now. If I fight him alone, it would just barely be an even match. I was an idiot. Fletcher never needed a templar. He'd kick my ass. But if you helped me—"

"Why? Why now, Lot?" Squatting down, Benedict looked him in the eye. "Is it because of Bianka?" Lot nodded silently. Benedict sighed and buried his face in his hands. "Jesus, Lot."

"He'll kill her, Benedict." When the blond vampire didn't reply, he reached out and grabbed him by the front of his frock-coat, dragging him forward. "He's going to kill her!"

"He won't! He needs to take her to the Archbishop."

"Does he?" Lot shoved Benedict away. "We're the ones who needed evidence against Fletcher. He doesn't need evidence against the Camarilla. He never has. Dyce will take his word."

"On something this big?"

"Maybe. Maybe not. I don't know if the Archbishop is going to be willing to punish all of the Camarilla in the Box." He looked at Benedict. "Will you help me?"

Benedict was silent for several moments. Finally he murmured, "She's just a Cammie, Lot. You can't throw everything away for—"

Lot's mouth twisted. "Why don't you just say no?"

"Because it's over, Lot. We've won, don't you see? Enough Sabbat know that you were the one to capture Bianka and send the Camarilla back to the Box that even without Bianka we should be able to convince Dyce that Fletcher is unstable and incompetent. We discovered the Camarilla rebellion, not him. Dyce will depose him. You'll be bishop, Lot. Fletcher will be gone."

"That's not important anymore, Benedict."

Benedict grimaced and abruptly leaned forward and reached out to slap Lot's face. Lot simply caught the hand and pushed it back. "Don't," he said dangerously.

"You're acting stupid. What about your discipline? What about the Sabbat?"

"You don't understand. That doesn't matter. I've got to find a way to get Bianka away from Fletcher."

"We've got to find a way to get you away from Bianka," muttered Benedict. He sighed again. "Look, Lot. Go to the Archbishop, talk to him—"

"It would take too long!" Lot snarled. The beast was surfacing again, trying to push past his discipline. He forced it down, forced himself to remain calm. More than calm. His fangs retracted as he made himself relax and think rationally. "It would all be over before I got back. There isn't time to go to Dyce!"

"Unless *you* want to fight Fletcher; he's the only one who could stop him."

"But there isn't—" Lot paused. There wasn't time to go to the Archbishop, but Benedict was right. Only Dyce could stop Fletcher. But maybe there was another way. Lot closed his eyes as he thought. How many times had he said himself that a good Sabbat needed to be subtle as well as violent? He opened his eyes again. "Benedict," he asked softly, "if you won't fight with me, will you at least play along?"

Benedict looked at him closely, then nodded. "What do you have in mind?"

"Just go back out to Fletcher. Tell him I'm on the phone with Dyce. I'll be out in a few minutes."

"All right." Benedict left. Lot looked at his watch and waited exactly two minutes, then followed him.

Just as he had expected, he ran into Fletcher in the corridor. The mingled stinks of burning propane, hot metal, and charred flesh clung to the bishop. Fletcher grabbed Lot and slammed him up against the wall. "You called the Archbishop?" he snarled.

"No. The Archbishop called here." Lot struggled to remain calm as the man he hated glared at him. "He's heard about the Camarilla leaving the Box. He wants to see you about it. Right now." He looked Fletcher straight in the eye. "He didn't sound happy."

Fletcher's eyes narrowed, but he slowly let Lot go. "Did he say anything else? Did he say anything about the woman?"

"Not really. But he wants you at his haven as soon as you can get there."

"Shit." Fletcher turned and walked back into

the main part of the warehouse. Lot followed him, almost afraid of what he would see.

It could have been worse. After all, Fletcher had only just begun the second round of his torture. Bianka lay chained face down across a crate. Her panties, stained with blood from the whippings, had been pulled off and tossed on top of her crumpled dress. Fletcher's blowtorch, the bucket of nuts and bolts, and a pair of long-handled tongs sat beside her. The smell of hot metal came from that bucket; the stench of charred flesh rose from Bianka's body. Two large bolts lay on her skin—one on her bare buttocks, the other on the back of her right leg—sizzling and smoking as they burned into her. She looked as if she were unconscious. "Benedict," snapped the bishop, picking up his whip and coiling it in his hand. "Wake her up. Get her ready to go."

"Wait," Lot interjected quickly. He glanced at Fletcher. "That would take too much time. The Archbishop is in a hurry. He can see her later. Why don't you take Benedict and go to him now? Benedict knows everything that happened." He picked up the tongs and used them to stir the nuts and bolts in the bucket. Bianka shifted at the dull, painful, rattling sound and moaned. Lot didn't allow himself to look at the beautiful vampire. "Let me finish with her."

CHAPTER ELEVEN

When Bianka came to, she had no idea where she was. Not that it mattered. She might have been underwater. Sounds billowed from a distance, swelling, weaving in and out, smoothly, waves that never quite broke. It was peaceful here, and safe—that was all that mattered.

And then one sound grew louder, not in

volume, which was already high, but in substance.

Bianka traveled from what she now realized enroute had been numbness to complete physical terror. The voice she heard pounded through her cells, awakening pain. Her arms and legs ached. Her back felt raw, a burning, now that she was aware of it, that throbbed endlessly. Every muscle felt damaged. Even her bones seemed bruised. She was excruciatingly weak from blood loss, and her veins had collapsed. Through it all, the Beast howled. Starving. She would kill for food. If only she could move.

Every second brought more sensation, and none of it was pleasant. She willed herself to stillness, like any creature whose life is threatened. But her body betrayed her. At first she thought there was an earthquake; she hallucinated that she was back on the island of Santorini, as black ash turned the sand gray.... The quaking escalated. She tried to crack her eyelids open and realized that they were swollen shut. When she did manage to see through a slit, her vision was too distorted to make out much. She saw two things clearly, though: It was not the earth that quaked, but her body, trembling violently, out of control. And then there was Fletcher—visible only from the waist down, mainly his legs: the arrogant, sadistic stance. The whip, wet with her blood, dangled from his hand.

"Why should I?" he was saying, his tone hostile, sending quivers through Bianka's body.

"Because you must meet with the Archbishop, and appraise him of the situation."

"Are you telling me my responsibilities?"

"No. Of course not. Simply reminding you of what you already know. Now is the time to continue, when she's close to breaking; but not here. Let me take her somewhere… private."

She felt the pause. Heard the laughter. "If I didn't know better, Lot, I'd think you wanted the bitch! She's not bad looking, or wasn't." More macho laughter.

"I want the truth, as do you, Fletcher. I can get it out of her, without killing her. The Archbishop may want to see her."

"Are you saying I can't do that?" The tone was aggressive. Challenging. Threatening.

"I'm saying you have more important things to do. Unless you'd prefer that I see the Archbishop, in your place."

Another pause. Reality faded away and with it the hot agonizing pain. She became cool thought. She needed blood to heal. They would not give her blood. She would not heal. She would die. The thoughts were simple ones, all she could manage. She clung to the black hole of unconsciousness as if it were a life raft. Only when an invisible hand forced it from her and she was plunged once more into awareness did she open her eyes as much as possible.

Someone was lifting her, trying to get her to stand on her feet. She could not feel her legs. Standing was impossible. She felt arms holding her, carrying her, as if she were a child again, a human child, in the arms of her mother or father, being carried to bed, to comfort, to safety.

Her body was slid inside something—a coffin? No, not so enclosed. A loud thud. It was cool here; the air cooled her wounded flesh, but not enough to freeze it to numbness. She could not speak, could not even cry out. The pain scaled the heights of her tolerance again until it felt overwhelming, yet this time it would not overwhelm her enough that she passed out. No mercy in this battered universe.

A loud sound. Motion. Her body bounced around, exacerbating the agony. Inside she screamed, but the sounds came out only as low moans, barely audible. Tears leaked from between her bruised eyelids, coating her face, cold tears that scorched her cheeks.

And then the motion stopped. Another thud. She lay alone, drifting on a cloud of pain, unable to do more than suffer.

Then another sound. Her body being moved to almost a seated position. A scent, human, flesh.

Blood.

The Beast in her demanded that blood and surged toward it, yet she knew her body could not move. But the blood came to her, warm for a second, then cooling, thick, rich. It tasted red. Earthy. Beautiful in its basicness. Swallowing was difficult, but she was motivated.

Even as she drank, she felt her wounds healing, her mind clearing. When she had the strength, still blind, she grabbed hold of flesh and bit. Instantly she realized she had pierced undead flesh. A sharp intake of the breath of the other, the flesh being jerked away. She tasted several drops of blood as the vampire cursed her. But it was the living blood she desired. Human flesh was pressed to her mouth. Her teeth cut into the struggling mortal, deeper with her fangs than the wound already there. She felt gluttonous in her thirst and sucked the blood from the veins until the flow diminished to a trickle.

And only when there was no more vitae, when she sucked and took nothing in, when she had healed enough that her eyes could open, her arms and legs could move, only then did her vision clear and she saw Lot's face. And then the face of the dead human.

Desperately, she glanced around, fearing she

would find Fletcher lurking, terrified that this had been some trick, that they had revived her only so that they could torture her again. An endless round of hurting and healing...

"Lie back," Lot said. "You're badly wounded. And you can't drink any more just yet."

She could not decide whether to be grateful to him or to hate him for forcing her to live, knowing she would again be Fletcher's victim.

She was in a car, in the back seat. Lot removed the empty shell that had been a burly body-builder and hurled the corpse into a dumpster in the alley nearby. He glanced at her, then closed the back door. She heard him get in the front. Then the car started up, and she felt the motion as he shifted into gear.

They drove for what seemed like a long time. She lay in discomfort against the soft leather seat, but not suffering the agony of before. Hunger still strangled her, and with the window open and the chilly night air wafting in, the scent of the warm bodies from the streets tormented her.

Lot turned off onto a road, gravel by the

sound of the crunching beneath the tires, and drove slowly. It was very quiet here and through the windows she could see trees above. The moon was closer to being full. Another night. Would she live to see it?

He pulled to a stop, got out, opened the back door.

"Can you sit up?" he asked.

She nodded and tried to speak. No words came out, just sounds at first, finally a whisper: "Yes."

He helped her out of the car. She was weak but able to stand with little assistance. They were in the cemetery, near the Capel crypt. Why had he brought her here?

They walked slowly across the lawn and up the stone steps. The carnage from sunset was still evident along the way—shreds of fabric, dark stains on the headstones, ahead, one of the grated doors ripped from its hinges. A chill passed through her that had nothing to do with the air's temperature.

Inside, the crypt showed more of the same. The hollow chamber stank of congealed blood.

The remnants of the Oriental carpet were saturated, although most of the Kindreds' blood on the marble beneath it had dried. One vault still lay open, the mahogany coffin shattered, the remains of the departed littering the premises. Feathers were strewn across the floor like black leaves, and Bianka wondered where Ravena was, if she was safe. She couldn't feel the raven's presence, but felt sure in her heart that the bird lived. And then she remembered that Lot had saved Ravena, at her request. Other fragments of memories flowed through her brain, and when she put them together, she realized that Lot had saved her, too.

"Why have you brought me here? Why are you helping me?"

she asked.

"Sit," he said.

A thick metal chain had been wrapped around his waist several times and secured with a heavy padlock. He used a key in the lock and began pulling the chain from his body.

Suddenly, she became afraid. "Are you going to chain me and torture me again?"

He paused. "I don't recall torturing you."

"No, you watched someone else do it."

Anger flashed across his face, but he had enough self-control not to let it get the better of him. "Yes, I might use the chain, if I need to secure you. Do I need to secure you?"

He waited, staring at her, the heavy links hanging from his hands.

"No. I gave you my word I wouldn't try to escape."

He dropped the chain onto the floor with a loud clank and motioned for her to sit.

She found a spot and slid down the wall, her back against the cold stone; she was sitting naked on her soiled dress, which he had brought along. Her body still ached. She was still weak and hungry. "Why is it you believe me? Trust is not a Sabbat trait."

"Because you can only tell the truth."

He stared down at her, directly into her eyes, and she felt as vulnerable as if he had stripped her naked. That he could see this, that her main weakness and strength was so exposed... that she had divulged this... that someone knew...

for only the second time in her existence, she had trouble making eye contact with a vampire.

He moved close and squatted in front of her. "I'm not going to hurt you, Bianka. I give you *my* word."

She smiled weakly. "It's not the same, is it?"

"If you mean am I capable of lying, yes, I am. But I'm not lying to you." He sat next to her, his back against the stones, his arm nearly touching hers, but not quite.

Silence encased them. Moonlight drifted through the small stained glass panels where the shirts and scarves had been torn away.

The Capel crypt; she remembered when she had been here before. It was a long time ago, in the last century, just after the tomb had been built. How odd that fate should lead her here once again.

All of Dameon's family lay moldering in these drawers, but there was nothing of him here. There had been nothing left to bury— there never is when an old one expires.

She was aware of Lot, sitting so quietly

beside her. "Why do you submit to him?" she asked gently.

Before he could respond, she said, "Oh, I know the Sabbat hierarchy. I understand you serve him. But there are those who do not deserve service. You are honorable, Lot. He's not."

Lot pulled his knees up and rested his forearms on them. He picked up a piece of the coffin's wood and began pulling it apart, as if the wood were composed of strands like hair.

Bianka watched his hands at work. They were strong, as befitted a highly placed warrior, but sensitive as well. The way he held the wood, and seemed to sense the energy in it— he might have been a sculptor. In a funny way, he reminded her of Giovanni.

Instinctively, she reached over and placed her hand on top of one of his. He flinched, as if she had struck him instead of touched him tenderly. In that moment, she knew that he had not been touched tenderly in a long time.

To save him, to save herself, she started to

pull her hand back. Suddenly he grasped it in his. He did not look at her but now looked straight across the crypt, his eyes intense, as if they were burning. He held her hand tightly, not painfully, at least there was no physical pain for her. If there was pain for him it was emotional, like the pain this contact made her feel.

"You can sense through the flesh, can't you?" she said softly.

"Yes."

"Then you sense me."

"Yes."

"You trust me."

He turned and looked at her, his face so close. His eyes, warm, almost human, but alive with the light of the undead. She studied his full lips, the shape of them, the definition, and wanted to know their taste.

"Yes. I trust you. I don't know who you are or why I trust you, but I do. Fletcher was about to kill you. I couldn't let that happen."

He appeared to be torn, by loyalties, by desire.

"Why did you come here?" he asked. "What were you trying to do, leading the Camarilla out of the Box? Didn't it occur to you that we'd track you?"

"Yes. I knew that. I suspected the Sabbat had an infiltrator in the Box."

He looked startled. He looked like he wanted to let go of her hand and move away. Instead, he gripped her tighter. "You... you led them into a trap."

"Yes."

"But why?"

"Because they had to rebel. I've already said—"

"The Camarilla want them back—"

"Yes. And the Sect would not accept them unless they showed some spirit—"

"I heard all that you told Fletcher. That doesn't explain why you wanted them to fail."

"It's not that *I* wanted them to fail. It's that they had to fail. For the greater good."

His brows knit in confusion. Before he could ask her the question she dreaded, Bianka said, "Please. Trust me on this too. I can't tell you why, but much depends on the Camarilla *not* taking these Kindred back. There's a balance, it's bigger than the Camarilla, bigger than the Sabbat, and if that's upset, it would affect all of you. Please. I'm asking you *not* to ask me why. I can't lie to you, but I cannot tell you the reasons."

He seemed to be going against every natural instinct in him. She knew he searched for truth, and was not afraid to face it. He felt compelled to face it; that made him appealing.

"I give you my word, Lot, I will tell you. But not now. When it's safe to tell you, when it won't matter that Fletcher, or someone like him, can get it out of you."

He didn't like it. She knew that. But he accepted it, and did not probe further.

Suddenly, they heard a fluttering. Bianka jumped to her feet. Ravena flew in through the broken window, circled the chamber once, squawking in excitement, then perched on the highest ledge.

Yes, my friend! I'm glad you're safe, too. Don't worry. He's helping me.

Ravena spread her wings and bent her head low, as if about to take off. But she only squawked, once, a long sound, making Bianka laugh and cry tears of relief.

Bianka sat down again, closer to Lot, wiping her eyes, feeling his skin next to hers, the heat of it—he had fed recently.

"How... why... ? The bird?" he said, and she laughed because he was so unsure of what he wanted to know. She found it endearing in one who was so strong and self-directed.

"Ravena came to me two hundred years ago."

"Are you going to tell me your age?"

"Nine hundred, give or take. Do you like older females?"

He grinned. "How do you know I'm not older than you?"

"Are you?"

His grin expanded. "No, I'm not."

They both laughed.

"We met in Baltimore, about 1744-45 or so—"

"'Once upon a midnight dreary...'"

She leaned back against the Ontario field

stones, and pressed closer to him. "I was in a cemetery, much like this one actually, but smaller—there were fewer dead then, as I'm sure you recall. I was seated on a curved stone bench. It was very dark. No moon. None of the wonders of electricity we have now."

"Were you alone? In the cemetery?"

She paused. "I've been alone most of my existence." She turned her face a bit and caught his eye. "But that's another story. For another time. Let's just say that it was a night when I felt particularly... mortal in my immortality."

"Meaning?"

"Meaning, I was lonely. Inconnu are... hard to know. Some say impossible. I could never fit with the Camarilla, or the Sabbat. I'm too different.

"Anyway, as I sat staring at the stars, reading the inscriptions on the headstones, I heard a fluttering. Suddenly, a large raven flew down and sat on the bench beside me. And began to talk to me."

"Talk to you?" He looked baffled. "How?"

"Not with words. It's difficult to explain. It's

as though I have a link with her... not brain... but spirit. I can read her emotions... um, her *urgings*, and translate them into thoughts."

"And you're not Gangrel? Yours is the strongest Animalism I've heard about."

"It's a power I didn't know I had."

"You're kidding!"

"No. I liked animals, when I was human, and after I was Embraced. But I didn't think I had any special affinity. Until Ravena."

"Why did you give her that name?"

"I didn't. She told me her name. That night. As we sat together. It was as though I'd found a twin I never knew existed. And when the sky began to lighten, Ravena hopped onto my shoulder and went home with me. She's been with me ever since."

Bianka looked into his eyes. "I haven't been lonely since then. 'Nevermore.'" She smiled.

Her focus narrowed until only his face existed. A face that moved closer to hers. Very close. So close she could no longer see him, but she felt his lips on hers, parting hers, and his tongue sliding into her mouth. The hunger that burned through her took a new direction, a new expression, and she matched the heat of his intention with her own.

They slept the day wrapped in each other's arms. When night fell again, they lay together yet apart.

Bianka was aware of a pain deep in her heart. Were they doomed lovers? He was Sabbat, and could be nothing else. She could not join him here, and he could not join her—where? She had no home. And then there was her mission, the entire reason she was in this place, at this time, what had allowed her to find him, and would likely cause her to lose him.

He touched her thigh, and it was as if he could read her fears. He drew her to him and they lay entangled together, neither believing what had occurred between them; and yet the reality of the connection was still potent.

He stroked her neck, her breast, kissed her lips, drinking her essence through the skin, reading her as if her body were a map to her soul.

She could tell he was weak, though. She saw it on his face, felt it in the strength of his touch—sleeping apart from his native soil had drained him.

"I have to go," she said.

His hand stopped.

"You have to let me go. I have to return to the Box and make sure they don't try to rescue me."

"Do you think that's likely to happen?" He sat up.

"Yes, I do. They tasted victory, then defeat. It's the first meal they've eaten. They'll want more. I have to keep them from leaving the Box again. You know your forces are on guard. The Camarilla will be killed if they step outside."

"Why do you care? You're not one of them. You said they have to fail. For the greater—"

She placed a finger over his lips to silence him. "You promised to trust me."

He reached for his clothing, stood and began to dress. She felt him moving away from her emotionally. He had other loyalties, and the lack of knowledge forced him to them.

She pulled her soiled dress over her head and got to her feet. "Don't turn away from me," she said, touching his arm.

His back to her, he said, "I can't let you go. I've sworn loyalty to my Sect—"

"And if you keep me prisoner, Fletcher will kill me. And it will be as if *you've* killed me."

He spun around, furious, frustrated. "Don't you think I know that?"

"Taste my blood."

The look of horror that passed over his face vanished before it could take hold. "Blood Bond? Are you crazy? I'm Sabbat—"

"Not a Bond like you think. I don't want you as a Thrall, but a Bonding of equals."

"That's not possible, unless all the blood is put together, the way we do it—"

"It *is* possible. I know. I've tasted your blood, in the car. Drink mine."

He took a step back, away from her. His

brows furrowed. "Why would you even suggest such a thing?"

"Why? One reason is, you're weak. Without your soil—"

"I'll recover."

"Isn't the most important reason obvious, Lot? Our connection is so... ephemeral. You have your loyalties. I'm such a loner. This," she waved a hand to include both of them, "will be lost. It will be the first thing to go."

He shook his head. "I can't do it."

She bit into her wrist until the blood flowed and held it out to him. "It takes three exchanges to form the Bond. This is only the first."

He focused on the river of red running down her arm. "You're trying to control me!" he said harshly.

"Is that what you think?" She stared at him for only a moment and, when he didn't answer, dropped her arm to her side. She pushed past him, toward the exit.

But Lot grabbed her and spun her around. He looked fierce as he pulled her wound to his lips and sucked in her essence, staring into her eyes, letting the taste and feel of her powerful, ancient blood blanket the fears that rocketed through him.

Bianka swooned under the pressure of the blood that barely filled her veins leaving. He didn't take much, but she felt the loss as if he had taken it all.

And when his lips came away from her wrist, their eyes locked. Something magical had been set in motion. Whether or not it would actualize was uncertain at this point. Only time would tell. If there was enough time.

Well before dawn, she chained him to the wall. It was as good a plan as any. When the Sabbat found him, he could claim that he had been Enthralled. Or that a dozen Camarilla came back and freed her. He could claim anything that would make sense, that would excuse him for losing a prisoner. That would save his own life.

"I'll come back for you," she told him, as Ravena left her perch and took her place on Bianka's left shoulder. "I give you my word." She kissed his lips, tasting flecks of her blood still lingering there, remembering the taste of his blood earlier, embedded with his power; remembering their lovemaking. Remembering that for long moments, she had not felt utterly alone in this world of endless darkness.

CHAPTER TWELVE

L ot let her bind him with the very chain he had brought to bind her. He let her leave, let her walk out into the night to confront the Camarilla.

In truth, he couldn't have stopped even had he been willing to try. Her blood sang in his veins. Her ancient blood, blood from a body that had walked the world nine hundred years ago, blood that could be only a few generations removed from Caine. To say that it sang was to say almost nothing. The music of it swelled into a grand, dark symphony, the age-blackened varnish of cellos and dull gleam of horns lifting him up and up. The blood was more: wild, abandoned drums under ancient skies; melancholy pipes in stone halls; harpsichords and violins in baroque splendor; deep thundering organs in cool, shadowy cathedrals; hard rock, driving beats in close, hot dance clubs. All of the music of every age washing through him, overwhelming him with ecstasy. His discipline vanished with the flavor of Bianka's blood. He was nothing. He lost himself in her dark night.

It had been all he could do not to keep drinking, to drink until he had tasted Bianka's heart's blood, until all of her precious ichor was his. He had finally pushed her away, however, and looked deep into her pale eyes. He loved this woman, loved her with all of his heart and all of his soul. He gave his love to her willingly. She had said that they could be united through a sharing of their blood. A Blood Bond that created not master and servant, but two masters and two servants. One spirit in two bodies. He wasn't sure he really believed her. He knew that he needed no compelling Blood Bond though. He loved her. A single draught of her blood was worth a hundred—a thousand—turns at the cup of Vaulderie.

When she drew herself out of his arms, he was still delirious, floating in the warm sea of his love and her blood. When she produced the chain, he smiled at her. There was, at least, no question of him taking her back to the Sabbat now. Not to Fletcher (there had never been a question of that), not to the Archbishop. When she pushed his arms back, like a gardener pushing back the branches of a rose bush, he moved with the gentle pressure she exerted and watched her loop the chain around his right wrist and forearm. There were big iron eyes sunk into the stone of the wall, holders for flag standards, a reminder of the funerals of the age when the crypt was built. The architect of the tomb had probably never imagined that his creation would be used to hold someone prisoner, but the eyes were perfect anchors. Bianka looped the chain through one eye, around Lot's waist, through another eye, then around his left arm and wrist, making sure the bonds were taut. She pulled him close to her so that she could reach behind his back and lock the ends of the chain together. He nuzzled her neck gently while she did it.

When she was done, she left him with a kiss and a promise. He whispered her name after her.

No sound came back. The cemetery was utterly silent. Not even the ever-present noise of the city penetrated its somber quiet. He pressed his head and back against the cool stone of the tomb, reveling in the memory of Bianka's blood. The sweet wonder of their intimacy swept through him again.

Every song must end eventually, though. After a time, Lot came back to himself. He tried to look at his watch, to see what time it was, but the chains and the cuff of his shirt masked the watch face. A thin sliver of moonlight fell through a chink in the makeshift coverings that the Camarilla had erected over the windows two nights before. Lot watch it change shape on the floor, growing shorter and narrower as the moon rose higher, then vanishing altogether as the moon passed entirely out of range. With even the moonlight gone, time seemed to stop. Darkness. Silence. Lot tested his chains, filling the silence with quiet rattling for a moment, but only for a moment. Bianka had bound him too well. The tension of the chains prevented him from reaching either of the iron eyes, and the loop around his waist prevented him from sitting to gain slack. Nor could he simply pull on the chains and hope to break either them or the eyes. The added tension would tighten the chain around his waist, causing him serious injury long before the metal gave way. And of course there was no way he could reach the lock behind his back. It was doubtful that he could have broken the chains anyway. In the haste and passion of the previous night, he had slept without the soil of his homeland around him. That mistake had left him weak. Not helpless by any means, but certainly weaker than he should have been, like a human who had not slept well. He was a prisoner of his own lack of foresight as well as Bianka's chains.

He had no choice but to wait.

Suddenly, though, there were footsteps outside the tomb. Lot had already called out "Bianka?" before he realized that what he was hearing was not one, but two sets of footfalls. He could smell something, too, a reek of old blood that penetrated even the smell of death hanging over the tomb. Light flashed around the edges of the crypt door. The door creaked open. Fletcher stepped inside. Behind him, carrying a battery-powered lantern, was Benedict.

Lot flinched before he could stop himself. Fletcher leered at him. "We missed you, Lot. You know, it's the strangest thing. When we got to Dyce's haven last night, the Archbishop wasn't there. Seems he'd been gone most of the night, too."

Damn. "She was manipulating me, Fletcher."

He rattled his chains. "Look. She chained me up and left me here!"

"And you called her name."

"I was afraid she was coming back!" Lot cursed himself silently for his mistake.

"Maybe," Benedict suggested from behind Fletcher, "she Blood Bonded him." The Ravnos avoided meeting Lot's gaze. Lot wasn't sure what to make of that—or the suggestion that he had already been Blood Bonded to Bianka. Fletcher might believe it or he might not. Even if he did, there was no guarantee that he'd let Lot off the hook for what had happened. Lot watched as Fletcher came closer.

"Blood Bound, eh?"

"The Vaulderie would break it," pointed out Benedict eagerly. Slowly, Fletcher nodded.

Then lashed out, snapping Lot's head back into the wall with a harsh punch to the jaw. Lot's glasses slid askew. "Then again," Fletcher roared, "maybe this bastard is just a fucking traitor to the Sabbat!" He slammed his other fist into Lot's belly. "How about that, Lot? Traitor? You and your fancy fucking manners and Tzimisce fucking meddling?" He stepped close, grasping Lot's shoulders. Lot guessed what was coming. He tried to spread his legs and lift himself up on tiptoe, making the extra space that would send Fletcher's knee cracking into stone. It didn't work. Fletcher's knee drove into Lot's balls. Lot retched and gagged, sagging in his chains. "It took us a long time to find you, Lot. Where's the woman? Where's Bianka?"

"Go to hell!" Lot spat. Blood dribbled out of his mouth.

Fletcher bounced his templar's face off of his knee. "We're the Damned, Lot," he said almost sweetly. "Of course, I'll go to hell. But you're going to be waiting around down there for a fucking long time before I show up." Face off the knee again. "Where is she?"

Lot kept his mouth closed, refusing to answer. He filled his mind with the sweet sensation of drinking Bianka's blood. The rich flavor, the swelling, majestic music... His eyes closed as well, he pictured her. Pale eyes. Dark hair.

He felt Fletcher drop his head, and then, a

moment later, take hold of his right hand. "It's not that hard a question," the bishop said. Lot's pinky finger snapped. The Tzimisce stifled a cry of agony, but a gasp still escaped him. "Awww… did that hurt?" Ring finger. "Funny, I didn't feel anything." Middle finger. "You must know, Lot." Fletcher pinched Lot's index finger almost gently, bending it slowly, inexorably backward. Lot choked. When the tendon across his palm finally snapped and the knuckle popped free, he screamed with the pain of the release. "Where," Fletcher whispered in his ear, "is Bianka?" With one hand he knocked away Lot's glasses and pulled up one of Lot's eyelids. With the other, he gripped Lot's thumb.

Benedict coughed. "Maybe she's gone back to the Box?"

"Shut up!" Fletcher snarled. "I want him to tell me that!"

Lot opened his other eye to glare at the bishop. "You already know where she is," he grated. Of course. If he didn't know where Bianka was going tonight, he would have guessed at the Box. Fletcher had to have guessed the same thing. It was obvious.

"Yeah, maybe I do. But here's a question you can answer for me." Fletcher's thumb pushed in bruisingly on Lot's eyeball. Half of the chained vampire's field of vision vanished in a haze of gray. Fletcher released his pressure. Lot gasped with relief. "Where in the Box did she go?"

Lot almost laughed. He had no idea where Bianka had gone to meet with the Camarilla. She might have gone back to the bar where he and Benedict had met DeWinter the other night. She might have gone to some other bar. She might have gone to some private Camarilla haven. He didn't know. And the irony was, that even if he had known, he doubted if telling Fletcher would have spared him any agony at all. He could buy Bianka time though.

Truth first. "I don't know."

Fletcher's fist slammed into his side. Lot was grateful the bishop didn't have his whip and blowtorch with him. "Try again," Fletcher hissed.

"I really don't know."

"Liar!"

Another pummeling, one that left Lot struggling to draw air for speech. "What are you going to do with her once you find her?"

Fletcher sneered. "Do those sound like the words of a traitor to you, Benedict? They do to me."

Lot ignored him. "Tell me!"

A sharp backhand cracked his head against the wall again. "Don't make demands, Lot." Fletcher slapped him again. "But if you really want to know, I thought I'd take a few Sabbat down into the Box and bring her back here. Maybe have a little reunion." He looked around. "I like this place. Isolated. Quiet." The sneer came back to Fletcher's face. "All I have to do is shut the doors and any mess is forgotten. Buried like shit in a litter box." He bent close. "What do you think of that?"

With a snarl, Lot lunged for him, fangs extended. Fletcher ducked back quickly, laughing, and all that Lot's fangs closed on was a mouthful of stinking air. "I'm never going to tell you where she is!"

Fletcher shrugged. "I didn't think you would."

"You're as crazy as a Malkavian."

"No." Fletcher tensed his hand. Talons grew. "Malkavians can't help their madness." He bared his ugly fangs, top and bottom. He plucked on either side of the chain around Lot's waist, hard enough to make Lot wince. "I like these. Convenient. Thoughtful of Bianka."

"Bastard."

The bishop ignored him. "Benedict, how long do I have before we meet the packs outside the Box?"

There was no answer. Fletcher turned around slowly. "Benedict?" he asked again menacingly. There was no sign of the Ravnos, however. Behind Fletcher's back, Lot reached out with his heightened senses. In the distance, he could hear the faint, rapid fall of running feet. The footfalls were too far way for him to be able to tell if they were accompanied by the rustle of

Benedict's velvet coat, but he was sure that they would be. Fletcher turned back again and Lot let his perceptions drop, looking at the foul bishop before him. Fletcher shrugged. "Just as well for him." He grinned. "I bet you two were up to something together, weren't you? I can hunt him down later."

He grabbed Lot's wrist and twisted it harshly to look at his captive's wristwatch. He snorted. "Lots of time." Lot tried to twitch his wrist away. Fletcher's grin grew wide and horrible. He reached out and drew his talons along the stone beside Lot's head. The sound was like fingernails on a blackboard, but much, much worse.

"So," asked Fletcher, "where would you like to begin?" He stepped closer. Lot's glasses crunched under his boots.

CHAPTER THIRTEEN

Bianka took Lot's car and drove to the western wall of the Box, stopping on the way just long enough to take vitae from a healthy human. She parked on Bathurst Street and walked the quarter block to Savage Garden. She figured the Kindred would be there. She was not wrong.

She had barely stepped inside the club when they surrounded her like a pack of wolves. Ravena flew up into the rafters and Bianka ordered her, *Stay there! You'll just make it worse.*

It was like being under the Sabbat's power, and Bianka knew that if the Camarilla weren't so set on blending in with mortals, they might have ripped her apart. As it was, they hustled her into a dark alcove, away from the bar, from the dance floor, out of view of human eyes. She still exhibited scars and bruises, but those didn't seem to affect them. They had their own wounds, many more severe than hers. They had had plenty of time to feed, and they still looked in terrible shape, she wondered how some of them could even be standing. There would be no sympathies from these undead.

Swan was the cruelest, and she could hardly wait to hurl invectives. "You betrayed us! You set us up!"

"What are you talking about?" Bianka said.

By way of an answer, the Brujah punched her in the face. Bianka stumbled backward, but didn't fall.

"That's enough!" DeWinter said, making his way into the group.

Bianka shook her head to clear it of the ringing, and tasted blood on her lips. Swan was no wimp; she had a powerful arm.

The Brujah in Bianka insisted she attack. She looked around and saw a dozen of the Camarilla, including Swan, Reg, Razor and, of course, DeWinter. The Toreador in her opted for reason, and diversion. "Where's Janus?" she asked, sucking in her wounded lip, wanting to add, and the others?

"Where do you think, betraying half-breed!" Swan snarled.

"He's not dead?"

"Of course he is! Four of us were taken out by the Sabbat. A couple of hearts ripped from the chest, one backbone broken and then the head snapped off—"

"But Lot told them—"

"Lot? Your buddy, the Terminator? I'm sure he told them to finish us off, and they almost did, no thanks to you, bitch!"

"Lot didn't tell them that. He gave me his word—"

Swan grabbed her by the throat and hurled her against the wall. The table she crashed into on the way shattered. It was all Bianka could do to stop herself from lunging.

"No more!" DeWinter said, his voice stern, for once. "I'm in charge here, in case you've forgotten." He spoke directly to Swan, but his words included the others. The authority in his voice was underscored by his words. "And if you *hadn't* forgotten that, and left the Box, our Kindred would not be dead, or near death now."

The fury in Swan's eyes gave way to guilt. If she hated Bianka, she hated herself more for believing in the possibility of freedom.

DeWinter turned to Bianka. "Why did you come here to betray us? Who sent you?"

Bianka got to her feet. Out of the corner of her eye, she saw Ravena hopping from beam to beam, edging closer. *No!* she told the bird. *Stay back!* Ravena ignored her.

"I didn't come to betray you. And I've told you why I'm here. It's the truth."

"The truth is," Reg said, "you killed Shadow."

"Me?"

"You left the building so we'd *think* it wasn't you. But you had time to attack her and drop her through the skylight, then get down here. If I could do that, you could."

"You asked her who did it. She said 'Sabbat.'"

"*I* said when you asked me, 'It was the Sabbat. Who else.' When I asked Shadow, she said, 'A Kindred.' She was a Neonate and didn't know the difference between them and us— she'd never even seen a Sabbat. She only knew it was a vampire of some kind. One she didn't know, or she would have named them. At the time I thought it must be a Sabbat. But she didn't know you, either."

"Well, it wasn't me." Bianka felt indignant that they didn't believe her. "I have no reason to lie." She almost told them she couldn't, but now was not the time to give anything away.

"You deceiving—" Swan began.

"Bianka," DeWinter said, the only one of

them with any sobriety to his voice—the others were drunk on grief and rage, "the Sabbat knew where to find you. Someone had to have told them."

She stared at him, watching his pupils dilate and expand. No, DeWinter, she thought, now is *not* the time to fade. "There's an infiltrator here. I found that out when the Sabbat were torturing me."

"Torture? You don't look like you were tortured," Swan sneered. "This is torture!" She ripped open her shirt and showed the deep gouges, like bullet holes, riddling her breasts. Wounds like that would take a long time to heal, and there might always be scar tissue remaining.

"I fed tonight. And healed some," Bianka said, not about to admit how she got the first of the food, or how much of it. They didn't know the extent of her injuries, or the power of her body to heal. Let them think what they liked.

DeWinter paused. "And the name of this infiltrator?"

"They only used the code name. Nightbird."

"That could be any of us," Swan said. "A stupid Sabbat nickname—"

"It could be, but it's someone specific. Someone with an affinity for bats, maybe," DeWinter said.

"Or a bird that flies at night," Swan said.

They all stared at Bianka. If looks could kill, she thought, I would be long gone. And then she saw it. Razor's bat tattoo, on her cheek. With the small ring through the bat's nose. And as she stared, the others turned their eyes as well.

"Why are you all looking at me?" Razor said, her voice rising.

"Because, you have a bat on your face," Reg said. "A very unbecoming bat. With a ring of ownership."

"Oh, come on! Am I the only Kindred with a bat tattoo? She's the one with the raven—you can't get much closer to a nightbird than that."

"Why weren't you injured?" Swan asked.

"I was!" Razor said defensively. "Look at my arm! They almost broke the damn bone."

"Almost. The rest of us were pretty banged up. You got off real easy."

"I was lucky. If you remember, I told you I got out of the crypt right away. Besides, none of us knew where she was taking us, so none of us could have warned the Sabbat. She's the only one who knew."

"Not the only one," Bianka said. She hated to do it, but she turned to DeWinter. Already his form was diminishing. "Damn it! Stay solid!" she ordered. "Tell them!"

"Yes, tell us," Swan said, her voice laced with disgust.

"It was either you or Bianka who betrayed us."

They watched DeWinter fade to translucency, then return to solid, over and over, as if he could not decide which way to go. Finally, though, he said, "Yes, I told them," and he went from barely corporeal to stable.

Stone cold silence fell upon the group.

"But I'm not the infiltrator."

"Then why the fuck did you sell us out?" Swan said through gritted teeth, her fists balled, her stance menacing, her voice dangerously low.

"Two Sabbat came here, into the Box, looking for Bianka. I was alone." He sat down backward on a chair turned away from them, rested his elbows on the top rung of the back and put his head in his hands.

"Coward!" Swan snorted.

His head jerked up and turned in her direction. "And you would be so brave? Two Sabbat, one with a gun, and no Kindred around? All of you were busy following this stranger outside the Box, breaking the Settlement I worked so hard to create so that we would have something here. As it was, Lot *knew* Bianka was here, stirring things up, talking of rebellion. He wanted to find her. Before you all left, Bianka told me where she was taking you."

"I thought he should know. In case... something happened," Bianka said. What she *didn't* say was the other half of this truth, but then, no one asked her. She had told DeWinter the larger concerns, and he had agreed to help her betray the Camarilla. That made him brave in her eyes. Now he was taking the heat. Playing the wimp. The old saying was true: There *is* wisdom in madness, and courage.

"I told them," DeWinter was saying, "because Lot promised to capture Bianka and send the rest of you back."

"If you didn't want us to leave," Swan said, "why didn't you try to stop us?"

DeWinter just shook his head. Clearly, Bianka's guess the night she led the Camarilla out of the Box had been correct: He had been afraid that if he took a stand against them—whether or not he believed in it—they would have gone anyway, and he couldn't risk losing leadership. And he couldn't admit that, even now, although Bianka understood his motives. That was why she had given him the information about the crypt, and about all the rest. She knew the infiltrator had told the Sabbat about her. It was the only way to make sure the Camarilla were thwarted. She felt sorry for DeWinter. Almost.

"How was I to know they wouldn't come after you right away?" he said.

"When did they come here?" Swan asked.

DeWinter sobbed softly. "Just after you left. I'd say, you would have just made it out of the Box."

"It's possible they saw us leave," Reg said. "Or maybe it's just coincidence, they came as we were leaving—"

"Or maybe they came when they knew we were gone," Swan said. "Maybe they couldn't get to their infiltrator—"

"Are you still on about that?" Razor said.

"And they decided to bide their time. They have an idea how many Kindred reside in the Box and they know DeWinter, so if they counted us leaving, they'd know he was likely the only one left, and two of those bastards could easily intimidate one."

Bianka wished she'd spent more time trying to get information out of Lot. Maybe if she hadn't been so busy—

"That doesn't explain why they didn't come after us until the next night," Swan said.

"But they did," Bianka assured her. "They followed us to the crypt. Watching. Waiting.

And when they realized we were spending the night, they slept in another crypt—likely the one we found open. That's the only way they could wake at sunset and surprise us."

Swan turned on her. "None of this explains my gut feeling. You led us out of the Box, not to encourage us to rebel, but to have our rebellion crushed. Deny it!"

Bianka took a deep breath. There was never a half-truth around when you needed one. "You're right. I wanted you to fail. But I didn't want the Sabbat to attack you the way they did. I didn't know that would happen. I knew about the terms of the Settlement, and that the Archbishop made a decree that no Camarilla can be killed—"

"Except if we threaten the Sabbat. Didn't you think they'd consider that a threat?"

"No, I didn't. They should have had to prove it to the Archbishop."

"Maybe they did."

"No. He didn't find out about it until *after* you were brought back here."

"And how do you know that, half-breed?"

Bianka did not want to implicate Lot in any way. She had already said too much. Razor would report all this to the Sabbat, and Bianka needed to protect him. "After he tortured me, the one named Fletcher was going to see the Archbishop and tell him about the situation. That was many hours after you all had been brought back."

DeWinter looked up. Bianka thought they were all stunned. They could hardly formulate the questions. At last Reg managed to ask, "Why? Why did you do all this?"

She didn't know how to explain it in a way that they would understand. "There are things going on in our world that require balance—"

"Cut to the chase!" Swan snapped. "Who sent you?"

"The Inconnu."

There was a very long pause. One of the Neonates whispered, "Who are the Inconnu?"

"Nobody knows," Swan said. "But they're not Camarilla and they're not Sabbat."

"We have our own agenda," Bianka said. "Much of it involves... monitoring the impending Gehenna. You're a part of the larger plan, and although it probably won't sit well with you, it's crucial that you stay here, in the Box. The events that have been brewing, since Reg's hand was mangled—we knew it was just a matter of time until you tried to get out."

Swan shook her head. "Why now? Why didn't you come last year? Or next year?"

"Because of the date. It's been a year and a day. A year and a day is a universal archetype, a metaphor for the dead in so many parts of the world. It's when the dead either rise, or stay dead. We knew something was being planned. Shadow's death was timed to happen just before one year and one day, and that's tonight, as is the full moon. The violence was designed to fester in you and provoke you to action tonight—it works on an unconscious level. That would justify the Sabbat wiping you out."

"So? I don't think a handful of Camarilla rebels matters to anyone," Swan said.

"You're wrong. You have to see this as part of the Sabbat's Jyhad against the Camarilla.

You're trapped in the Box, but what happens here has far-reaching consequences. If the Sabbat wiped you out, the Camarilla outside Toronto would then have had to act, and that would mean war. There are other factions that would have joined in—Toronto is a major territory, and a lot of favors are owed. It's a domino effect. Certainly the east and midwest would have been engaged in this war, and it could very easily spread throughout North America and then further, to engulf the world."

"Let me get this straight," Swan said, her words rapid-fire. "If we rebelled on our own we would have been wiped out, which would have started a war, leading to Gehenna. So, you come in here and try to get us to rebel—"

"A controlled rebellion. With a controlled conclusion. I would have left here, gotten word to the Camarilla princes of Chicago, Vancouver and Boston about what you'd done. They would have laughed, called you pathetic, and said they weren't going to lift a finger to help you. Once I came back and told you that, it would have reinforced your despair."

"Right! Keep us down. We're the scapegoats. You'd have hung us out to dry!"

"No. I couldn't do that. When I came back, I planned to help any of you who wanted to escape; I was going to set up a kind of underground railroad out of here. If you escaped, it wouldn't change the balance because the other Camarilla wouldn't have seen a need to be involved, and the Sabbat would either have killed you individually in the attempt, or you would have been out of here."

"Then why in hell didn't you just do that in the first place?" Swan yelled.

"Because," DeWinter said, "any of us who escaped would be Caitiff. No sect. No territory. An outcast."

"At least you would have been free," Bianka said.

"This is all bullshit!" Swan said. "You're trying to manipulate us. We stay here, we're the walking dead in a roach motel. We leave, we're tortured to death by the Sabbat. Well, I say I want death before dishonor. I'm gonna take that fucking crypt, and if the Sabbat kill me in the process, then at least I'll die the True Death knowing I wasn't a coward or a plaything! Who's with me?"

Voices from the crowd shouted, "Me!" "I'm ready to die tonight!" "Yeah! I won't be a stinking prisoner or clanless!"

"All right!" Swan shouted. "We go now, and do it!"

"Don't!" Bianka warned them, but none of them listened. They had no idea what they were doing, the terrible repercussions. Taking the crypt was obviously symbolic to them, a way both of reclaiming their lost self-esteem and reversing the defeat they had just suffered. But another complication was that Lot might still be in the crypt, waiting for her. They would disembowel him first thing and feed his liver to the cemetery rats.

"You with us, DeWinter?" Swan demanded amidst the general pandemonium.

The leader nodded hesitantly.

"A great plan," a voice boomed. "But one

you'd better rethink!" The temperature plummeted as the voice surrounded them like barbed wire.

Bianka froze at the sound. It was Fletcher. While they had been arguing, he had sneaked in, and with a veritable army. Her heart raced. The Kindred were boxed in. *She* was boxed in. Her cells began to react with stark terror and hatred for this insane one. And now she would be in his merciless hands again!

Fletcher strode into the center of the Camarilla, unafraid. "Bianka, baby! You're everywhere, aren't you? It's a shame your lover isn't here, but he's kind of hung up right now. I wouldn't count on him or his white horse."

Roughly, he grasped her jaw and turned her face up to his. His eyes were black with violence. "You're a fast healer. Thanks. A clean slate for me to work on!" He squeezed her jaw until she felt the bone just on the edge of snapping.

Suddenly, from above, Ravena swooped down. Her talons dug into his scalp and her beak found his flesh. "What the fu—!" he cried.

No! Bianka screamed at the raven. *He'll kill you!*

The raven had made a severe dent in his skull, one that instantly gushed blood—obviously she'd hit an artery—but managed to fly out of range before Fletcher or any of the Sabbat could react.

Instinctively, Ravena flew almost straight up, past the rafters, up into the darkest parts of the high ceiling.

"Where is it? Find the damn thing and strangle it!" Fletcher yelled. Several of his gang pulled out handguns and fired shots toward the ceiling.

Hide, precious one! For my sake as well as your own! Bianka called.

The gunshots sent the humans screaming from the room. Several of the Camarilla tried to bolt but were stopped short.

"We should get out of here!" a craggy-faced Sabbat said to Fletcher.

"Why? Because a few mortals know about us? Let them know! We're vampires! We don't hide from humans like these insects!" He knocked

Reg hard with the back of his hand. The Toreador hit the wall and his head went through the plaster. "Let them get on their knees to their masters!" Fletcher sneered.

"That may be, Bishop, but they will bring others. With guns. If we stay, we're going to be in trouble. They'll call the cops and—"

"Chicken shit!" Fletcher spat, grabbing his guard by the throat.

Bianka saw that the madness had escalated. If only Lot were here! He would be able to overthrow this barbarian.... The thought of Lot and what state he might be in caused her more pain than it was safe to feel at the moment.

The music pounding through the room ended abruptly. It was clear that most of the humans were gone. They *would* have called the police. Even Fletcher could now see that. As stubborn as he was, as bent on his whims, his face showed that he was shrewd enough to want to escape unnecessary injury.

He noticed Bianka staring at him. "Bitch!" he cried, and grabbed her long hair hard. He shoved her onto her knees. She knew it was the way she looked at him that infuriated him, as though he were nothing, as though he held no value in her eyes. An ego like his demanded constant feeding, and she had no intention of feeding him.

"I've got what I came for," he said, twisting her hair until she felt her scalp would come away from her cranium. "We'll take this bitch with us. But before we go, we'll teach these wimpy Cammies who owns them."

He yanked Bianka to her feet.

"Say goodbye to your friends, Bianka, baby. The next time they see you, it'll be in ash form, floating from the funeral pyre."

Bianka scanned the faces of the Camarilla. Their emotions ranged from terror to impotent fury. They were outnumbered three to one. The Sabbat would show no mercy. They would be more than vicious, and they could justify their actions. The Camarilla would sustain more losses, that was clear, and the ones who would be left would be worse than dead.

All this, Bianka saw in a flash, and she knew they knew it as well. "Don't give up," she said to Swan firmly, using her lips to convey what her hands could not. "Not to them. Never. They are unworthy opponents, and if you die at their hands, make sure your death has meaning."

Whether it was her words or the reality of their meaning that struck home, Bianka did not know. The Brujah's face altered, hardened. Out of the corner of her eye, Bianka watched DeWinter turn more solid than she had ever seen him before.

"Don't worry, sister B. They won't take me alive."

Not all of them, but a small cadre of the Camarilla felt the same way. Enough that the Sabbat might not have felt threatened, but they did become alert to this new energy.

"Perfect!" Fletcher mocked. "The slugs slither at your command. And I'll make you slither at mine! We'll see just how diseased your blood is, because I'm going to test it and then drink it as I watch you die. You!"

Fletcher pointed to a tiny Camarilla girl with black and blue hair. The Neonate looked terrified and froze. One of the Sabbat shoved her forward, glancing behind him, obviously jittery that Fletcher had not given the order to leave this place.

With a nod in Bianka's direction, Fletcher said, "Hold her!"

Two Sabbat grabbed Bianka from behind. Fletcher pulled a knife from one of their belts. He yanked her hair so that her neck stretched out and sliced the vein in her throat.

"Drink!" he ordered the Neonate. When she didn't move, he forced her lips to the wound and used his other hand to pry open her jaw. She had no choice but to swallow.

After two gulps, the young Camarilla was pulled viciously up. Her lips were smeared with blood. Bianka focused on her eyes, willing her to collapse—the blood was far too strong for her, and already she was swooning, staring at the Inconnu with adoration.

Fletcher, though, knew what Bianka was trying to do. He forced the Camarilla to turn away.

There was nothing to do but heal the wound in her throat, so that's what Bianka focused her energy on. Fletcher would know soon enough that this young one had hit gold. Bianka watched his face as he watched the girl.

"She is truth, pure truth and light, and can say nothing but the truth," the young Camarilla whispered.

Fletcher laughed. "Diseased blood! Lot never used to have a sense of humor. Bianka, drinking your ancient vitae must have been good for him. I'll take it myself, eventually. All of it!"

The neonate turned slightly, her face angelic, a look of rapture and devotion directed back toward Bianka. "I believe you, Mistress, because you cannot tell a lie."

Fletcher's shrewd eyes narrowed. "I see," he said slowly, the implications of the girl's understanding slowing sinking in. And Bianka knew that her strength, now that he had uncovered it, would be her downfall.

"Snap her neck!" he snarled at a muscular guard, meaning the Neonate.

In less than a minute, a tall, bulky Sabbat had torn the young Camarilla's head from her shoulders. The scream coming from her lips was cut short. Her dead body dropped like a log. Her eyes stared at Bianka with love.

The Camarilla and even many of the Sabbat were struck dumb with the horror of this act. But Bianka, still held firmly by strong Sabbat, knew that what was next on the agenda was even worse, for her, and tried to steel herself against the onslaught.

Fletcher used the knife to cut into his stomach. "Prepare to submit to your Regent!" Blood bubbled out of the vein, so dark it seemed black. He grasped Bianka's head with both hands and forced her face down and forward until her lips touched his wound. Then he held her there, and pressed her nostrils closed, until she could do nothing but gasp to take in air. Against her will, his blood trickled into her mouth. She spit most of it out, gagging, but some she could not help but swallow.

Fletcher's vitae was tainted. It sent chaos through her veins. Snippets of violent visions raked her insides, and it was like entering the special place in hell to which all the criminally insane had been relegated. Amidst the heat of evil, she could barely hold onto herself. Tidal wave after tidal wave of rot and corruption crashed over her. And this, she knew, was only the beginning. Fletcher would make her drink the three times, until he possessed her will. And then he would drain all her blood and drink it for the power he could absorb as he killed her, slowly, painfully. But by then she would beg for death.

"Follow your master, slave!" Fletcher said to Bianka.

She straightened immediately, not able to resist his command. And yet she felt the power of his blood subsiding. But it did not vanish, and would not, as long as he remained alive.

Swan stepped in front of him. Instantly, two burly Sabbat grabbed her, one twisting her arm so hard she nearly cried out. "Are you afraid to take us all, vampire?" she sneered at Fletcher. "Or can the Sabbat only torture one at a time?"

Bianka shook her head, still too wobbly to speak; this was *not* the type of resistance she meant. Swan had lost her mind, putting herself in harm's way. Challenging the mad leader like this, before his men, would make them more vicious. Whatever Swan would suffer here from the Sabbat in the Box, whether or not she resisted, would be far less in scope than what he would suffer at Fletcher's haven, inflicted by guards hell-bent on defending their honor. This kind of blatant resistance would mean that the Camarilla would be wiped out. When the Camarilla outside the Box heard about it, a chain-reaction would be set in motion....

Fletcher laughed hard. Bloody spit flew from his mouth and sprayed across Swan's face. "I can torture you both at once, and kill you in the same instant. Would you like that, Cammie slut?"

"Take me too," Swan snarled, "Sabbat mutant!"

"And me," DeWinter said.

Reg and some of the others joined in.

Fletcher laughed in delight, like an insane but dangerous child, a hysterical laugh that took too long to bring under control. Even some of his gang looked concerned. "But, that's what I planned all along!" he gasped. "I just wanted you all to beg to die!"

His laughter stopped abruptly and his face turned to stone, like the most sinister gargoyle that Bianka had ever seen. From outside, the sound of sirens drifted in, still far away, but close enough to be detected by the more acute undead hearing.

"Scrape up the scum and bring them!" Fletcher hissed, a demented god, proclaiming the end of the world.

He turned to Bianka. "And I'll bring my new Thrall."

CHAPTER FOURTEEN

The half dozen vehicles—two vans, a Jeep, a battered pickup truck and two sports cars—reached the cemetery at midnight. Ahead, a full moon hung over the Capel house of the dead. The air felt statically charged, but then Bianka's nerves were already frayed.

She was afraid of entering here. Afraid of

what she would find. Lot was probably dead, and Fletcher was sadistic enough to make her look at his corpse while he tortured her again. It was unfortunate that her compulsion to honesty extended to herself as well. She faced the truth, and not even reluctantly: Tomorrow night, she would have to drink from Fletcher again, and the night after that. And very soon, she would no longer be alive.

Bianka met the realization of her impending Enthrallment and demise with both calm and terror. She hadn't given up. She *wouldn't* give up. But the situation seemed hopeless.

Besides the many Sabbat dragging the twelve kicking and screaming Camarilla along, another two dozen met them at the cemetery.

Fletcher gave orders for most of the guards to remain outside. The Camarilla were marched in, or the ones who could still walk. The Sabbat had hurt them all during the ride and through the grounds, and some, like Reg and DeWinter, were incapable of standing unaided.

Swan was tough, and Bianka felt a love

borne of admiration for the Brujah. It saddened her to think that such a strong spirit would be crushed by this mad Bishop.

Bianka was the last to enter. She had been virtually unharmed en route—Fletcher had ordered it. He obviously wanted her all to himself.

As she mounted the stone steps, the smell of blood slammed her as if she'd walked into a wall. This was not the faint odor of the congealed mess that had been left over from the night the Sabbat had surprised the Camarilla here. This was fresh blood. And a lot of it.

Lot hung by the chains above the alter. Upside down. Naked from the waist up. His broad back was riddled with stripes from Fletcher's whip. His wrists had been slit and the skin clipped open, not to the arteries, but to the veins, so that he would bleed slowly.

The silence that filled the crypt was tangible. Even the hardened Sabbat guards cut short their bravado.

"I think he makes a bitchin' martyr, don't

you?" Fletcher said from behind her, and Bianka knew he was talking to her. "It's why he's attractive to you, isn't it?"

He shoved her forward, toward Lot's body. She could tell Lot was not dead, but he was very close to Torpor.

Fletcher grabbed Lot's hair and twisted his head around. "Look at your lover," he goaded Bianka. "Doesn't all that suffering make him beautiful?"

Lot's face was ravaged by pain. His eyes did not open. His wide bones pressed against the pale skin. Dried blood, the color of rust heated by fire, coated his lips and nose, and the flesh was discolored there, and swollen. Fletcher had done a job.

"Tell me," Bianka said to the Bishop. "Were you like this when you were human? Did you go around crushing little animals, holding a glass over insects, so the sunlight could fry them?"

He dropped Lot's head, which was why she was distracting him; she didn't want Lot hurt any more. She braced herself. He was about to hurt her.

But a sound, outside one of the crypt's little windows above, caught Fletcher's attention.

Stay out... Bianka began, but the message to Ravena didn't get finished.

The blow sent Bianka reeling, knocking backward into a Sabbat, who shoved her forward again. The force of that shove caused her to fly across the room, crashing into Lot, knocking her head against the altar.

Through an audio haze, Bianka heard Swan's voice, then Fletcher ranting. And the sound of slaps and punches and screams as the Camarilla were attacked.

Bianka could barely clear her mind, but she managed enough that she could say to Ravena, *I need your help, my feathered friend.*

The bird, circling the roof of the crypt, listened carefully.

Lot needs my blood to recover. I'm wounded. Bianka felt the split in her lip and the crimson seeping out. *Come. Take vitae to him. But you must be careful! They will try to stop you.*

But Ravena had no time to take action. Bianka was hauled to her feet. Dazed, she stared around her in shock. The Sabbat were dealing with the Camarilla in the way they knew best. She turned away. But Fletcher forced her against the wall, forced her head around. "Open your eyes!" he commanded, and inside her, something of him forced her to watch.

Swan, who stood the tallest, took the worst of it. The ones who were down, who were no longer conscious, or close to that state, were weak prey, and the Sabbat liked adversaries who fought back. The Brujah wouldn't give up, and that infuriated them and inspired them to greater depravity.

Soon, her body was as red from blood-flow as if they had stripped her skin, exposing the muscle beneath. Her face became unrecognizable. And it took a long time before they felled her. She toppled like a proud old oak, and then Bianka was only one of two standing who was not Sabbat.

"See where you've led them, Bianka? To

their doom. And now there will be war between the Sabbat, and those cowards

outside Toronto. A war that the Sabbat will win!"

He laughed and strolled around the crypt, kicking bodies, eliciting moans.

Be ready to act swiftly and discretely, Bianka told Ravena. She heard the raven enter through the broken stained-glass window and perch on the high ledge above the alter. Bianka did not dare look at her.

She hated to do it, but someone had to be sacrificed. And she knew just who that someone would be. "If you're going to go to war," Bianka said, "I suggest you train some decent spies."

That caught his attention. Fletcher turned. Curious.

Bianka nodded toward Razor. "Your infiltrator. Ask her who else she reported to. Besides the Sabbat."

Razor stood in a corner, unscathed. Only when Fletcher turned on her did her features alter. "What? The bitch is lying! I reported to you, Bishop, you know that. And Benedict, but you told me to do that."

Fletcher still faced her, but he paused, considering.

"Don't believe me," Bianka said. "Ask DeWinter. He'll tell you."

DeWinter lay with his head twisted at a painful angle. His face, like all of the other Camarilla faces, was bloody, his eyes dazed. He was dimmer than usual, but didn't have the strength to dematerialize.

Fletcher strode to him and stared down. "Well, leader of the wimps. What is it?"

Now! Bianka said.

Ravena moved cautiously, edging along, hopping down, all of it quietly. Bianka leaned back against the stones, a Sabbat to her right.

"The hot dog vendors knew about it all along," DeWinter mumbled.

Fletcher kicked him in the side, making him groan. "Don't talk gibberish to me, crazy Malkavian! Did Razor betray the Sabbat?"

"I didn't—" Razor began.

"Shut up!" Fletcher said. He nodded, and

one of the Sabbat women leapt over an unconscious Camarilla and slammed Razor into the wall.

"When the Bishop wants to hear from you, he'll ask!" the guard said.

Ravena hopped down and balanced on the handle of a drawer above Bianka's head. The bird paused, then hopped to the handle of the next drawer down, about level with Bianka's face.

"Answer me!" Fletcher shouted, kicking DeWinter again.

The raven jerked her head around, watching.

Bianka glanced surreptitiously around the room. *I think it's safe. But hurry!*

DeWinter opened his one remaining good eye. If he had the energy, Bianka knew, he would have faded long ago. "She told them you were crazy," he said. "She was right."

Fletcher turned on Razor. The guard held her while he worked her over, while she screamed, while the other Sabbat looked on, laughing. While Bianka turned her head to the left and Ravena plucked a drop of blood from her cut lip and held it carefully in her beak. *And a message*, Bianka said. *Of endearment*.

The punishment went on a long time, until Razor dropped to her knees, at which point the Bishop nodded and the female guard took over.

Bianka was careful to look away, so that she would not lead any of the guards' eyes in the direction of Ravena. But from the corner of her eye she occasionally sneaked a glance. The raven dropped down, behind Lot's body, out of view.

Careful, friend, she said.

She could not see Ravena deposit the drop of blood between Lot's lips, into his mouth. She could not read his mind, and did not know if Ravena could pass the message to him, or if he could receive it. But she knew that her blood was powerful enough to heal him. And while a drop could not replace all that he had lost, at least his wounds would be far less severe, and he *might* have the strength to free himself. There were no mortals around for sustenance, but there were plenty of vampires in this necropolis. He could drain a few of them, if he had the will to do that.

Ravena had enough time to hop back up to the ledge and edge her way along it until she was back on the handle next to Bianka's face. Bianka turned her head, asking the questions she'd been asking the raven as she returned. *What?*

Suddenly Ravena bobbed her head forward and deposited a single drop of blood onto Bianka's bottom lip.

Bianka's tongue flicked out and caught the precious liquid. It was cold and congealed, but it tasted of Lot and his essence. Ravena had taken it from the mass of vitae that had leaked from his body onto the floor under him. Already, Bianka could feel it swirling inside her, filling her with him until from across the room she felt him throb with life. It was as if invisible silk threads stretched between the two of them, with currents sliding back and forth. Each time it reached her, she sent it back with more potency, and she knew that when it reached

Lot, he did the same. She felt their separate and combined energies swelling, as if they were not feeding off each other so much as recharging one another.

Once Fletcher tired of watching the guard beat Razor into unconsciousness, he ordered her to stop. He was a hands-on madman; not one for vicarious thrills.

Lot's throat was numb. His discipline had deserted him again near the end and he had howled in mindless agony. He wished that the rest of his body was as numb, though. Fletcher had had his whip, it turned out. When he had finished and gone to meet the other Sabbat outside the Box, Lot had been too weak, too tormented, to even think about trying to escape. He had hung in the darkness of the Capel tomb, as alone as when Bianka had left him here earlier. Now, however, every moment in the darkness passed like a breath of eternity. And he had sound to listen to, as well: the slow patter and splash of his blood as it dripped onto the altar of the crypt. He had heard the Sabbat gathering outside, and the return of Fletcher with Bianka and the Camarilla. Helpless, he had heard the vampires of the Box tortured (it was a stupid, insane thing to do, but there was no question of Fletcher's madness now, was there?) as the other Sabbat cheered.

He had heard Bianka's voice. Had heard her struck. He wished he could see her. He wished he could rescue her, come to her aid and comfort her. But he couldn't. He was too weak. His strength, even his anger, had been flayed away by Fletcher's whip, had pooled on the stone altar. And his eyes were gummed shut with his own bloody tears.

Something touched him, a sudden weight coming to rest on his inverted crotch. In his soul, Lot shrieked with renewed terror. No more! His body didn't move, too exhausted. The weight shifted and left his crotch. Lot heard the soft rustle of wings.

Ravena.

Abruptly, Lot was glad that his body could no longer respond to his mind. He had already betrayed himself once tonight by calling out Bianka's name. The bird was up to something. He didn't want to betray himself—or Bianka or Ravena—a second time. Ravena came to roost again, clinging upside down to his chin and neck, claws digging into his skin. It hurt, but the pain was sweet. Lot struggled to open his eyes, working against the encrusted blood. Finally the lids of his left eye parted with a thin wet tear and a sensation like the slash of a hot knife. Lot strained to look up toward Ravena.

She cocked her head. A black gem of an eye met his gaze. Devotion filled him. Devotion and love. Lot knew the message came from Bianka. Below his head, Lot's good hand convulsed into a fist of impotent rage. A scream that would never sound built in his throat. He wanted her! He needed her! But he would never have her again! He wanted desperately to sob. He could hear Fletcher ranting in the background.

Bianka would be there somewhere as well. And he could do nothing. Nothing!

Ravena pecked at his lips. Lot didn't look at her. Fletcher had hung him so that he faced the wall, the better to whip him. Now his body masked Ravena's presence, but it also denied him a view of anything but cold stone. Ravena pecked him again. When he didn't respond a second time, she thrust her beak between his lips.

The taste of Bianka flooded Lot's mouth. The shock of it brought both his eyes snapping open, his right eyelids pulling apart sharply but with no pain that he could feel. Once again, he was drowning in Bianka's potent blood. Ancient blood. Only a single drop, carried by Ravena, but it was enough. Energy rushed back into his body. His mind was alert again, his strength renewed. Sweet blood. Powerful blood. He almost sighed with the ecstasy of it. Almost, but not quite.

He felt everything again. He was aware of everything again. He was strong again, but nothing had changed. He was still dangling upside down, surrounded by Sabbat. There was still nothing he could do! The moment he moved—the moment he made any sound—Fletcher would notice. He clenched his teeth in frustration. Ravena tilted her head, as if expecting him to do something. He could have laughed. He caught the raven's eye.

Can't, he tried to communicate silently, straining to convey words. *Too many*. He projected an image of Bianka. *Love*. Let the bird carry a message back to Bianka.

Then he thought of something else. Bianka had wanted to share a Blood Bond with him. They had fed from each other once. He had fed from her a second time. They wouldn't have the opportunity to feed a third time, but he might be able to let her taste his blood again.

Down, he told Ravena. He formed a picture in his mind, Ravena plucking some of his spilled blood from the surface of the altar below and taking it to Bianka. *Go*.

Ravena understood. She dropped... not onto the altar where she could be seen, however. She dropped down behind the altar. A pool of his blood was slowly dripping over the edge and onto the floor. Lot watch dizzily from above as Ravena waited patiently for the next drops of blood. When they came, she caught them deftly. Intelligent bird. Then she waited until Fletcher's ranting and the shouts of the Sabbat rose to another crescendo. In the moment of noise, she took wing again, climbing swiftly up past Lot's body and out of his sight.

A moment of distraction. That might be all he would need to cover his escape as well—if such a moment ever came.

No. Lot refused to give up on new-found hope so easily. He knew how much Bianka loved Ravena. She had risked the bird to get blood to him. A few minutes later, he knew that Ravena had been successful in taking his blood back to Bianka. He could feel her. Without even being able to see her, he knew exactly where she was in the room. He could almost feel her will and energy pouring into him. He returned love to her. His strength... her strength... their united strength grew. It was like the loyalty to the Sabbat that came through the Vaulderie, but more intense and more intimate. Bianka was with him. He was with Bianka. Two tastes of her ancient blood. A Blood Bond took three tastes, he had been told. What would happen if he tasted Bianka's blood a third time? He wanted to know, but at the same time the idea frightened him.

But none of that would matter if they didn't escape. Lot closed his eyes, turning his finely tuned senses inward, concentrating on the tactile sensations that his body fed him, trying to figure out how Fletcher had bound him. He focused past the lingering pain of his torture. Bianka's blood would allow his to heal those weeping wounds, but the moment he did, the Sabbat would notice something was amiss. Except... he healed his slashed wrists and, with effort, straightened and rejoined the bones of the hand that Fletcher had broken. He couldn't afford the loss of any more blood and he would almost definitely need the use of that hand.

There was a constriction around his feet and

lower legs. Something hard and cold wrapped around him. The chain. He opened his eyes again, rolling them as far as he could to see what Fletcher had hung him from. He couldn't quite see, though, and risked moving his head just a little. He caught sight of a heavy old lamp suspended from the high ceiling over the altar. He was hanging from the lamp. The chain was wrapped around and around his feet and ankles. He gritted his teeth. It would take more than a little distraction to give him the time he needed to get out of this.

He got it. Suddenly, there was shouting outside the crypt. Someone came charging in. "They're coming for us!"

"Who?" snarled Fletcher. Lot heard a wet crunch. He suspected that the bishop had struck the messenger. "Who's coming for us? Who would dare?"

"Border packs!" The shouting outside was intensifying. Lot could hear the wet sounds of battle as well, but distantly. Out across the cemetery, vampires were fighting vampires.

"Stracharn and the border packs." A murmur rippled through the Sabbat inside the crypt. The border packs never came downtown. Their territory was the suburbs at the edge of the city. "And the Archbishop! We broke his edict!"

There was a scream.

Chaos erupted inside the crypt. Lot heard the rush of vampires pushing at each other to get at the door. "No!" Fletcher roared. "Get back! We can hold them off! We're justified! The Camarilla violated the Settlement!" Someone hissed at him or at someone else. Someone yelped. Someone shrieked.

The Sabbat thrived on violence. Violence fed on fear. There was only so far loyalty to the sect would hold. Sabbat began to tear at each other in their terror. The crypt, a haven before, had become a death trap. One door. High, narrow windows. If they didn't escape before the border packs arrived, they would be helpless. Fletcher's roaring was drowned out in the madness.

Lot bent himself upward, grasping at his legs, then at the chains binding him, dragging himself up his own body. His wounded flesh screamed in protest. He let it heal itself a little and allowed himself a moment to look around. To look for Bianka. He spotted her, struggling with two Sabbat who were trying to restrain her in spite of the confusion. Ravena screeched and swooped through the air, half in attack of Bianka's captors, half in sheer panic. Lot turned back to the chains around his legs and tore at them, trying to work them loose. If he could, he might be able to wriggle free. The bonds were too tight, though. And even with Bianka's blood in him, he wasn't strong enough to break them. If the chains wouldn't break or loosen, there was only one other possibility for him.

Grimly, he flexed one foot, pointing it as far as it would go. That helped a bit, but not much. Wrapping a hand around his heel, he squeezed.

The leather of his boot made it difficult, but leather and flesh and bone were still a lot weaker than metal. Bones grated and snapped and popped. Agonizingly, his foot compressed. Someone yelled his name. He had been noticed. Weight hanging from one arm, he slipped the broken foot out of his boot. The chains went slack. His empty boot fell to the floor. His other foot came free easily. Without looking, Lot let go of the chains and dropped.

Bianka caught him, lowering him gently to the floor. There was blood on her hands and on her face. For a moment, Lot stared into her pale blue eyes, then he wrapped his arms around her and kissed her red mouth. She kissed him back, then pushed him away. "What now?" she asked.

"We have to get out of here."

"Why? The Archbishop… "

"No. I don't want any of the Sabbat to get their hands on you." Lot winced. Wasn't he Sabbat? "Not Fletcher. Not the Archbishop. If he's called in the border packs, he's angry. Who knows what he'll do?" Lot gripped his foot and forced the bones back into their proper positions, willing blood to flow and bones to heal. The pain was sharp, but he would be able to walk. He pulled on his boot then pushed himself into a crouch. Bianka caught him, pulling him back down for a moment.

"Wait." She was looking up into shadows near the crypt's ceiling, searching.

"Ravena?" he asked. She nodded.

"She's terrified. There's too much commotion by the door." Bianka's eyes went distant for a moment. Ravena swooped down out of the shadows. She screamed once and flew for the broken window, tucking her wings to dive through it.

Lot shook his head. "Too bad we couldn't leave that way, too." He peered up over the edge of the altar.

Fletcher's talons hooked through the air just in front of his face. "Bastard!" he howled. "Traitor!" Red-flecked foam dripped out of the bishop's mouth, as if he was rabid. Lot scrambled back, pushing Bianka behind him. Fletcher lunged over the altar, reaching for them. "Fucking bloody templar! You fucked everything—I almost had them! The damn Cammies were as good as dead!"

Lot grabbed at him, trying to force him back. It was no good. In his frenzy, the bishop was unstoppable. He raked at Lot with one hand, lifting the other vampire by his very flesh and throwing him back against the crypt wall. "Traitor!" he bellowed again. Draped over the altar, he stretched forward, talons dripping.

Bianka's foot slammed into his backside. Lot threw himself aside as the blow shoved Fletcher forward hard, propelling him face first into the wall. Bones cracked. Bianka knelt down. "Are you all right?"

New blood ran down Lot's chest, but he nodded. "Well enough." He pushed himself to his feet and ran for the door, jumping over the unconscious bodies of the Camarilla that littered the floor. He saw Bianka pause beside one, a blond woman. He grabbed the Inconnu's hand. "Don't worry. The Archbishop will take care of them."

There was still a mob at the door. Many Sabbat had managed to pour through the narrow exit already, but some still struggled to escape. They screamed and yelled in their terror, ripping at each other with claws and fangs, lost in panic.

"How do we get out through that?" Bianka shouted in his ear.

Lot glanced back at Fletcher. The bishop was already climbing to his feet. He looked back at the door. "Straight through." He took a couple of steps back, then charged forward, lowering his broad shoulders like a football player.

The crush of vampires was too thick for him to break all the way through, but his charge punched him to within a few feet of freedom. Bianka was right behind him, biting and pushing at the Sabbat around them, holding them back. Lot realized that both of them had a significant advantage over the other vampires: They hadn't succumbed to their fear. The Sabbat were simply tearing at each other, hardly moving forward at all. He and Bianka worked their way toward the door.

Fletcher's angry roar surged over the chaotic din. Lot looked back. Fletcher was striding forward, but with each stride, he changed shape. He dropped onto all fours, fur sprouting from his body as he took on his heavy-jawed wolf-shape.

The wolf would be able to slip through the struggling vampires just as easily as it slipped through forest undergrowth. "Hurry," Lot hissed at Bianka. He began to lift the vampires in front of them, thrusting them out of their way. One more vampire. Two more. Then they were out.

The night spread around them. There were still screams and shouts and struggling vampires here, but the anarchy was lost in the consuming darkness. The Sabbat that Fletcher had gathered fled—or tried to flee. The fierce Sabbat of the border packs stopped them—or tried to. Sabbat loyalty was strong, but the instinct to survive was stronger. Sabbat justice was swift and harsh. Lot didn't doubt that many of the Sabbat who had entered the Box with Fletcher tonight would come to regret their choice.

Archbishop Dyce came pacing out of the shadows. Benedict was with him. Lot froze. That was where the Ravnos had gone after he fled from the crypt. To summon the Archbishop, perhaps with hopes of rescuing his friend. Lot bit back a snarl. He grabbed Bianka's hand and pulled her away, running from Dyce and Benedict. "Come on!" Out of the corner of his eye, he saw Benedict grabbed at the Archbishop's arm and point at him. The Archbishop, though, was looking elsewhere. His eyes seemed to be on the door of the tomb. Lot kept running, drawing Bianka into the darkness.

They had managed maybe forty or fifty feet when Fletcher emerged from the crypt with a deep howl. Lot risked a look back. The bishop was taking human form again, still moving after them.

"Fletcher!" Dyce called sharply.

There was command in that voice. Fletcher froze. Everyone froze—border packs, panicked Sabbat, even Lot and Bianka. The night was silent again. All eyes turned to look at the Archbishop. Dyce's face was harsh and cold. "You've abused your power, Fletcher. Explain yourself."

Fletcher gestured wildly toward the crypt.

"The Cammies." His other arm came up to point after Lot and Bianka. "Lot... "

"I've heard about the Camarilla rebellion, Fletcher." The Archbishop's eyes were narrow. "I've also heard that you captured the leader, but allowed her to escape."

"Not me!" Fletcher protested. "It was Lot. He betrayed the sect."

"Perhaps. But tell me why it was necessary to gather so many Sabbat to raid into the Box. Tell me why you abducted the Camarilla and brought them here." He snapped his fingers. Stracharn stepped forward. He held a Sabbat in each hand. They were battered and bruised. Lot guessed that they had sided with Fletcher earlier tonight, but that Dyce had had a talk with them since. "Tell me why I will find a dozen tortured Camarilla in that crypt." The Archbishop didn't give Fletcher a chance to reply. "You've exceeded your authority, Fletcher. You are no longer my bishop." He snapped his fingers again, gesturing for Fletcher to come to him. "You will be punished."

Bianka gripped Lot's hand. Lot squeezed

back. His chest ached where the bishop's talons had raked him. The strength that Bianka's blood had lent him was ebbing. He watched the scene by the crypt intently. Fletcher didn't move.

The Archbishop snarled. "Come here!"

Fletcher's mouth twisted. His eyes, piggish with red hate, glared at the Archbishop—then shifted to stare at Lot. "You... *traitor!*" he howled suddenly. He leaped after them.

Lot ran, pulling Bianka after him. The shadows rang once more with shouts and calls and Fletcher's roars. Lot ran as fast as he could, as fast as he dared, dodging, twisting, weaving among tombs and monuments. The moon was bright and that aided their flight. Even so, he knew he could see better than Bianka in the shadows.

Even so, Bianka was moving ahead, pulling him after her.

Suddenly there was a tombstone in front of him. Bianka had dodged around the thin slab of marble. Lot crashed into it. He fell, bringing the stone and Bianka down with him. Bianka got up again. "Are you okay?" she asked quickly.

The cool stone felt good under him. His strength was gone. He couldn't run anymore. He didn't say anything. He knew how he must look to her: wasted, thin, nothing more than the corpse that he was. He reached up for her hand.

"Bianka."

She glanced back the way they had come. Lot could hear Fletcher, but he was distant. They had lost him—for now.

"Go ahead. Give me a minute," he told Bianka. She shook her head and bent down, picking him up easily. There was a big Romanesque crypt nearby. She stepped behind it and lowered him to the ground, holding him gently. She held out her wrist.

"Take more of my blood, love," Bianka said.

Lot shook his head. "I'll heal. I just need time."

"We don't have that luxury. If they find us—"

"Don't," he said, pulling her close. His flesh was too cool. It would take him days to recover. If only he weren't so stubborn—she could heal him with very little—

"I need to tell you this," he said.

"I'm listening."

"At the warehouse. When Fletcher was torturing you..."

His features twisted into a mask of agony that she knew was not physical.

"I... I wanted to stop him—"

"I know."

He held a finger to her lips and looked into her eyes. His dark orbs drew her in like a bottomless well. She wanted to spend eternity diving into those waters. She kissed his finger and he pulled her close until their lips met.

And then he pulled back, the tortured look returning to his face. "I very nearly let you die." It was as if he couldn't say anymore. She could see the pain deep in him and knew that long after she forgave him—and he would need to hear her say it—he would still be blaming himself.

"You are precious to me," he finally said. "All that my existence has lacked. Yet even now I feel torn."

"I know that, Lot. It's understandable. You've been with the Sabbat for a long time. You've bonded with them, and now you've almost bonded with me."

"I'm like an outlaw, in hiding. Where can we hide? They'll find us."

"There are places outside of Toronto—"

"I won't be Caitiff! That's not an existence."

"You don't have to be. The Sabbat and the Camarilla aren't the only sects, and besides, they're different everywhere. I've met so many—"

"And they'd take in a Sabbat traitor? And an Inconnu? I don't think so."

She inhaled slowly and deeply and looked at him. "I don't have any answers, but I do have a question: Do you want to go back?"

"I want to feel that I *could* go back. With you."

"Maybe that's still possible."

He shook his head. Then he looked at her again. Her blood in his veins sang to her, the way his blood flowing inside her resonated for him. Even after only twice sharing, it was a given that they would always be inside one another, always be connected. He felt it as much as she did.

He touched her face tenderly. "I don't want to lose you."

"You already have!" The voice was Fletcher's. He'd found them.

Bianka jumped to her feet. Lot did as well, but she was keenly aware that his movements were not as fast or as coordinated as they normally were. And Fletcher noticed, too.

"What's the matter, Lot? Has she drained all your strength? Or was it me?"

"Fuck you, Fletcher! Your minutes are counted."

"I don't think so. But then, I'm not some wacko Sabbat traitor, hopelessly in love with a Thrall."

"Thrall? What the fuck are you talking about?"

Bianka shifted uneasily.

"Didn't you tell your lover?" Fletcher chided, taunting her. "You can't lie, so this must be an evasion—"

"Tell me what?" Lot turned to her too.

"I... I tasted his blood."

Lot looked shaken.

Fletcher, on the other hand, howled in glee. "The bitch two-timed you! What a sucker! I am her regent."

"That's a lie!" Bianka said quickly. "He forced me to take his, earlier tonight—"

"There's a standard line," Fletcher said.

"It's nothing like what we've done. He didn't drink from me—"

"But you drank from me."

"Once."

"And once can be enough, can't it, Bianka?"

Lot turned to her, startled.

"Can't it! Tell him!"

Bianka hesitated. "In certain circumstances, when powerful rituals are used, yes, but—"

"Then you and I have already Blood Bonded," Lot said, looking dazed.

"No. What we've done takes three exchanges—"

"And with him?" Lot said. He looked guarded, and Bianka felt her heart pulse in pain.

"Trust me, Lot. You know I can't lie."

"Couldn't," Fletcher said. "Until you became my Thrall. And now you're under my power."

"I'm not your Thrall!"

But Lot looked very unsure. Confused.

"Tell you what," Fletcher offered. "Let's write all this bullshit off to the full moon. Come back with me, Lot, we'll talk with the Archbishop, enact the Vaulderie, and break whatever ties you have with her, and all will be forgiven," Fletcher said. "She's a Zillah. It's not your fault. Hell, the Archbishop himself thinks she's sexy."

What's Fletcher trying to do? Bianka wondered. She and Lot had been there when the Archbishop condemned him. Did he think they would forget that? But even as those thoughts and others like them swirled through her, Bianka saw the longing on Lot's face, the pull of his desire to return to the pack, to his place, to belong.

"Lot, don't listen to him! You know what happened back there. The Archbishop is probably out looking for Fletcher right now."

"Get over here, Bianka!" Fletcher snarled. He reached out toward her, and moved a step closer.

She could feel the intangible pull, like a weight that she had to struggle against, fighting for enough balance to keep from falling in his direction.

And while she concentrated on resisting, while Lot, depleted, so that his senses were dull, watched her, and while she observed the look of horror on his face, they were both too preoccupied to realize what was happening. Until Lot's features shattered and reformed, reflecting excruciating pain.

At warp speed, Fletcher extracted Lot's bond-handled knife from the sheath and embedded it deep into Lot's chest, all the way to the hilt. The wide blade cut up, through muscle and connective tissue and entered the heart.

"No!" Bianka screamed.

Lot crumpled instantly, and sank to the ground. His body was already too weak. And this blow was too severe.

Bianka fell beside him. She cradled his head in her arms.

He was barely conscious. She was afraid to pull out the knife, afraid of further damage. "Drink from me!" she cried.

"Twist the knife," Fletcher told her.

The ragged sound of his voice was a command that moved in a circuit into her brain and down her body, through her arm and back up again, gaining power each time it did the loop. Against her will, she found herself reaching out for the knife handle.

Tears swelled from her eyes. Lot could barely keep his open. His lips moved, as if he were trying to kiss her, but no words came out.

"Please! Drink!" She lowered her head and bit into the wrist of the arm that encircled him.

"Grab the knife!" Fletcher's words cut into her like sharp blades, the pain forcing her to actions she did not want to perform. Her fingers curled around the handle.

"Lot! Can you hear me? I'm going to give you blood. Please! You must accept it. Will you accept it?"

"Twist the fucking blade, bitch!"

Her hand trembled as she held the knife. Through the handle she could feel the weak quiver of Lot's heart around the steel. She fought the urge to turn the blade, but it all hinged on Lot. "Take my blood!" she cried. Her wound at his lips seeped, waiting for any sign that he would accept the red life that would heal him and bind them. And give him the strength to defeat Fletcher. That *might* be enough to bond them forever, the potence of her blood completing the connection in two nights instead of three. She hoped.

"Will you accept this Bond?" she whispered.

Lot nodded once. Slightly. But she saw it and quickly pressed her wrist to his mouth.

And then his heart stopped beating. It just stopped.

She felt the absence of the beat through the knife. It took a second for her to take that in. *No! I cannot bear this pain!* she said to Ravena in a too-calm, too-lucid fashion, because she could tell no one else. Ravena, on a tombstone, stood perfectly still.

It was as though time had stopped. The longest moment of Bianka's existence came into being. Her blood falling on the lips of her dead lover. Fletcher's macabre laugher. The heavy black curtain that closed over her heart, that kept her heart from shattering into a million pieces. That kept the pain in so that the rage could spray out like acid at anything or anyone in its path.

In a second she was at his throat, tearing out Fletcher's windpipe.

The Sabbat was thrown off-guard, but not for long. He hurled her across the cemetery, into a black marble Celtic cross that topped one of the gravestones.

The Beast in her, so long in check, scrabbled

at the door, and she threw it open with glee. Blood, red, darker red, black flowed over her vision, and the power of nine hundred years of consumed vitae surged in her veins.

Fletcher screamed, "Kneel at my feet!" But it was too late for that. The Beast in her gobbled up the power and influence of his blood. He bent, but before he could pull the knife from Lot's chest, Bianka leapt onto his back. Her teeth sank into the jugular at the side of his throat.

Fletcher tried to throw her off and they both fell, Bianka onto her back, Fletcher on top of her, his back to her front.

His face twisted with murderous fury. In a split second, his nails extended into the longest talons she had ever seen. He used them to claw her in the side, bisecting her liver with one stab, slicing into her right kidney with the next.

Bianka's hand reached around front, grabbed his genitals, and yanked.

Fletcher screamed. He used the daggers at his fingertips to chop at her hand and quickly severed fingers from it until she was forced to let go.

They rolled and tumbled down a slope and at the bottom they crashed into an old tombstone that knocked them apart. Bianka was on her feet immediately, the Beast going after the one thing it ever wanted and needed—blood.

She tore and ripped at Fletcher, the deranged animal in her bent on destruction. Fletcher, though, had a Beast of his own, unleashed, determined to survive.

Bianka grabbed a stone and bashed his head until the skull cracked. Despite the injury, he pushed her down and straddled her hips. Fletcher had honed his skill at using his claws. As with Lot, he found her heart easily. He jammed his talons into her chest hard and deep, and up. And then he twisted them.

The sharp claws nearly severed the right ventricle. Little blood would be flowing in. Their eyes locked. And through the Beast haze, Bianka felt she might be on the verge of joining

Lot soon, wherever he had gone. But she was determined that if she did, the three would meet in that place and finish this battle on that other plane.

With all the strength remaining in her, she grabbed onto the sides of his head and pressed. For her. For Lot. For the well-being of all the undead throughout the world. Fletcher's talons exited her body. His hands came up and tried to pry hers away, but she had the strength of a hundred.

Fletcher's head exploded. Gray matter popped out of the ruptured sutures that had knitted the three pieces of his skull together. The brain material and blood oozed over his face and her hands. The shocked look on his face wasn't enough, though. Bianka wanted to be certain he could not come back.

She felt her strength dimming, and gathered it together for one final onslaught. With a severe twist, she wrenched his head from his neck and pulled until the vertebrae snapped apart, the muscle shredded, the skin tore. His eyes bugged out, and his mouth opened in a silent cry. She pitched his head aside, and his body dropped backward.

Blood from the artery in his neck spurted out, bathing her feet. She hungered after it but did not have the strength to move.

DreamYouMe! It was Ravena, the first time Bianka had heard the raven speak in more than impressions. *TheyEmerging.*

The wound to her heart was close to being fatal, Bianka knew. The Sabbat might kill her— that's what Ravena was trying to say. Even now Bianka could hear them searching through the grounds, trampling down flowers for the dead, knocking over monuments to loved ones. Loved ones. Lot's body was just up the rise. Surely she should feel his presence—

Danger! Ravena squawked to reinforce the message.

The raven came and sat on her chest, and the slight weight felt like a ton and forced her to lie back.

"I've found Lot!" one of the Sabbat called. "He's dead!"

Footsteps, moving quickly. "That's Lot's

knife!" another said. "Fletcher must have killed him with his own knife!"

"Lot only died a few minutes ago. Let's get Fletcher!"

Benedict's voice was low, close to the ground, carried by the breeze. "Lot!"

Freedom! Ravena said in her bird-way.

She opened her beak wide, very wide. Her head turned slightly, and Bianka stared into her eye. An eye of one color, the color of midnight, of black skies and dark oceans. Of death and decay. And eye so dark that to enter there must surely lead to light, to resurrection.

Bianka closed her eyes and felt her essence gathering within her damaged body.

"They're down here!" one of the Sabbat called.

A sound rumbled from low in Ravena's throat, and Bianka knew she meant *Hurry!*

Bianka felt her life-force fold into her damaged heart. Her heartbeats were irregular. She had enough blood in her that healing was already taking place, the ventricle was knitting together, but she could not repair in nearly enough time to escape the Sabbat running down the hill.

Like a cloud forming, her inner being fused. Her lungs exhaled and the vapor she was moved up through her esophagus, past her windpipe and out of her mouth.

Ravena bent forward.

Feeling left Bianka's body, from the toes up, and the last thing of a physical nature she felt was the raven's beak against her lower lip, kissing her body as she received Bianka's soul.

CHAPTER FIFTEEN

Benedict was the first to reach the bodies. He went skittering down the grassy slope, pushing his way past the other Sabbat. The sight of Fletcher and Bianka's final remains stopped him. Both vampires were covered in blood, their own and the other's. Bianka's flesh was torn, shredded by Fletcher's claws. Fletcher's body was battered as well, but his head was gone completely. It lay upside down against the base of a tombstone, a malignant, pulpy ruin, empty eyes staring up at Benedict. Accusingly.

He looked away, looked at Bianka. Her eyes were closed. A raven perched on her chest. It cocked its head at him, then screeched and leaped into the air. It came to rest again on the tombstone that towered over Fletcher's head. There was peace on Bianka's blood-streaked face. Frightening peace. Benedict didn't know which was worse—Fletcher's last expression or hers.

Benedict scrambled back up the hill even as other Sabbat made their way down to gawk at the bodies. Dyce was waiting above. "Well?"

"Dead." Benedict swallowed. "True death." He fell to his knees beside Lot. "All of them."

The Archbishop touched Benedict's head as if in blessing. "You tried, Benedict." The Ravnos said nothing. Bloody tears were running down his face. Dyce stroked his hair for a moment more, then added, "Fletcher violated my edict. His body will be exposed to sunlight and his ashes smeared over my door."

"What about Lot?" He gestured behind him, down over the hill. "What about Bianka?"

"What more do you want me to do?"

Benedict's reply was washed away by the sudden screaming of the raven and the shouts of the Sabbat below. Someone whooped with glee. Benedict and the Archbishop both turned to look. The bird was flapping madly around the vampires clustered about Bianka's body. One of them had his face buried in Bianka's neck. The Archbishop snarled. "What are you doing?"

The vampire looked up. His face was red. "There's still blood in her!" he called. "It's potent. She must have been ancient—no wonder Lot wanted her."

Benedict climbed quickly to his feet and caught Dyce's arm. "I want you to destroy their bodies, too. Don't let this happen to them." Dyce looked at him questioningly. "Please," Benedict begged. The Archbishop was silent. Then he nodded slowly.

"Leave her alone," he ordered the vampires

below. The Sabbat hissed and muttered, but stepped away from Bianka's body. The raven settled on it protectively. The Archbishop looked up at the sky. There was a pearly glow in the east. He turned.

"Bring all of the bodies back to the crypt." A renewed murmur passed through the Sabbat. "Bring them!" the Archbishop snapped.

Grumbling, two vampires bent to pick up Bianka's body. Three took Fletcher's, with another carrying the former bishop's head. Benedict knelt down and picked up Lot's abused body himself. Carrying their burdens, they followed the Archbishop back through the cemetery. Morning dew soaked their shoes. The raven flew overhead, circling in the gradually vanishing shadows. Benedict walked last in the procession. Blood still ran from his eyes.

Stracharn was waiting for them. "We have most of the Sabbat who went with Fletcher tonight," he said gruffly. "What do you want us to do with them?"

Benedict watched as the Archbishop looked over the border packs' prisoners. None of them would meet his gaze. There were so many of them, Benedict realized, so many who had followed Fletcher, eager to fight the Camarilla. Surely there were too many for Dyce to kill them all. It would be a stupid thing to do. The Archbishop must have been thinking the same thing, because he frowned. "Let them live," he told Stracharn. "But tomorrow night, they're all to come to my cathedral. They will be branded as punishment for what they've done." Stracharn nodded. The captive Sabbat closest to Dyce, the ones who could hear their judgment, looked relieved. Branding was still a harsh sentence, but their punishment could have been much worse.

"What," Stracharn asked, "about the Camarilla?"

Dyce's frown grew deeper. "Bring them out."

The vampires of the border packs dragged the battered Camarilla out of the crypt. Most could not even stand upright. Benedict wasn't sure that some of them were still alive. The Archbishop pointed at one. Stracharn seized him and dragged him forward. DeWinter. Dyce tilted the gaunt vampire's head up tenderly so that they looked at each other face to face. "I'm disappointed, DeWinter."

The Camarilla mumbled something, then turned his head slightly. A broken fang fell from between his lips. He looked back at Dyce. "So am I. Fletcher invaded the Box."

"You left it."

DeWinter managed a crooked smile. "We're pawns, Dyce. Pawns to you, pawns to Fletcher, pawns to the other Camarilla, pawns to the ancients. I'd think the Sabbat would have sympathy for that."

"I have sympathy. You could still join us, DeWinter." He nodded toward Bianka's body and Lot's. "The Sabbat and the Camarilla have both lost bright stars tonight. Lot tried to warn me about Fletcher. If I had acted sooner… " He shrugged. "Will you join us now, DeWinter?"

The gaunt vampire shook his head. "No. I can't." He sighed with sudden pain. "Let us go back to the Box, Dyce. We've been beaten down. Half of us have died in the last two nights. We're your prisoners. We've been punished."

"You realize I'm going to have to appoint a new bishop?"

DeWinter nodded. The Archbishop looked up. "Benedict," he called.

No. Benedict's arms tightened around Lot's body. *This was supposed to be you,* he told his friend silently. *That was the plan.* He stepped forward, past the vampires holding Bianka's body. For a moment, he hated the dead woman. *If it wasn't for you, he might still have been here.*

The raven was perched on Bianka's cold breast. It glanced at him, black eyes gleaming. There was silent reproach in those eyes. Then the bird vaulted into the sky. Benedict's gaze dropped down to Lot's face. *If it wasn't for me,* he told the dead vampire with bitter guilt, *you would be with her.* He looked up again and stepped forward.

"Stracharn," the Archbishop said, "witness this." He bit into his thumb. Blood welled up. He smeared it across Benedict's forehead.

DeWinter nodded again. "Good choice," he murmured. The Camarilla reached out to lay a hand on Lot's head. "I'll remember you. Like gold in my memory." Then he pushed himself away from Dyce to totter over to Bianka. "And you. Like gold as well." He stumbled and collapsed.

Dyce gestured. "Take him and the rest back to the Box." He looked up at the sky again. "Make sure they're inside somewhere, safe from the sun." He looked around. "Everyone go." He pointed at Benedict and the vampires holding Bianka and Fletcher. "Put them inside the crypt, then find cover for the day."

Benedict was the closest to the blood-stained tomb. He led the way inside and laid Lot across the altar. The slab was against the west wall. When the sun rose, its first rays would come through the eastern windows to illuminate the altar. He motioned the vampires with Bianka to lay her on the altar as well. Fletcher was dumped unceremoniously on the floor.

The other vampires left. The Ravnos stayed.

"Benedict?" The Archbishop was standing

just inside the door. "Stracharn and I are taking refuge in one of the other tombs."

"Give me a minute."

He didn't hear the Archbishop go. He just stared at the bodies on the altar.

Bianka-Ravena looked down through the same eyes, eyes that were sharp enough to see detail clearly. They stood on the ledge below the broken window, head cocked, watching. On their tail feathers, they felt the heat of the sun as it threatened to melt over the horizon.

Benedict stood very still, staring down at the three bodies for a long time. He was the last of the Sabbat in the tomb, and Bianka-Ravena waited impatiently for him to leave the crypt.

He crouched and moved Lot's remains closer to Bianka's body, then he bent and pulled Bianka to his friend. Her damaged shell, now soulless, had tried desperately to heal, but had entered extreme Torpor; it seemed unable to regenerate for lack of incentive. No soul meant no will, Bianka-Ravena knew.

Ravena-Bianka squawked loudly, hoping to hurry the Sabbat along. Perhaps, if Bianka's spirit could reenter her own physical form...

Benedict looked up briefly, and they thought they saw pink-tinged tears on his cheeks.

He turned back to the two bodies—Lot and Bianka—and folded them together, arms around backs, chests and pelvises close, until they were pressed to one another, in an embrace, until it looked as though their lips were meeting.

Suddenly, in a ragged voice, Benedict quoted one line from Romeo and Juliet: "As one dead in the bottom of a tomb."

He shook his head, trying to remember the whole passage. He could sense the rising sun. Even in the faint predawn light that filtered through the stained glass windows, his skin stung as if he were being attack by a hundred invisible wasps. But he had to speak. He had to say something. Then the words came to him.

"'O God, I have an ill-divining soul! Methinks I see thee, now thou art below, as one dead in the bottom of a tomb. Either my eyesight fails, or thou look'st pale.'

"'And trust me, love, in my eye so do you. Dry sorrow drinks our blood. Adieu, adieu!'"

"See, Lot," he whispered, "I can be poetic, too." He kissed his fingers, then bent forward to touch first Lot, then Bianka, their faces close. He smiled in black humor and murmured, "As one—dead in the bottom of a tomb."

He turned his back on the altar and went to the door. The eastern sky was ablaze. He would have to hurry. He glanced back one final time at Lot and Bianka. "I hope you two are happy together."

Benedict pulled the door shut and ran for the last embracing shadows of night.

The fireball lit the sky. The raven body could tolerate such heat and light, but was no longer accustomed to it. It instinctively longed for darkness and shelter. And rest.

As light crept through the fractured stained-glass windows, the bodies of the dead undead incinerated quickly. Fletcher burst into blue-yellow flame and burned fast, like refuse that needed to alter from solid to gas, that needed to evaporate until there was no trace.

But the other two bodies, joined as they were, burned as one. This glow flamed red-gold as passion. The heart inside Bianka-Ravena beat very fast and mist clouded their avian eyes. "As one dead in the bottom of a tomb." The words reverberated through the tomb

Suddenly the raven turned and flew out the window and soared straight up, toward the sun, wings spread wide, flying blind for a moment. And then it headed down and away from the

411

cemetery, toward the west, the direction in which the sun would set. Where the gargoyles live.

ABOUT THE AUTHORS

Nancy Kilpatrick has published six novels, including NEAR DEATH. CHILD OF THE NIGHT (set in the NEAR DEATH world) will be published by Raven Books this May. Approximately 100 of her horror, dark fantasy, fantasy and mystery stories have seen print—she has one collection of her stories out, and two more on the way. She has also written four issues of a comic for the VampErotica series. In addition to writing, she is the editor of four erotic horror anthologies. Nancy has been a finalist twice each for both the Bram Stoker Award and the Aurora Award, and she won the Arthur Ellis Award for Best Mystery story. She lives in Toronto, Canada, not far from the Box.

Don Bassingthwaite comes from Meaford, Ontario, but currently lives and works in Toronto. He is a graduate of McMaster University and of the University of Toronto with degrees in anthropology and museum studies. His short stories have appeared in the World of Darkness anthologies published by White Wolf, and he is the author of the dark fantasy novel SUCH PAIN. His most recent novel from White Wolf Publishing is titled BREATHE DEEPLY and is based on the collectible card game RAGE by White Wolf Game Studio.

THE MASQUERADE OF THE RED DEATH TRILOGY

Blood War

For ten thousand years a race of immortal vampires has waged a secret war to control mankind. Beings of incredible supernatural potency, they are driven by a lust for power...and human blood.

They are the Kindred.

The first volume in a trilogy focusing on the vampires of the World of Darkness™, *Blood War* is written by Robert Weinberg.

ISBN 1-56504-840-7
WW 12400
$5.99 / $7.99

Unholy Allies

The Red Death, a powerful vampire thousands of years old, has made a blood bargain with monstrous fire creatures from another dimension. With their aid, he plots to rule the world as Master of the Undead.

The only two people who can stop the Red Death are Dire McCann and Alicia Varney. Racing against time as the Red Death comes closer to achieving his goal, they desperately need to find the one historian who knows the vampire's identity.

The second novel in the trilogy about vampires in the World of Darkness. Written by Robert Weinberg.

ISBN 1-56504-841-5
WW12401
$5.99 US/$7.99 CAN